Faith's Crossing

Carrie Carr

Yellow Rose Books

Nederland, Texas

ISBN 1-932300-12-0

First Printing 2003

9 8 7 6 5 4 3 2 1

*This story was initially published, along with the story *Destiny's Bridge*,
under the title *Destiny's Crossing*. Some parts have been changed from the
original version.

Cover design by Donna Pawlowski

Published by:

Yellow Rose Books
PMB 210, 8691 9th Avenue
Port Arthur, Texas 77642-8025

Find us on the World Wide Web at
http://www.regalcrest.biz

Printed in the United States of America

Acknowledgments:

So many people have helped me with this book, and I hope they all know how grateful I am. I would like to thank a few of them personally, though. My editor, Day, whose hard work has been invaluable, as well as fun and educational. The talented Lori L. Lake, and her selfless acts of teaching me new writing skills every day, while still creating her own wonderful novels. Cathy, whose patience and understanding allowed me to hone my craft, while also allowing me to live my dream. And my wonderful AJ, who also gave up long nights and weekends while I edited and rewrote so much of this book. Thank you all.

This book is dedicated to:

My parents, because without their example of love, I'd never be able to write about it.

My brother, who no matter what, has always stood beside me, lending his love and support. Be loved and be happy, K.

And, of course, my AJ. The woman who I get to spend the rest of my life loving, and being loved by. I will gladly marry you again and again, sweetheart. Forever and always.

Chapter One

LEXINGTON WALTERS WOKE at her usual time—before the sun had the opportunity to rise. Groaning at the early hour, she used her right hand to rub her weary eyes, while she mentally debated with her more practical side that told her to get out of bed. Just when she had decided to listen to that annoying little internal voice, she felt the body draped across hers snuggle closer. Lex sighed. *Not like I have a good reason to leave this.* Her lips turned upward into a small smile. *Not like I'd leave this even if I did have a good reason.*

The blades of the ceiling fan rotated at a leisurely pace, sending just enough of a breeze to cause the window's lace curtains to billow gently. The same soft breeze caused a slight chill to the woman stirring in Lex's arms. Lex lovingly caressed her partner, easing her awake. "Morning," a sleep-roughened voice grumbled, before soft lips kissed Lex's throat. "I've got to figure out a way to make you sleep in until at least sunrise, just once."

Lex worked her hand under the soft material of her lover's sleep shirt, gently scratching Amanda's back. "I dunno if you can, but it will certainly be fun watching you try."

Amanda eased up the relaxed body until their faces were inches apart. "You're on." She dropped her head slightly and brushed her lips against Lex's. When she felt strong hands run underneath her shirt, along her spine, Amanda deepened the kiss, and the body under hers trembled. "Mmm. Cold?" She loved the way her lover responded to her touch, just as she responded to Lex's in much the same way.

"N...n...no...not...at all," Lex stammered, unable to control her voice when she felt Amanda's hands exploring under her shirt—hands that had already come to know the right places to touch, leaving behind an almost electrical charge. "Amanda," she cleared her throat, "we shouldn't." But her body happily rebelled by arching upward. "Your, ah, grandparents." She lost the battle as a gentle touch traced down her stomach, closely followed by insistent bites and small licks. "They might...oh, God."

"Shhh. It's okay, sweetheart. They're at the other end of the hall, and won't be up for hours." Amanda slowly worked the shirt up Lex's quivering body. "Besides, the risk of getting caught is half the fun." Then she stopped talking, having found something much more enjoyable to do with her mouth.

CONTENT, LEX FOLLOWED Amanda down the stairway a couple of hours later. It had taken all of her considerable willpower not to climb into the shower with Amanda after their pre-dawn activities, especially after her lover went into great detail as to what she would be missing. *She is such a little tease.* She was unable to take her eyes off the gently swaying hips in front of her. So engrossed in her perusal, Lex didn't realize when Amanda stopped, and she had to grab the railing to keep them both from falling when she bumped into the lithe form.

Amanda turned around to peer into her lover's eyes. "Hey, there. Everything okay?"

The question brought Lex back to reality, making her a little embarrassed that she had been caught daydreaming. "Yeah, sure." Her brows creased into a questioning gaze when Amanda put her hands on her shoulders and directed her to stand on the step below her on the landing midway down the staircase. "What?"

With a mischievous smile, Amanda leaned forward and wrapped her arms around Lex's neck. "Much better." She looked directly into her partner's eyes before she captured Lex's lips for a sweet moment.

"Ahem."

Breaking off the kiss reluctantly, Lex slowly turned around to find the source of the interruption. "Busted."

At the bottom of the stairs stood a cheerful Anna Leigh. "Good morning, you two." Seeing her granddaughter wrap her arms around Lex did her heart good. She couldn't remember ever seeing Amanda so happy. "I trust you both slept well."

Amanda propped her chin on the shoulder in front of her. "Oh, yeah. Like a baby." She tugged Lex closer. "But, then again, I had a pretty good nap on the sofa last night."

Lex leaned back into the embrace and entwined her hands with those splayed across her torso. "Well, you looked so peaceful that I didn't have the heart to disturb you."

"Yeah, but you could have made me get up, instead of carrying me up the stairs.

Knowing the good-natured argument could go on forever, Anna Leigh waved to the couple. "Come on. I was just on my way up to tell you breakfast is ready."

"Mmm. I was hoping that's what the great smell was."

Lex began her descent again, but was bypassed by Amanda, who skipped down the stairs as she said, "Great! I'm starving."

Anna Leigh laughed as Amanda darted past her, and headed for the kitchen table. Then she quipped, "You'd better hurry, too, Lexington. No one cooks a better breakfast than my Jacob, and we Cauble women are known for wielding a mean fork!"

Lex and Anna Leigh entered the kitchen laughing, causing Jacob to turn around at the counter from where he was pouring a cup of coffee. "Good morning, ladies." He pulled two more mugs from the cabinet. "Coffee?" Hearing affirmative answers, he filled the cups, then turned back toward the women and set the mugs on the table.

"Good morning, Grandpa Jake." Amanda slipped her arms around his waist, squeezing tight. Snuggling her face into his chest, she released a heavy sigh. "I've really missed this." Closer to him than even her own father, Amanda needed the physical assurance that Jacob was really recovered from the automobile accident that had almost taken him from the family months prior.

Jacob enveloped her in his arms, returning the hug and kissing the head beneath his chin. "Me, too. Did you sleep well?" He looked to Lex and Anna Leigh. "Have a seat, ladies. Breakfast is ready." With a final hug and kiss to his granddaughter, Jacob turned back to the stove. "Wanna help, Peanut?"

Lex gazed at Anna Leigh, wondering if she should offer to help with the final preparations. Even though she wasn't very good at it, she felt bad just standing there while Jacob did all the work.

Anna Leigh shook her head. "Better do as he says. Sit down, or he'll never serve us." She pointed at a chair opposite her and watched as Lex sat down gingerly.

While she and Lex seated themselves at the table, Jacob and Amanda brought over platters of food. Fluffy eggs filled with vegetables covered one plate, while crisp strips of bacon and sizzling sausage links were on another. Before sitting down, Amanda topped off Lex's steaming cup of coffee and gave her shoulder a tender squeeze. "Here you go. I hope you're hungry. Grandpa makes the best omelets I've ever tasted." She winked at Jacob as he sat down next to his wife.

They spent the majority of the meal talking of the events occurring over the past week at the ranch, with both of the elder Caubles expressing their shock and concern. While driving over Lex's bridge during a storm, Amanda's car had been tossed into the swollen creek, and Lex dived in to save her. Then, a few days later, while they were riding on horseback in the remote sections of Lex's property, they came upon a group of cattle thieves. The men started after them, and only after a frightening chase did Lex and Amanda get away from them.

"...and then, after we get back to the house, Martha and I discover that tough-stuff over there," Amanda pointed at Lex with her fork, "got shot sometime during all that running and never said a word to either one of us."

Lex set her coffee mug down on the table. "You're telling it all out of proportion." She gave Jacob a pleading look, hoping he'd understand and intervene on her behalf. He looked calmer than the Cauble women, whose faces had both paled as the story progressed. "I really didn't notice anything until later. It barely grazed me."

Amanda gave her companion a dirty look. "Yeah, right. A scratch that even now, several days later, still bleeds. Which is why we're going to see Doctor Anderson right after breakfast, right?"

Rolling her eyes, Lex let out a heavy sigh. "Amanda."

Anna Leigh looked across the table at Lex. "Is that true? Lexington, you run the risk of infection with a wound like that, if it's not infected already."

"That's what I've been trying to tell her, but she's just so darn stubborn." Sensing another ally in her ongoing battle with Lex, Amanda added, "She wouldn't even let me change the dressing on it this morning."

Lex gave one more pleading look to Jacob, who simply shrugged his shoulders as if to tell her she might as well give up right now. When he didn't come to her defense, Lex tried to change the subject. "Mr...ah, Jacob, do you know of a good detail shop around here?"

"Sure, Lex. Shuman's on Fourth does excellent work. Why?" Jacob had finished his breakfast and was leaning back in his seat, one arm casually draped across the back of his wife's chair.

Amanda pushed her chair back and stood up. "Oh, that's right. You can't see the driveway from here. Since everyone's finished eating, why don't we go out front, and we'll show you." She took Lex's hand, helped her from her seat, and led the group through the house.

Also hand in hand, Jacob and Anna Leigh followed the younger couple outside, stopping in shock when they saw the Mustang sitting in the driveway, muddy, but whole. "Oh, my." Anna Leigh placed her free hand over her heart. "How—"

Jacob turned to look at his granddaughter. "But I thought you said it was lost?"

"Lex pulled it out of the creek and then got it running again. She gave it to me the night all the excitement happened." The "excitement," that Amanda alluded to so calmly occurred when the cattle thieves broke into the ranch house because the leader wanted to settle the score with Lex. The rancher had disabled their getaway vehicle, and he wanted retribution. Amanda wrapped an arm around her embarrassed friend. "Excitement" was a mild word compared to what really happened. Lex, alone on the main floor of the darkened ranch house and armed with only a frying pan, took on half of the cattle thieves after they had shut off the electricity and broken in. With Amanda and Martha hiding in the basement, she disarmed one of the men and narrowly missed being shot by another, as well as by a good-intentioned deputy. That was more excitement than Amanda cared for.

"Didn't do that much, really. Just let the car dry out," Lex mumbled, not at all enjoying the attention that was focused on her.

Jacob came up on her other side and gave her a hug. "Uh-huh. And just how *did* you get the car out of the creek? Whistled, and it followed?" He enjoyed the look on both young women's faces— Lex's, which was one of pure embarrassment, and Amanda's, who looked as if the idea had never crossed her mind.

"He's right." Amanda looked up at her lover, who wouldn't meet her gaze. "The car was on the far side of the creek. How did—" What Lex must have done to retrieve her car dawned upon her. "You didn't?" Although she didn't say a word, when Lex closed her eyes, Amanda knew exactly what she had done. "You went *back* into that cold, heavily running stream with bruised ribs? Are you *nuts*?"

Jacob limped to where his wife stood, quietly watching Amanda take Lex to task. He whispered, "I think we should go in and take care of the breakfast dishes, don't you, sweetheart?"

Anna Leigh nodded, and the two of them went back into the house, leaving their granddaughter and her lover alone.

Hearing the emotion in Amanda's voice, Lex opened her eyes to see it matched by the look of concern on her face. "I, um, it's just that you were so sad about losing that car, and I wanted to do something to cheer you up, especially after the story you told me about how you got it." She gazed into Amanda's eyes, which shone with unshed tears. It took her breath away to see not just concern, but also the love Amanda had for her.

"But, God, Lex. You could have asked me to help you, at the very least." Amanda felt her control slipping, and then Lex's callused hands cradled her face gently. "When did you—"

"The day I went to get the Jeep. I used the winch on it to pull your car out of the water." She kissed Amanda on the nose. "Piece of cake."

Amanda moved her arms up until they were around Lex's

neck. "Yeah, right. And just how did you attach the winch to the Mustang?" She saw Lex trying to think up a good answer. "Magic?"

"How'd you guess?" Lex felt her head being pulled downward. "Not buying that, huh?" she asked, as she leaned down to meet Amanda halfway. Their lips touched, and to Lex, time ceased to matter. It was as if the sounds around them stopped, and all she could hear was the rapid beating of her own heart. A motorcycle suddenly roared by, reminding her where they were standing, so she slowly broke off the kiss.

Amanda brought her arms down and placed one around her lover's waist. "Don't think for a minute that I've been distracted from our little discussion. We'll finish it later." She led Lex back inside. "But right now, we've got a doctor's appointment to keep."

EVEN THOUGH SHE protested having to go, Lex liked Doctor Anderson. The elderly physician had taken care of her assorted injuries and illnesses her entire life, and he was one of the few people she trusted completely. She and Amanda arrived at his office shortly after the doors were unlocked, which made them the only people sitting in the painfully cheerful waiting room. Since Dr. Anderson was a family practitioner, his office had brightly colored scenes adorning every wall. One wall had a circus theme, making the chairs look like they were inside the Big Top, with animals everywhere. Another had a large mural of sporting events, while the last looked like a corral, complete with several horses. Lex chose to sit in the "corral" area, to her companion's amusement.

"Always the little cowgirl, huh?" Amanda couldn't help but tease Lex as she sat down beside her.

The rancher looked around and smiled sheepishly. "Uh, well actually, I just like looking at the women athletes." She pointed to the wall across from them.

Before they could continue their conversation, the interior door next to the receptionist's window opened, and a small, gray-haired man bent with age stepped into the main room. "Little Lexington Marie! It's been awhile, hasn't it, child?" he greeted with a strong voice. "Now get yourself in here, and bring your little friend, too." He turned and headed down the hallway, gesturing to a door on his left.

Amanda enjoyed the chagrined expression on her lover's face as she followed Lex and the doctor. The brightly lit hallway was almost as blinding as being outside, and the white tile floor shone as if no one had ever walked on it.

Lex stopped at the door and waited for Amanda to enter the room, whispering as Amanda walked by, "Don't you start." She knew her lover was getting a little too much enjoyment out of her discomfort, and she hoped that at some point, she'd be able to return the favor.

"Come in, come in," the small bespectacled doctor commanded as he took his seat on a small rolling stool. "Close the door behind you. Now get over here and hop up on the examination table, Lexington." He chuckled when she rolled her eyes. "Don't give me that look now, or I'll have to call Martha."

Lex sighed and grimaced slightly as she took her place on the padded table. "It's probably just a waste of your time, Dr. A., but—"

Ignoring her protests, he turned to the young woman who stood by the door. "Come over here and sit down, honey." He cocked his head at her, trying to remember if they'd ever met. "I don't believe we know each other, do we?" he asked, holding out a wrinkled hand.

Amanda grasped the offered hand, faintly surprised at the strength in it. "No, I don't think so. I'm Amanda Cauble."

The doctor held her hand in both of his. "Jacob and Anna Leigh's little Amanda?" Seeing her blush and nod, he laughed. "That's grand! They speak of you all the time. They are so proud of you, my dear." He allowed her to sit down, then turned his attention back to his patient. As he checked the clipboard his nurse had left in the room, he asked, "Well, then. What have you gotten yourself into now, Lexie?"

Amanda grinned at the fatherly way the doctor treated Lex. When Lex furrowed her brow at Amanda, she cleared her throat and pretended to be paying attention to the medical posters on the wall.

Dr. Anderson laid the paperwork on the stool and adjusted his glasses. "Broken ribs and a gunshot wound?" The doctor held the end of his stethoscope to warm it up a bit. "I'll bet you really set Martha off with that one!" He waited patiently while Lex unbuttoned her shirt, then he gently placed the listening device to her chest. "Did you make her mad?" He began to palpate the area over Lex's ribs. "You look like you've lost a bit of weight."

"No, just been real busy. Martha will fatten me up again in no time." Lex flinched when he probed the bandage on her side.

"Hurts, huh?" He shook his head. "Got a nasty scrape here, too." He poked the muscular side gently. "Why aren't your ribs wrapped up? It'd probably hurt less, even though they're just bruised. I'd hate for you to injure them further and risk another punctured lung."

Neither of them noticed Amanda's reaction to the doctor's question. Her face paled as she considered Lex's propensity for injuring herself. While she was quickly resolving to do what she could to keep Lex from more pain, the old man pulled the taped bandage from Lex's side.

"Ow!" Lex skittered sideways on the table and reached to steady herself against the wall to keep from falling off. "Could you please leave me some skin?"

Ignoring his patient's complaints, the elderly doctor finished removing the gauze and let out a low whistle. "That doesn't look good at all," he mumbled, shaking his head in dismay.

Amanda rose from her chair and moved to stand next to him. "What? What's wrong?" She peered around the doctor, trying to see where he was looking.

Running a hand down his face, Dr. Anderson pushed Lex onto her back, then helped her raise her legs until she was lying flat on the examining table. "Might as well get comfortable, girl. We're going to have to open it back up to take care of the infection." He patted her leg. "Let me go get Laura, because she's going to have to help me." He left the room to search for his nurse.

Amanda took a close look at Lex's side. She could see that the area around the wound was very swollen, and the skin had an unhealthy red shine to it. The bruising on her chest was fading, only showing mottled yellow and light purple, and the gash she received in the creek was almost completely healed. Lex was lying still with her eyes closed. Not knowing what else to do to soothe her lover, Amanda brushed the dark bangs off her forehead. "Are you in much pain?"

Lex opened her eyes to meet Amanda's concerned gaze. "No, that's what's so strange. It's only a slight ache." She captured the hand running through her hair and brought it to her lips. "Is this where you tell me, 'I told you so?'" she asked, trying to get a smile from the worried young woman.

"No, Lex. This is where I say, 'I wish I wasn't right' because I hate seeing you go through this." Amanda looked at the wound again. "That looks really bad. I can't believe it's not hurting you because I hurt just looking at it."

Doctor Anderson came back in the room, followed by a young woman about the same age as Lex. "See?" he told the waiting women. "I told you we wouldn't be long. Laura, this is—" he was about to introduce Amanda when the small red-haired nurse spoke up.

"Amanda? How's your grandfather?" Laura walked over and gave Amanda a hug.

"He's doing great, thanks." Amanda stepped back, but kept one hand on the nurse's arm. "Grandpa talks about you quite a bit. He says you're the best nurse he ever had."

Laura laughed. "That's just because I would sneak him a milk-shake every now and then." She glanced at the woman lying on the exam table. "Lex. It's been a while, hasn't it?" Laura gave Amanda's hand a gentle pat, and then walked closer to look at Lex's side. "What have you done to yourself this time? Wreck a car? Fall off a horse?"

Doctor Anderson put on rubber gloves and pulled a rolling tray next to him and Laura. "No, actually something different, this time. Gunshot." He grinned as his nurse paled slightly.

"*Gunshot?* " Laura looked at the wound. "Dear Lord, Lex, do you thrive on trouble?" She gave the rancher's shoulder a slight squeeze, then turned to Amanda. "You don't have to watch. We can come and get you as soon as we're done."

Amanda shook her head. "I'd rather stay for moral support. That is, if I won't be in the way." When she saw the look of relief cross Lex's face, she was glad she made the offer. As tough as Lex tried to be, only Amanda knew how scared she was. *Don't worry, my love. I'm not going anywhere.*

"No, not at all." Laura pulled on her own gloves and then pointed at a chair by her patient's head. "You can sit right over there. Maybe with you here, we won't be subjected to your friend's bad language." She almost laughed out loud at the nasty look the woman on the bed was giving her.

"Hey, it wasn't my fault. That needle was huge!" Lex countered, glad that Laura was helping her in the effort to distract her worried friend.

Laura reached over to the rolling cart. "You think that one was big." She took the protective cap off the syringe she was holding. "I get to give you three of these!"

The doctor laughed. "Laura, don't tease my patient." He gave Lex a friendly pat on the leg. "Now, we're going to give you a local anesthetic, so try not to kick my nurse, okay?"

Rolling her eyes, Lex nodded. "Okay. But she could at least *pretend* not to enjoy it so much. I don't remember you being this sadistic in school, Laura."

"That's just because you didn't know me like you do now," the nurse retorted. "Now sit still, and I'll see if I feel like being gentle."

Chapter
Two

"DO YOU REALLY think that's such a good idea, Lex? The doctor said you should just lie down and take it easy for the rest of the day." Amanda was driving because the shots Doc Anderson had given Lex made her drowsy. Amanda sat up straighter, straining to see over the steering wheel. She felt somewhat dwarfed by the large hunter-green customized Dodge pickup, which they had picked up before going to the doctor's office. Her Mustang was now at the detail shop, only a block or so away from the mechanic where Lex's vehicle had been in for a tune-up.

Lex turned her head to look at Amanda, who was sitting with her leg tucked under herself. "My bank is on the same street as the pharmacy, and it won't take me but a minute to go in."

Stopped at a light, Amanda examined her passenger. Lex was unusually pale, and her eyes appeared slightly glazed. "Why don't you let me take you home, and then I'll go get your prescription?"

"I really need to get that paperwork from the bank. When I called Mr. Collins yesterday, I told him I would be in today to meet with him." Shifting in the seat, she closed her eyes as another wave of dizziness washed over her. *Damn shot. I felt better before I went to the stupid doctor.*

Amanda reached across the truck to touch Lex's arm. "I'm sure he'd understand."

"Maybe. But I won't be able to get any rest until I can look at those papers." Lex adjusted her arm until she was holding Amanda's hand. "Please, Amanda. I promise to make it quick." Seeing her friend begin to waver, she added, "You can come in with me to make sure, okay?"

Amanda didn't say anything, but she pulled the truck up to the bank and turned off the engine. "Five minutes, Lex. Then we're going to pick up your prescriptions, and I'm taking you home and putting you to bed." Seeing the smirk on Lex's face, she hurried to amend her remark. "You know what I mean."

"What? I didn't say a word." After slowly getting out of the vehicle, Lex stopped at the entrance to the bank and held the door open so Amanda could enter before her.

A short heavyset man in an expensive suit met them just inside the door. "Ms. Walters, what a pleasure to see you again." He grabbed her hand and began to shake it wildly. "Please, come into my office." Pausing, he looked at the woman standing next to one of his favorite customers, and it didn't matter to him what people said about the Walters woman. "Oh, excuse me, miss...?"

Lex turned and motioned to Amanda. " Forgive my lack of manners, Mr. Collins. This is a very good friend of mine, Amanda Cauble." She gestured at the banker. "Amanda, this is Mr. Collins, the president of this fine institution."

The introduction brought a blush to the banker's features. "That is too kind of you to say, Ms. Walters." He led them to a glassed-in office in the corner of the building and waited for them to step inside. "Please, have a seat." After Lex and Amanda each took a chair, the slightly balding man closed the door and sat down behind an ornate oak desk. "I received your email, Ms. Walters and personally gathered up the information you requested. And," he pulled out a small attaché case from under the desk, "not only was I discreet in my research, but I put everything in this case for you." His pudgy hands shook slightly. "You don't believe that anyone here at the bank would be involved in any illegal activities, do you?"

Lex waved a hand in the air to cut him off. "No, of course not, Mr. Collins. I just felt that the fewer people who knew about this, the better off we would all be."

The bank president visibly relaxed. "Ah, that's fine. Just fine. We will do anything to keep one of our best customers happy."

Amanda cleared her throat discreetly to get Lex's attention. Now that they had what they had come for, she was determined to make her lover keep her end of their deal.

Struggling to keep a smile from her face, Lex slowly stood up and extended her hand across the desk. "Mr. Collins, it's been a pleasure doing business with you, but I'm afraid I have another appointment." *And a girlfriend to appease. Besides, Amanda's right. I feel like I'm about to fall asleep standing up.*

"No problem, Ms. Walters. You have my home number if you need anything else, right?" Unaware of Lex's recent visit to the doctor, Collins pumped her hand enthusiastically.

Lex winced, then disentangled her hand from the beaming banker's grip and picked up the attaché case. "You'll be the first one I call, Mr. Collins." Before Amanda could "remind" her again, Lex led her partner from the room and out of the bank.

AMANDA RUSHED OUT of the pharmacy as soon as she was given Lex's prescriptions. Absorbed in her thoughts, she didn't see the large man about to go through the door. "Ooof! Excuse me." Stumbling back, she glanced up and saw who it was.

"Well, well. Hello there, sweet thing," a deep voice drawled. "Fancy meeting you here. Did you come in to pick up your birth control pills?" Rick Thompson, the manager from the realty office where she worked, blocked her exit by standing in front of Amanda with his thick arms crossed over his chest. "No, wait. I guess you don't need to worry about that sort of thing anymore, do you?"

Why do I have the sudden urge to go home and shower? Yuck! "It's really none of your business, Rick. So if you'll excuse me, I have someone waiting for me." She tried to edge past him, but was halted again when Rick grabbed her arm.

"Wait! I just want to talk to you for a minute. When will you be coming back to work?" Rick let Amanda wriggle out of his grasp, confident that she wouldn't go anywhere. He was having so much fun with the confrontation that he decided to see just how far he could push her. "So, have you had a nice *vacation*?"

Amanda pulled her arm back and slapped him, hard. "You sonofabitch!" Knowing that he had sent her out to Lex's ranch as a cruel prank, and nothing more, brought out Amanda's anger. She had come to care for the rancher a lot, and the thought of the man in front of her trying to hurt the woman she loved set her off.

Rick had actually been knocked back a step. "Why you little bitch. You're going to wish you'd never done that." He lunged forward and reached for Amanda, only to be stopped by a strong grip on his shoulder. Rick spun around, ready to pound on whoever had decided to interfere. "What?"

Bloodshot and angry eyes glared into his. "Problem?" Lex inquired coolly, even though it took all she had not to knock the an into the middle of next week.

"Mind your own damn business, Walters." Rick tried to pull away from Lex. "The little whore deserves whatever I want to do to her. She slapped me!" His tirade ended when Lex grabbed two handfuls of his suit coat, and got right in his face.

"So? From what I saw, you started the whole thing. Wanna try picking on someone your own size?" Although close to the same height, the realtor outweighed Lex by sixty pounds or more. She wasn't worried because she knew Rick was basically a coward. Not to mention how much she'd enjoy taking him down a peg or two.

"Why? What's it to you?" With his bravado fading, Rick's tone turned more wheedling.

Lex could feel her heart pounding in anger, which in turn caused her newly stitched wound to throb painfully. "She's a friend of mine, asshole."

Amanda took the opportunity to step around Rick, and moved to stand behind her agitated lover. Placing one hand on Lex's back, she whispered, "Let it go, Lex. He's not worth it."

Only for Amanda's sake, Lex released her hold on Rick's jacket, then stepped back and took a deep breath. When she saw the big man begin to smile, she moved forward until they were inches apart. "If I *ever* hear of you speaking about her that way again, they're gonna have to use glue to put your sorry carcass back together." Believing she made her point, Lex allowed Amanda to escort her away from the scene.

Three passersby had stopped to stare. "This ain't over yet," Rick yelled halfheartedly. "Not by a long shot!" He aimed a fist at the departing women. "You'd better be careful who you're threatening around here."

Neither woman turned around, but Lex raised a hand over her head and waved it in the air. "Yeah, right." She followed Amanda back to the truck and climbed inside.

Amanda closed her door and leaned against the steering wheel. She looked over at Lex who was slumped in her seat with her eyes closed. "Are you all right?"

Lex pulled herself together and sighed. "Yeah, but that jerk has always been able to yank my chain." She turned her head and did a quick visual inspection of her friend. "He didn't hurt you, did he?"

"Nah." Amanda gave her a strained smile and then started the truck. "Only the palm of my hand when I slapped him." She flexed her hand to ease the stinging, and then pulled the vehicle out of the parking lot. "Let's go home, so that I can tuck you into bed."

"Mmm, I think I can handle that." Lex's eyes closed and her head fell back against the seat, almost against her will. "Damn, Laura must have given me some sort of sedative. I can barely stay awake."

"Yeah, she did say she was going to give you something to help you relax." Amanda quieted when she saw Lex had fallen asleep. She felt a strong protective urge come over her. *Rick's real lucky he didn't start anything with her, or I would have done more than just slap him.* She drove the rest of the way home in contemplative silence, taking her time and avoiding the main streets and their potholes. The last thing she wanted was for Lex to be jarred anymore than necessary.

Amanda saw her grandparents walking out to their Suburban as she pulled up into their driveway. She got out of the truck and met them halfway.

"Mandy." Anna Leigh embraced her granddaughter in a loving hug. "We were getting concerned since you've been gone for hours." She looked to the truck, barely able to make out the still form in the passenger's seat. "Is Lexington going to come inside?"

Jacob joined the two of them. "You just caught us on our way to the car dealership. They called to say your grandmother's new car is ready." He had been driving his wife's car when a drunk driver hit him six months before. They had waited to order her a new one until Jacob's doctor had cleared him to drive, not seeing any sense in having an extra vehicle with only one driver.

"Hi, Grandpa." Amanda stepped into his welcoming arms. "I take it you've finally been given a clean bill of health?"

"Yep."

Amanda backed off a step. "That's great news." She pointed to the truck and its sleeping occupant. "Lex dozed off on the drive back. They had to reopen the bullet wound because it was infected, and Laura gave her a sedative to keep her calm."

Jacob smiled. "How is Laura? She was such a sweetheart to me, although I think I gained a few pounds from those contraband milkshakes she kept sneaking to me." Jacob looked at the sleeping figure in the truck. "Do you need any help getting Lex into the house?"

Amanda followed his gaze, and her eyes softened at the picture her lover made. "No, I'll wake her up in a minute. At least I should be able to get her to rest today." She gave both her grandparents a hug. "You two go ahead and pick up that new car. I can't wait to see it."

Once Jacob and Anna Leigh had driven off, Amanda walked back over to the 4x4. She opened the passenger door slowly, so as not to startle the woman sleeping inside. "Lex? Honey, it's time to wake up." Amanda tenderly brushed the hair away from Lex's eyes, which slowly opened at her touch. "Hey there."

Lex looked around, somewhat disoriented. She cleared her throat, before attempting to speak. "Hi." After blinking a couple of times, she finally recognized where they were and wiped a shaky hand across her face. "I'm sorry. I didn't mean to drop off like that."

"Don't worry about it." Amanda unclipped Lex's seat belt. "Do you think you can make it into the house?"

Rolling her eyes, Lex sat up and swung her legs out of the truck. "Relax, I'm fine. Just a little drugged up."

Amanda took a step back, but stayed within arms' reach. "Okay. Well, I'm staying right here, just in case." Her tone dared the other woman to argue with her. She saw how woozy Lex was.

"Waste of time." Lex slid out of the truck, but her legs buckled as soon as she put her weight on them. "Whoa!"

Amanda jumped forward and caught Lex before she fell. She

wrapped an arm around her partner's waist and struggled to slam the truck door. "Teach you to not listen to me." She started toward the house slowly, grumbling all the while. "Of all the stubborn, pig-headed, obstinate things—"

"It's not my fault," Lex complained, but never released her grip on Amanda. "I just wasn't awake yet." The battle lost, Lex allowed Amanda to guide her into the house and up the stairs.

Walking into the bedroom that they shared, Amanda led Lex to the bed. She pulled the comforter back and pushed Lex down gently. Silently, Amanda lifted her lover's feet up, removed her boots, and began to unsnap Lex's jeans.

The silence was beginning to bother her, so Lex attempted to joke to ease the tension. "If you wanted to get me into bed, all you had to do was say so." Reaching down to help with her jeans, she was startled when her hands were batted away. "What?"

Amanda tugged the jeans down the long legs, then folded them neatly and placed them on a nearby chair. "Hush." She rooted out a soft cotton nightshirt from Lex's suitcase and draped it over the bemused woman. After lifting the covers over Lex, Amanda went into the adjoining bathroom and brought out a glass of water. On her return, she stopped by her purse to grab the prescription bottles. "Here, take these. I'm going to go downstairs and get you something to eat."

Puzzled, Lex did as she was told, then set the glass down on the bedside table. "Okay. Are you mad at me?"

Stopping at the doorway, Amanda realized how it must seem to the other woman. "No honey, I'm not." She walked back to the bed and sat next to Lex. "I'm sorry. I just wanted to get you settled before you fell asleep again." She brought a hand up and caressed her lover's cheek before standing up. Amanda bent down and kissed Lex on the top of the head. "I'll be right back, so try and behave yourself for a few minutes."

Lex realized she wasn't going to win any arguments today, so she decided not to even try. "Yes ma'am. Could you do me a favor and bring the bank papers with you? I'd really like to start looking them over."

"Sure, if you promise to get some rest first." Amanda countered, standing at the doorway. "I'll even help you if you want."

Lex leaned back against the pillows. "It's a deal." She felt another wave of lethargy wash over her. *What in the hell did they give me? I feel like I could sleep for a week.* She closed her eyes and didn't even notice when Amanda slipped from the room.

SOME TIME LATER, Amanda sat at the kitchen table nursing a

cup of coffee, when Jacob and Anna Leigh returned from the dealership.

Jacob sat down next to her, his strong face etched with concern. He didn't see Lex anywhere and found it hard to believe that the two women, who had been practically inseparable since they arrived, would be apart. "Peanut, is everything okay?"

"Hmm? Oh, sure, Grandpa." With everything that had happened so far, Amanda's day was shaping up to be less than stellar. "It's just been one of those days. Mother called while you were gone."

Anna Leigh sat down on the other side of her granddaughter. "Oh? Is there anything wrong?"

Amanda shook her head. "No, she called to see how Grandpa was feeling, and to find out why I haven't called *her* for so long. I told her that everything was great, and that you'd gone to pick up your new car." Now came the hard part. "Mother says since I'm 'not needed' here anymore, she wants me to come back to Los Angeles and help her with the gallery."

Jacob put a strong arm around Amanda's shoulders. "Help with the gallery? She rarely spends any time there, herself, these days." He looked at his wife. "I wonder what she's up to now?"

"Maybe she just misses you, Mandy." Anna Leigh tried to be tactful. The fact was, Elizabeth Cauble only seemed interested in her children when she needed something from them. To her, there were things much more important, like traveling to Europe, handling her many business dealings, and looking good at community functions. "Did she give you any other reason for wanting you to come back?"

Amanda ran her hand through her dark blonde hair in agitation. "Not really. She did say she and Dad were about to go out of the country again. But she usually leaves Jeannie in charge of the gallery, so I don't know why she wants me there." Her older sister had rarely come to visit, spending most of her time traveling, much to Jacob and Anna Leigh's dismay. Amanda wiped a tear from her eye. "I told her I wanted to stay here permanently, because I've found someone I truly care about, and I'm happy for the first time in a very long time."

Anna Leigh squeezed her hand. "What did Elizabeth say about that?"

"She said I was too young to know what I wanted, and that this was probably just a 'phase' I'm going through." Amanda sat up straighter and gave her grandmother a resolved look. "It's not a phase, Gramma. I've never felt anything more right in my entire life. And I'm not giving this up."

Jacob pulled her close. "We're both behind you one hundred

percent." He shared a look with his wife. "Funny thing is, I think your grandmother was told the same thing when we first started dating."

Wealthy and about halfway spoiled, Anna Leigh Winston literally ran into Jacob one summer at the lake. He was nineteen and worked for the maintenance manager, while she was there with her well-to-do family. The seventeen-year old Anna had knocked the lanky youth to the ground, scattering the wood he carried, and the moment her green eyes met his blue ones, it was love at first sight. They spent the entire summer together, and while she thought he was there as a guest, he never realized she was part of one of the rich families who took over the lake in the summer.

At the end of the summer, when Jacob removed his grandmother's silver ring that he wore on his pinkie and proposed, Anna couldn't have been happier. Unfortunately, her family didn't see it the same way and forbade them to have any more contact with each other.

"She was the most gorgeous woman I'd ever seen," Jacob related to his granddaughter. "Her father didn't think I was good enough, and so, to keep us apart, he put Anna on a ship to Europe, knowing I didn't have the money to follow. But I ruined that, didn't I, my love?"

Anna Leigh laughed. "I'd forgotten all about that." She looked down at the small silver band on her right hand. Seeing Amanda's questioning look, she explained, "My family was considered to be in the upper echelon of Austin society at that time. Father thought your grandfather was 'beneath my station,' and he even went so far as to send me to Paris for one summer. I had been there for six miserable weeks when a certain young gentleman showed up on my doorstep."

"Grandpa?" Amanda whispered, mesmerized by the story. "How did—" She looked at her grandfather, who had a slight blush on his face, much to the delight of his wife.

"Well, since Jacob didn't have the kind of money needed for passage, he worked his way across on a ship. I believe it was a cattle ship, wasn't it dear?"

Jacob finally laughed. "Oh yes. I shoveled sh...er, by-product for almost five weeks. Talk about an adventure." Seeing the delighted smile on his granddaughter's face, he knew they had successfully sidetracked her from her previous depression. "To this day, I can't even look at a bag of fertilizer without traumatic flashbacks."

A scratchy voice spoke up from the doorway. "Guess that means you won't be out to visit the ranch anytime soon, huh?"

"Lex, what are you doing up?" Amanda rose from her chair at

the table and hurried to her lover. "You should be in bed."

The tired woman allowed herself to be steered to the table and guided into a chair. "I feel much better now, especially since I've finally got all that medication out of my system. But remind me to get even with Laura the next time I see her."

Jacob chuckled. "She's pretty good at that, I remember." His concern for his granddaughter's companion caused him to turn serious. "You really should be in bed resting, Lex. You still look pretty pale."

"No, I hate lying in bed. It makes me feel like I'm sick or something." Lex raised a hand to stop Amanda before she could add anything. "I really feel fine. Besides, I've got some paperwork to start looking over."

Amanda realized she would not win this round. "Okay, but only for a little while. Then you're going to get some more rest—or else." She shook a warning finger at Lex, who seemed amused by her protectiveness.

"Or else what?" Lex smirked. She glanced over at Jacob, who was trying not to laugh.

Watch out, my young friend. Our little Amanda's a lot tougher than she looks. Jacob met his wife's eyes, which were also dancing with merriment.

Amanda placed her hand on Lex's shoulder and gave it a light squeeze. "Or else I'll call Martha and tell her you're not taking care of yourself." She loved the scowl that replaced the cocky smile on Lex's face. "I'm sure she'll be glad to haul you back out to the ranch for a little TLC."

"You wouldn't," Lex sputtered. It annoyed her to no end how quickly Amanda and Martha had joined forces against her, at least in her mind. Even though they only wanted what was best for her, she hated being treated like a recalcitrant child, first by the house-keeper, and now by her lover. And seeing Jacob and Anna Leigh both fighting to keep from laughing out loud, she knew when she'd been beaten. "You would, wouldn't you? All right. You win, for now, anyway."

Trying to stop the battle, Anna Leigh decided on another tact. "Lexington, you are quite welcome to use our office for your work. The desk is more than large enough to spread everything out on, I believe."

"Thank you, Mrs. Cauble, uh, I mean Anna Leigh." *That's going to take some getting used to, I think.* "I really appreciate you allowing me to stay here while I get some business taken care of, especially since my brother and I are not getting along very well right now, and I couldn't very well stay at his house." *Yeah, that's an understatement.*

"Come on." Amanda grabbed Lex's hand and helped her to her feet. "I'll show you where the office is, and help you get settled." She smiled at her grandparents as she tugged her friend out of the room.

AMANDA LED THE way through the house, bringing Lex into a spacious room off the main hall. Expansive bay windows with flower-patterned curtains brightened the room, which had a large antique cherry wood desk sitting in front of the windows, and several oversized chairs in complementary colors that were scattered around the room.

"This is where Gramma keeps track of things at the real estate office, even though she officially retired a couple of years ago." Amanda showed Lex the state-of-the-art computer occupying one whole side of the desk. "She keeps after me to take over for her, but until recently, I really didn't have any good reason to live here permanently." The smile she gave her companion told of Amanda's change of heart. "Let's relax for a minute before you get too engrossed in paperwork." She guided Lex to a sofa, then dropped beside her with a sigh.

Lex watched as Amanda nervously played with their clasped hands, and a small tremor of fear ran through her. *Something's bothering her, but what? Bite the bullet time, I think.* "Amanda?" Lex used her free hand to caress Amanda's cheek, until they were looking eye to eye. "What's the matter?" Seeing a small sparkle of tears in the eyes so close to hers, a lump formed in Lex's throat. "You know you can tell me, right?"

"I know, it's just that, well, my mother called today." Amanda struggled to put her feelings into words. "I'm twenty-three years old, and yet every time I talk to her, I feel like I'm sixteen again." She felt the reassuring grip on her hand tighten slightly. "She wants me to come back to Los Angeles and work in her art gallery."

Lex stiffened. "And," she had to clear her throat, "what do you want?" Although her heart was pounding, she tried to appear calm for her lover's sake. She realized that Amanda must have noticed, because she scooted closer until she was almost sitting in Lex's lap.

"I want," Amanda pulled their linked hands up to her lips, "to stay here." She kissed the hand in hers. "I want to tell my grandmother that I would be glad to run her office for her, and—" Amanda was unable to finish her thought, as she was pulled up into Lex's arms, and her mouth was captured in a passionate kiss. She tangled her hands in Lex's hair and pulled them even closer together. Amanda trembled as she felt Lex's hands roam across her shoulders, mapping across her shirt with sweet urgency. Pulling away to look at Lex's face, she whispered, "I just found you." Seeing answering tears shine in those incredible eyes so near hers, she continued, "And I'm not ready to give you up. Not for my mother; not for anyone."

Lex looked into Amanda's face and saw a determination so fierce, it almost took her breath away. *She really means this.* Feeling her misgivings crumble beneath that gaze, Lex tried to think of words to convey what she was feeling in her heart. "I love you." Those three little words felt woefully inadequate to Lex, when what she felt was so much more. But when she saw the answering smile break across Amanda's face, she realized it was more than enough.

"I love you, too." Amanda leaned forward to place a soothing kiss on Lex's mouth. It was not the heated kiss of a moment before, but one affirming the commitment Amanda had made to Lex in her heart. The kind that lovers give to each other when all questions of belonging have been settled. Breaking off, she snuggled her face into the tan neck, happy to simply absorb the feeling of love that seemed to surround her.

They sat there quietly for a while, content just to hold one other, until a ringing phone made them both jump. The moment broken, Amanda slid off Lex's lap and had just curled up next to her again when Anna Leigh came into the room.

"I'm sorry to disturb you, Mandy, but your father is on the phone, and he wants to talk to you."

"Gramma, are you okay?" Amanda stood and walked over to her grandmother. "Did he say something to upset you?" She felt Lex come up behind her and place a hand on the small of her back, which comforted her somewhat.

"I'm fine, dearest." Anna Leigh didn't want to upset her granddaughter any more than the day already had. "God knows I love my son, but he can be so small-minded at times. I've often wondered where we went wrong with him." But, in her heart, she did know. Her parents, trying to make up for losing their daughter to a "working man," gave young Michael the best of everything, even when Jacob and Anna Leigh strenuously argued against it. His grandparents showered him with expensive clothes, fancy cars, and contributed to him deciding at an early age that money was the most important thing in the world, no matter how much his parents tried to tell him otherwise. And when his grandparents introduced him to a young socialite from a wealthy family, Michael immediately saw his opportunity and proposed. Anna Leigh often wondered how Amanda could have come from such a business-like merger.

"Guess I'd better get this over with." Amanda went to the desk and picked up the phone. "Hello, Daddy." She listened for a few minutes, her normally cheerful demeanor becoming more clouded by the minute. Looking across the room, she saw Lex and her grandmother were in a deep discussion. Putting her hand over the mouthpiece, she whispered, "Lex." No other words need be spoken. Her lover crossed the room quickly to take Amanda into her arms.

Looks like she's in good hands, now. Anna Leigh left the room quietly, closing the door behind her.

"I know what Mother wants, but as I told her earlier today, I'm staying here in Somerville." Tears welled up in her eyes as she listened to her father's tirade. "I'm a grown woman, Dad. I love you and Mother, but there's nothing there for me anymore." She took a deep breath as Lex pulled her tight, kissing her lightly on top of her head. "I've found someone I love very much, and I'm very happy here." She leaned back into the strong arms that now supported her. "Yes, Gramma and Grandpa know about us. She's staying here with us right now, as a matter of fact." Amanda pulled the phone away from her ear as he father began to rant in earnest now. "No! She's not like that. Gramma and Grandpa have accepted my choices, why can't you?" Amanda felt the tears of frustration fall down her face. "I'm sorry you feel that way, *Father*." She slowly placed the phone back on its base, then turned and tucked herself into the strong body behind her and began to cry. "Oh, God."

Lex was at a loss. *What can I say to her without sounding like a selfish fool?* She leaned down and whispered into Amanda's ear. "Shhh. It's going to be alright, sweetheart."

Amanda cried herself out, feeling a deep sense of loss. "He doesn't want anything to do with me until I 'come to my senses.' He thinks that all you want is my money, and that you're just using me." She looked up, expecting to see anger. The emotion that greeted her was even more surprising.

Laughing out loud, Lex gave Amanda a strong squeeze. "You're kidding, right?" She released her hold and moved over to a small table, where the attaché case from the bank had been placed earlier. After a short search, Lex pulled out an envelope and handed Amanda a piece of paper. "Read the balance on the statement."

Once her eyes scanned the page, Amanda couldn't help but echo Lex's words. "You're kidding, right?" According to what she'd read, the woman standing before her had more money than both her parents combined.

Lex shook her head. "Nope. My mother's family did okay for themselves, and with the investments I've made in the past few years, it's safe to say that I won't be trying to clean out your bank accounts in the middle of the night."

"Not that I ever had any worries in that regard, Lex. I don't use my parent's money. Which has caused its own share of arguments." Amanda stepped into Lex's arms. "I don't care if you were just a poor ranch hand, I'd still be in love with you."

"I know. And you should know that I fell in love with you the moment I pulled you out of the creek. I had no idea who you were, but there was just something about you I couldn't resist." Lex pulled Amanda closer and then kissed her on the temple. "So, are you going to help me read all these damn reports? Maybe you can figure out where all the money is going."

Amanda allowed herself to be led back to the desk, where she sat on a nearby chair. "Sure. I help with the bookwork at the office all the time. I love numbers."

Happy with the answer, Lex handed her a pile of papers. "Maybe I should hire you to do my paperwork at the ranch? I hate sitting in an office when I can be outside doing something instead."

"I'd love to." Amanda started to sort the papers into some semblance of order. Not able to resist tweaking her friend, she couldn't help but ask, "What are you willing to pay?"

Lex gave her a sexy look. "I think we could work something out." After getting the expected blush from Amanda, she also started dividing the papers she had into neat little piles.

They worked quietly for almost two hours, each woman studying the papers before her. Amanda finally found a pattern to the losses. She handed a paper to Lex, pointing out her find. "Look. This is the third time I've seen this."

"Now that you mentioned it, I've seen it a couple of times myself." Lex dug through a pile, then jumped to her feet. "That sonofabitch!" She threw the papers down and began to stomp through the room. "I'll kill him!"

"Lex, wait!" Amanda jumped up from her chair and caught the enraged woman before she could reach the door. Latching onto a strong arm, she forced Lex to turn and face her.

Spinning around, Lex was about to sling off the annoyance when a quiet voice cut through the red haze of her fury.

"Lex?" Amanda spoke quietly, hoping to calm the angry woman as one would a wild animal. "Hey, come back in here and sit down, please?" She thought at first Lex was just going to brush her aside and continue out the door, but the eyes burning with rage softened, and she allowed herself to be guided to the sofa.

Leaning back, Lex closed her eyes and took a shaky breath. "I'm sorry." She felt the anger ebb away, leaving only weariness in its place.

Amanda sat next to her, feeling her own heart slowly return to its normal rhythm. She watched as Lex finally calmed down, seeing the tense lines on her face gradually soften. Picking up the hand clinched into a tight fist, she coaxed it open, entwining their fingers together. "Shhh. There's nothing to be sorry about."

Lex pulled their joined hands up until they were against her chest. Bending her face down, she placed a very light kiss on Amanda's knuckles. "I'm sorry you had to witness that." Opening her eyes, Lex looked down at their hands, still unable to bring herself to meet her lover's gaze. "But better you know now how I can be, I guess."

"Look at me."

The quiet demand was something Lex couldn't refuse. She took a deep breath and slowly raised her eyes, expecting to see fear or disgust for her lack of control. Lex was surprised at the amount of love and understanding she saw through the shining eyes across from her. Opening her mouth to speak, she found her lips gently covered with a soft fingertip.

"If that's the best you can do to scare me off, you're in big trouble." Seeing Lex take a breath to speak, Amanda shook her head. "No, wait. I know you have a temper. But if you ask anyone in my family, they'll tell you I have a pretty short fuse myself." Taking her hand away from Lex's mouth, she used it instead to caress her lover's cheek. "So, between the two of us, everyone else had better watch out." When she saw that Lex's eyes were turning watery, Amanda threaded her fingers behind her partner's neck and pulled her head forward. She gave Lex a gentle kiss, then leaned back. "Would it help you to talk about it?"

Lex bent forward again until their foreheads were touching. "It's kind of hard to explain." Her voice dropped to a hoarse whisper and her eyes involuntarily closed. "It's about the missing money." When her hand was released, she felt a heavy weight descend onto her chest, until strong arms wrapped themselves around her body. Pulling Amanda into her lap, Lex snuggled close. "It's not the amount of money that bothers me, honestly."

Amanda stroked the dark head tenderly. "Shhh. I know that honey." Even though they'd only known each other a short while, Amanda could say without a doubt that money was the last thing Lex ever thought about. She felt the body under hers tremble slightly.

"My own brother." Lex sniffed, trying to control her emotions. The feeling of betrayal hurt almost as bad as the knowledge of who was behind the loss of money. "How can my own brother be embezzling money from the ranch?"

No wonder she's so upset. Amanda could feel the quiet shuddering that told her of Lex's hurt. She had never seen Lex cry, at least not like this. "Maybe there's another explanation."

Lex pulled herself together and reclined slightly so she could look into Amanda's face. "I could probably handle the fact that he's taking money from the ranch, since he really never got over the fact that Dad signed it over to me." She gave Amanda a weak smile, as delicate fingertips wiped the tears from her face. "But the way he's done it. I really never thought the slimy bastard was that smart."

"He can't be too smart, since you've caught him at it," Amanda remarked, relieved to see her companion was feeling more like herself.

"That's just it, Amanda. Looking at the statements and receipts, we haven't caught him." She helped Amanda get off her lap, then picked up several papers from the desk. She showed her partner a signature on the withdrawal slip. "Look right here." It read *Lexington M. Walters.* "We've caught me."

Chapter
Three

LATER THAT EVENING, Amanda convinced Lex to tell her grandparents what was going on, since each of them had been running their own businesses for years. She was hoping their different perspectives would help them find an easier solution, one that didn't include Lex having to testify against her only living sibling, and possibly sending him to prison. *I think she'd feel more guilt than anything else, not to mention the embarrassment of dragging all of this out in public*, Amanda reasoned.

"So, he's been withdrawing money by signing your name to the slips for the last few months?" Anna Leigh asked, while she looked at the receipts from the bank. "And since all the statements had been sent to him, you're just now finding out about it?"

Lex sat in a nearby chair with her head propped in her hands. "I know. It was totally irresponsible of me not to have copies of the statements sent to the ranch every month." She was feeling more and more foolish by the minute.

Amanda, who was perched on the arm of Lex's chair, rubbed her lover's back to try and comfort her. "I think what Gramma is wondering is why the bank hadn't figured out that anything unusual was happening." She looked at her grandmother, who nodded in agreement.

"Goodness, Lexington. I never meant for you to think I was questioning your business sense." She waited until Lex looked up at her. "It's just that the only time I can see you've withdrawn money without using a check is when your brother has done it. And then, it was for fairly large amounts. I just can't believe they actually allowed this to happen without some sort of authorization."

Jacob looked up from the stack of papers he studied. "She's right. Those idiots at the bank should have realized something was wrong a long time ago. Unless someone there is in on it, too."

Lex closed her eyes as a sudden wave of exhaustion washed over her. "I've already called Mr. Collins and told him not to allow

any more withdrawals from this account without verifying that the
person that's doing them is authorized." She leaned her head back
against the chair. "I'm going to take your advice and go down
tomorrow to open a new account, so Hubert won't have access to
the ranch funds anymore."

Anna Leigh and Jacob both eyed the rancher with concern.
Amanda gazed down, seeing that Lex had closed her eyes. "Lex?"
She ran a hand gently through the dark hair. "I believe you've done
all you can today." She waited for her lover to look up at her. "It's
getting pretty late, so why don't we head upstairs to bed?"

"Yeah, I think you're right. I'm beat." Lex slowly stood up and
looked self-consciously at her feet, addressing the couple at the
desk. "I really appreciate all your help today. I don't know what I
would have done without you." She raised her head and rubbed
her eyes. "I was just so shocked when I found out who was behind
all of this, I couldn't think straight."

Anna Leigh moved around the desk so she could wrap her
arms around Lex. "Oh, dearest, you're part of the family. We'll
always be here for you."

Jacob stood beside them, giving Lex's shoulder a gentle
squeeze. "That's right, Lex. Now get yourself upstairs and get some
rest."

Lex stepped back and gave them both a heartfelt look. "Thank
you. I wish I had known my own grandparents. But I have a feeling
they couldn't have held a candle to you two." She then allowed
Amanda to steer her out of the office and up the stairs.

When her lover placed an arm around her shoulders, Amanda
quickly became worried. "Lex, are you all right?"

"Yeah, I'm fine. Just enjoying the company." The answering
swat on her rear elicited a small chuckle from Lex. "And I am a little tired. It's been one hell of a long day." Weary, she let Amanda
guide her to the bed, where she sat down and enjoyed the attention
she received.

Amanda unbuttoned Lex's shirt. "Have you taken your medicine this evening, Lex?" Not waiting for an answer, she efficiently
stripped her partner and then reached into their suitcase and
picked up a clean nightshirt for Lex to wear. "Here, put this on."
Once again she dressed Lex as if she were a child. Before Amanda
could finish buttoning the shirt, she felt her hands gently captured.

"Amanda." Lex spoke quietly, so as not to send the wrong
message to the woman she loved. "Please stop fussing so much.
You're going to wear yourself out." She brought Amanda's hands
to her lips and placed a soft kiss on the delicate knuckles. "Why
don't you get undressed and join me?"

Amanda blinked, suddenly self-conscious about what she had

been doing. "Oh. I didn't even realize—" She pulled away and grabbed her own nightshirt from a nearby dresser. Stripping efficiently, Amanda didn't notice the appreciative eyes watching her until she had slipped the long tee shirt over her head. "What?"

"Have I ever told you how beautiful you are?" Lex asked, in a reverent tone. "Just looking at you makes my heart beat faster."

"Oh, come on. I think that medication you're on is affecting your eyes." Amanda thought it was funny, until she noticed the expression on Lex's face. She moved over to the bed to join Lex. "You really think so?"

Lex pulled her close, then rolled over onto her back and tucked Amanda against her left side. "Oh, yeah. Most definitely."

Amanda felt an unexpected surge of happiness flow through her with that thought. *Wow.* "Thank you," she murmured, absorbing the feeling with joy.

"You're welcome." Lex pulled her even closer, if that were possible. "Love you." She managed to say before sleep claimed her.

"I love you, too," Amanda whispered, then she kissed the shoulder underneath her cheek and closed her eyes to join Lex in slumber.

THE EARLY MORNING sun burst brightly through the windows, causing Amanda to open her eyes and groan. In an attempt to ward off the impending day, she buried her face back into her pillow. Feeling the pillow move, she reopened one eye and realized the surface her head was propped up on was actually breathing. *Amazing. I actually woke up first.* Reaching up with one hand, Amanda touched Lex's forehead. *No fever. That's a good sign.* She thought about getting up, but Lex had her arm wrapped possessively around her shoulder, and Amanda really didn't have the heart to disturb her. *So I guess I'll just suffer here in bed. What a hardship.* Amanda wrapped her arms tightly around the firm body beneath her and drifted back to sleep.

Lex awoke sometime later, pleased to note that the fuzzy feeling from the medication was gone, and the wound in her side didn't hurt at all. Amanda was still sprawled against her with her head snuggled up under Lex's chin. Looking out the window, Lex could see the late morning sun streaming in. *I can't believe I slept so late.* She peered fondly at her companion. *She's not gonna let me live this down for a while, I'll bet.* Pulling her friend close, Lex kissed the top of her head. "Amanda." She felt one arm squeeze her tighter. "Come on, sweetheart, time to get up. We can't lounge around in bed all day."

"Mmm, no," Amanda grumbled. "Don't wanna." She buried

her head deeper into Lex's shoulder.

Desperate times call for desperate measures. Lex slowly edged a hand under Amanda's nightshirt and tickled her ribs.

"Hey," Amanda squealed, moving back quickly. "That's not nice." Sitting up, she rearranged her shirt. "You act like you're feeling better today."

Lex rolled over onto her left side and propped her head up with one hand. "Yep, good as new."

Amanda mirrored her posture. "I wouldn't go that far. You still need to take it easy for a few days. Doctor's orders." Seeing the decidedly evil grin that broke out across Lex's face, Amanda quickly rolled out of bed and started for the bathroom. *I don't know what she's thinking, but I'll bet I won't like it.* "Don't give me that look," she warned, not even bothering to turn around. She was almost to the doorway when she was caught from behind. Quick hands reached under her shirt and began tracing a gentle pattern on her stomach, revving up Amanda's libido.

"Want me to scrub your back?"

Amanda felt her legs weaken as Lex's lips started a tender assault on her neck. "Umm." She lifted her arms back over her head to tangle her hands in the Lex's hair. The searching hands began to drift upward, then took a firm grasp on responsive flesh. "Oh, yeah. Sharing is good," Amanda murmured, then allowed Lex to guide her into the bathroom.

By the time they made it downstairs, the kitchen was strangely quiet. Amanda steered Lex to a chair at the table. "Looks like I finally get to cook your breakfast." She brought over a mug of coffee and placed it in front of her lover. "Here, you can start with this."

Lex took a sip of the brew and watched as Amanda turned on the griddle at the stove to heat. "Thanks. You really don't have to wait on me hand and foot, or cook my breakfast. We can always stop and get some doughnuts or something."

"No way. Those things will kill you. Besides, I like taking care of you, and I've never had anyone to pamper before. So get used to it." Amanda shook a finger at her, indicating that no more arguments would be heard, then turned and started to pull items out of the refrigerator.

Anna Leigh walked into the kitchen to refill her coffee cup. "Good morning, girls." She gave Amanda a hug, then kissed Lex on top of the head as she joined her at the table. She missed the startled look on the rancher's face, which turned into a relaxed smile. "What kind of trouble are the two of you planning on getting into today?"

Amanda turned away from the counter where she was stirring

pancake batter. "Funny you should ask, Gramma. I was going to talk to you about that."

"Really? Well, here I am, so ask away. Do you need me to do something for you?"

Even though the conversation was serious to her, Amanda kept her concentration on her cooking. She poured the batter onto the griddle using a gravy ladle, so that the pancakes would all be the same size. "Actually, I was hoping it was something I could do for you." Keeping one eye on the griddle, she partially turned to look at her grandmother. "Since I've decided to live here in Somerville on a more permanent basis, I was wondering—"

Her sentence was cut short as Anna Leigh leaped to her feet, rushed to the stove, and wrapped Amanda in an exuberant hug. "You're staying? That's wonderful, Mandy!" She leaned back to look her granddaughter in the eye. "Does this also mean I have a new office manager? Two people have called in the past week to give notice because of Rick." Anna Leigh felt bad that things had gotten this much out of hand, but her thoughts had been focused on Jacob's health. The real estate office had been on the bottom of her priority list after her husband's accident.

Giving her grandmother a squeeze, Amanda returned her attention to the pancakes. "If you still want me to, then yes." Flipping them over, she turned to Anna Leigh. "But," Amanda pointed the spatula, "only if you think I'd be the best person for the job."

"Absolutely. When can you start?" Anna Leigh clapped her hands and then resumed her place at the table across from Lex. "Would you two mind meeting me at the office this afternoon? I can't wait to get rid of that sorry excuse for a human being." Although normally fearless in business, Anna would rather have as many witnesses as possible when she dismissed the hulking Rick Thompson, just in case he took his termination in a bad way.

"I can't speak for Amanda, but I would love to be there when you give the ax to that worthless son of a...goat." Looking at her partner's back, she decided to share an anecdote with Anna Leigh to show the older woman just how gutsy her new manager was. "Did Amanda tell you she had a run-in with him yesterday? He probably has a nice little bruise to show for it, too."

"Really? What happened?"

Amanda groaned. Her escapade with Rick was the last thing she wanted her grandmother to hear. "I couldn't help it. He started mouthing off, and I just lost my temper." Amanda placed the pancakes on plates and brought them to the table.

"And?" Anna Leigh drew out the word, expectantly.

"I slapped him." Embarrassed at her loss of control, Amanda sat down next her lover. *You are in so much trouble when we're alone,*

Lex. I can't believe we're sitting here discussing this.

Lex snorted. "More like knocked him silly. He nearly fell over."

"Good Lord, Mandy! That man is huge. He could have seriously hurt you," her grandmother scolded.

Amanda made it a point to look over at Lex. *All right, Miss Tough Stuff. Two can play this game.* "I wasn't worried. Lex got into his face and nearly made him wet his pants." They all burst into laughter at that thought. "But please, Gramma, wait until we get there before you do anything. I really don't trust him."

"Certainly, dearest. That would work out better, anyway. Jacob has been going stir crazy, so he's decided to work in his shop for a little while, and he's gone now to get supplies. He's just so glad to be able to drive himself around again."

"I can sympathize, since I nearly drove Martha crazy when I broke my leg a couple of years ago." Lex recalled the incident with humor, although at the time she had been ready to gnaw the cast off so that she could become more mobile again.

"How did—" Amanda shook her head. "Never mind. I don't think I want to know."

Anna Leigh gave Lex a sympathetic look. "Wasn't that when you rolled your truck during that nasty ice storm?"

"Yes, ma'am. That whole mess is the reason Martha insisted that I start carrying a cell phone. She gets pretty upset when I forget to take it." *Like the night I went to check the fence in a thunderstorm. Well, at least that worked out.* Seeing Amanda's questioning look, she shrugged. "It happened on a Friday afternoon, and they didn't find me until Saturday night."

"I remember. I swear, she almost called out the National Guard." Anna Leigh turned to explain to Amanda, "Martha called everyone on the Historical Committee and had nearly every ablebodied man in the county combing every inch of the roads between here and the ranch."

Horrified, Amanda touched Lex's arm in an attempt to connect with her lover. "Dear God, that must have been horrible for you."

"It really wasn't that bad. I don't remember much about it." Lex tried to appear nonchalant.

Anna Leigh slapped Lex on her other arm. "That's because you were unconscious for most of it, silly." When she heard the news, Anna had been surprised that the rancher survived the ordeal. She didn't know if she herself had that kind of strength. Then she remembered nursing Jacob through his own injuries. *I suppose we all have that strength, somewhere. I just hope these two don't ever have to find out.*

"See? I told you it wasn't that bad." Lex stood up and put her plate in the dishwasher. When she was done, she leaned back against the counter and asked Amanda, "Are you about ready? I'd like to get my business with the bank done as soon as possible."

"Yeah, I'm done." Amanda put her dishes away, then kissed her grandmother's cheek. "See you at the office around one o'clock, Gramma?"

"That will be perfect. You two try and stay out of trouble until then, if that's possible." When both women rolled their eyes, she couldn't help but add, "I know it's a lot to ask, but—" Their laughter as they left was the best sound Anna Leigh had heard in a long while. She loved seeing her granddaughter so happy, and if it also made a certain young rancher more content, Anna was all for it.

AS THE COLD from the bank's air conditioner caused goose bumps to break out along Amanda's arm, Mr. Collins sat across the desk from them, sweating profusely.

Lex sat ramrod straight in her chair with her arms crossed over her chest. She was tired of the banker's pitiful excuses, and she silently glared at him, daring him to contradict what she had already told him.

"I...I...swear to you, Ms. Walters," he stammered, wiping his forehead with an already damp handkerchief, "I honestly don't see how this could have happened." His face got redder by the minute, and Amanda was afraid the poor man was on the verge of passing out or having a stroke. And her lover's present attitude wasn't helping matters.

"Are you doubting my word, Mr. Collins?" Lex asked quietly. Her intense eyes bored into the bank president's face, though all she wanted to do was yell and scream about his employees' obvious lack of training.

"No," he practically shouted. When he realized his raised voice irritated the woman across from him even more, he softened his tone. "I mean, of course not. But our policy on any withdrawal is to get a visual identification. Especially with such large amounts."

Lex leaned forward in her chair. "Then," she paused, lowering her voice, "unless my brother has changed drastically—" Lex looked down at her own body, "I suggest that one of your employees is either not following policy or is in on his little scheme." She glanced back up, catching the sweating banker staring at her breasts.

"M...m...m...Ms. W...ww...Walters." He flushed scarlet and pulled his collar away from his throat. "I can assure you we will be investigating this matter thoroughly. And these papers," Collins held up several documents, "will insure that only you—" He looked at one page somewhat puzzled, "and Miss Cauble here," not hearing Amanda's gasp of surprise, "will be the only people who have access to this account."

Lex nodded and stood. "That's fine. But if anything happens to this account," she gave him an icy stare, "I will hold you personally responsible." Lex got a certain amount of enjoyment out of seeing the banker's face suddenly pale. "Have a good day, Mr. Collins." Lex gestured for Amanda to precede her through the office door.

After Amanda signed the necessary papers, Lex ushered her out of the bank and back to the truck. Amanda didn't say a word as Lex helped her into the passenger seat and closed the door after her.

Getting in behind the wheel, Lex sighed. She looked over at her silent friend with concern. "Are you all right? You seem really quiet."

Amanda turned away from the window, her voice laced with wonderment. "You didn't tell me you were going to do that."

"What?" Lex asked, puzzled. "Oh. That." She met Amanda's eyes with a hopeful look. "I'm sorry. I guess I wasn't really thinking. Does it bother you?"

"No. I mean, it's not that. I was just really surprised, that's all." Amanda offered her hand to Lex. "But why put anyone else on the account, after all the trouble it's already caused? And why me?"

"Because I know you would make sure Martha was taken care of if anything ever happened to me."

"Please don't talk like that! I don't think I could survive if anything ever happened to you." Amanda took a deep breath in order to keep herself from crying at the turn in the conversation. "If that's what you're worried about, why not put Martha's name on it?"

Lex pulled Amanda's hand up and held it to her cheek. "I'm afraid if I do, Hubert will somehow find out. But he'd never suspect that I would give authorization to someone I've only known for a short while." Lex kissed the hand she held. "And because I'm totally in love with you and want to share all that I have."

"You know that I have all I really need right here, right now, don't you?" Amanda tenderly cupped her lover's cheek. It took all she had to resist the urge to crawl across the seats and wrap herself around Lex's body. "I'll try not to ever break this trust you have in me." Breaking free of Lex's grasp, Amanda sat back and buckled her seatbelt. "It's almost time to meet Gramma at the office. Are you ready?" She knew this was neither the time nor the place for such a deep conversation, and could also see her companion had been made more than a little off balance by the whole thing.

Somewhat at a loss, Lex struggled for words. "Yeah. This ought to be fun, huh?" She backed the truck out of the parking space in front of the bank then drove to the real estate office. Part of her was looking forward to Rick finally getting his comeuppance, while an even bigger part of her just wanted to go somewhere and curl up with Amanda, and let the day go by.

LEX FOLLOWED AMANDA into the small building, ignoring the curious looks that passed her way. She was led into a brightly lit room with several partitioned cubicles and then was guided to a maroon fabric-covered office chair next to a cluttered desk.

"I would apologize for the mess and try to tell you it normally doesn't look like this, but I refuse to lie." Amanda sat down at her desk, wishing she had spent time cleaning it last week before she left.

Lex leaned back in the chair, crossing her legs at the ankles and resting her entwined hands on her stomach. "They say a cluttered desk is the sign of a busy mind. So, when do you find time to sleep?"

Amanda stopped her cleaning efforts, and wadded up a piece of paper. She threw it at her smirking friend. "Oh, you!"

Lex caught the paper in mid air and tossed it back only to have it hit Amanda on top of her head and then ricochet over the partition. "Oops!" Lex then tried to look innocent as a woman glared over the wall. She had short, sandy-blonde curls framing her round face and appeared to be a few years older than Lex. Her gray eyes flicked to the desk with a scowl.

Her demeanor instantly changed when she saw who was sitting at the desk. "Amanda. It's about time you got back." She disappeared, then reappeared a moment later in Amanda's cubicle. In a flash, she had Amanda wrapped in a hug. "You look great." When she finally noticed they weren't alone, she gave Lex a tentative smile. "Oh, I'm sorry, I didn't know you had company." She studied the seated woman from head to toe. From the expressive eyes, denim shirt, pressed jeans and worn but well cared-for boots, she had a pretty good idea who it was. "You must be Lexington. The whole office has been buzzing about you."

"Really?" Lex stood and held out a hand. "You can call me Lex."

The older woman smiled, more genuinely this time as she shook Lex's hand. "Lord, my manners are horrible. I'm Wanda Skimmerly. It's really nice to meet you."

Amanda hated to break up the introductions, but her curiosity had gotten the best of her. "What do you mean, the whole office is buzzing?"

"Well, when your grandmother called to say why you weren't

coming in for a while, she said something about how you were literally pulled from the jaws of death. That's Janet talking, not me." She looked at Lex. "She's the one who spoke to Mrs. Cauble when she called."

Lex laughed, then sat back down in her chair. "I'm afraid it wasn't that exciting. I just helped Amanda out of the creek and then held her hostage until the bridge was rebuilt."

Wanda shook her head. "Uh-huh, if you say so." She could tell by Amanda's demeanor that she had pretty much worn out her welcome. *I should just leave these two lovebirds alone. Amanda can't take her eyes off of Lex. Not that I blame her much for that. If I weren't a married woman...* "Well, I'll let you get back to it, then. Nice to finally meet you, Lex." As quickly as she had arrived, Wanda was gone.

Lex glanced over at her companion, who had a smirk on her face. "The 'jaws of death'? Good grief! These people need to quit watching so many talk shows."

Amanda was kept from answering by the buzzing phone on her desk. "Amanda Cauble." She listened, and then broke into a wide smile. "Hi, Gramma. Sure. We'll be right there." She raised her eyebrows at Lex after she hung up the phone. "Show time." Offering her hand to the reclining woman, Amanda pulled her lover out of the chair and led her out of the cubicle maze, and to the rear of the building.

When they walked into the manager's office, Lex and Amanda noticed Anna Leigh was sitting behind the desk, while Rick lounged in a visitor's chair with a sullen look on his face.

Hearing the door open, he turned and then jumped to his feet. "I should have known," he sneered as Amanda walked by him to sit on the corner of the desk. "This is about yesterday, right? You went crying to grandma because I hurt your little feelings?" Not getting a response from Amanda, Rick turned to Lex, who casually leaned against the door with her arms folded across her chest. "She's got you on a pretty short leash, eh, Kentucky?" His use of the old high school nickname was meant to taunt Lex, but she refused to rise to the bait. "Maybe you'll do a few tricks for us, huh?"

Before Lex could reply, Anna Leigh spoke up. "That's quite enough, Mr. Thompson. Now please have a seat."

Lex wisely kept quiet. Personally, nothing would make her feel better than trying to see if Rick's head would bounce off the desk that Anna Leigh sat behind, especially after his comments to Amanda. But from the look on Anna Leigh's face, she figured his time working at Sunflower Realty was about to come to an end. *I'm really gonna enjoy this.* She could see the angry set to Amanda's jaw and knew that it was on her behalf. *It's nice to have someone take up for me for a change.* Wanting to ease the tense lines on her friend's face, Lex winked and got a small smile in return. *That's better.*

Anna Leigh stood up and walked around the desk. "Mr. Thompson. First, let me assure you this meeting has nothing to do with the events of yesterday. That was outside of this office, and I feel my granddaughter is more than capable of taking care of herself." Seeing him relax, she continued, "However, it has been brought to my attention that as of late, you have been abusing your position."

"Abusing, my ass," he sputtered, ready to jump to his feet once again.

"Mr. Thompson." Anna Leigh held out a hand to forestall his outburst. When he stayed where he was, she walked back over to the desk and returned to her seat. "I have had several complaints about your treatment of the employees of this office." She pulled a stack of papers from her briefcase. "These are the complaints from this past week." Handing the papers to Rick, Anna Leigh watched as he read over them.

"Harassment? Lewd comments? Intimidation?" He looked up at the older woman, his face reddening with anger. "What the hell is this? Some sort of goddamned witch hunt?"

Anna Leigh shook her head. "No, Mr. Thompson, it isn't. And we're not even going to go over what you did to Amanda last Friday."

"What? I sent her on a call. It's not my fault the little brat can't read directions."

Pulling a discolored paper from her purse, Amanda handed it to her grandmother, and spoke for the first time. "Funny. Even though it's kind of water-stained, you can still make out the client's name. 'L. Walters,' and in the space below are the directions, in your handwriting."

Anna Leigh held on to the piece of paper and narrowed her eyes. "Mr. Thompson, as a woman who almost lost her granddaughter due to your petty games, I am furious. And, as the owner of a business who nearly lost a very valuable employee, I have no other recourse than to terminate your employment with this agency."

"What?" Incensed, Rick jumped to his feet. Glaring at Amanda he yelled, "It's all your fault. Things were just fine around here until you showed up." He pointed his finger at Anna Leigh. "You old biddy. You've always looked down your nose at me. Well, I'm not gonna sit still for this." He took a step toward the desk, but was stopped by a hand on his arm.

"That's far enough," Lex informed him quietly.

"Get your damn hands off me, you meddling bitch!" Rick ducked his shoulder and slammed an elbow into Lex's side, causing her to grunt and fall to her knees, with her arms wrapped around herself in agony.

Then Rick turned a murderous gaze on Anna Leigh. "You're next, old woman."

Amanda saw Lex fall to the floor, and then everything around her slowed. Rick started for the desk, but his head suddenly snapped upward. His chin wore the perfect imprint of the bottom of Amanda's shoe.

Amanda readied herself for another kick but Rick toppled, and his eyes rolled back in his head. He was unconscious before he hit the ground.

Lex was able to raise her head just in time to see Amanda knock Rick out. Still kneeling, she concentrated all her attention on staying conscious. Closing her eyes, she swallowed several times, fighting a wave of nausea brought on by the excruciating pain from her abused ribs, and the wound that Dr. Anderson had just recently reopened. *This hurts worse than when that damned barn hit me.* She focused on taking very small breaths, then felt a gentle hand on her shoulder.

"Lex? Come on, love, look at me." Amanda brushed the hair away from Lex's bowed head, frightened by the loss of color on the normally tan features.

Anna Leigh was on the phone, calling the sheriff to come remove Rick from the office. "Mandy? Should I ask for an ambulance?" She was extremely concerned, because Lex hadn't moved since she had dropped to the floor.

"Honey? Do you want to go to the hospital?" Amanda was still running her hand nervously through Lex's hair.

"No," Lex managed to get out, hoarsely. Finally able to look up, she gave a slight smile. "Just...let me...catch my breath."

"Okay. Why don't you let us help you up." Amanda waved her grandmother over, and the two of them helped the pale woman into a nearby chair.

The sheriff and two deputies stepped into the room. Seeing the big man out cold on the floor, the sheriff raised his eyebrows. "Well." He looked over at Lex. "Did you do this?"

She shook her head and inclined it Amanda's direction.

"Amanda?" He took off his hat and scratched his gray head. "Well, I'll be damned. What did you use? A two-by-four?"

The young woman blushed and looked down at Lex. "Umm, no." She felt her lover grasp her hand, which had been resting on Lex's shoulder. "I, uh, kicked him."

Anna Leigh joined in. "That's right. Mandy took karate lessons one summer when she stayed with us. I had no idea she still remembered any of it, though."

"Remind me never to make you mad." Charlie watched as the deputies pulled a groggy Rick to his feet and out of the room. "I know he's a jerk, but do you have any other charges to press? I'll need something to put down on the report."

Amanda spoke quietly, and with a touch of anger, with her eyes still on Lex. "Assault. He hit Lex in the side, unprovoked."

Lex shook her head. "No. I'm not pressing charges." Still in agony, her words were hard to hear.

"But—"

"No, Anna Leigh." Lex turned her pain-filled eyes to the sheriff. "Tell him if he'll leave Mrs. Cauble and Amanda alone, I won't press charges."

Charlie nodded. "Gotcha." He looked closely at her pale face. "You gonna be okay?"

"Yeah, fine. Do you need me to sign something?"

"Nah. I'll handle everything. Take care of yourself, Lex." He moved toward the door, donning his hat, then turned and tipped it to Anna Leigh and Amanda. "You ladies just give me a holler if you need anything."

Anna Leigh walked over to him and shook his hand. "Thank you, Sheriff. I certainly appreciate your quick response. Let me walk you out."

"Thanks, Mrs. Cauble."

Amanda watched them leave and then squatted down beside Lex. "Are you feeling any better?" She was relieved to see the color returning to Lex's face.

"I'm doing fine. I just didn't know you could pack such a wallop."

"I really don't know what came over me. I saw you go down, and then he was coming toward Gramma." She pulled Lex's hand up to her face. "I guess I just snapped." *The idea that I could easily take down someone that size without thinking scares me.* "What kind of person am I to do something like that?" she whispered aloud.

"A very brave person, who will stand up for their family and friends when they're being threatened," Lex answered. Not getting a response, she tried a different approach. "But damn, Amanda. You're something else. Wanna be my bodyguard?"

That did it. Amanda finally broke out of her contemplative mood. "Oh, Lex." She laid her head down on her partner's lap and wrapped both arms around Lex's legs.

Anna Leigh walked back into the room, then stopped next to Lex's chair and placed one hand on the seated woman's shoulder. "Lexington, are you certain you're going to be okay? I'd feel a lot better if we took you to the doctor. That was quite a blow you took."

"I'm okay, really. Just sort of got my attention, that's all." Lex glanced down and watched as she ran her hand through the silken hair in her lap. The motion soothed her, and once again she thought about how lucky she was to have found this woman who held her so tight.

As much as she hated to disturb them, Anna Leigh cleared her throat. "Mandy? Everyone is in the conference room. It's time to make the announcement."

Amanda lifted her head. "Well, it's got to be easier than what we just went through, right?" She climbed to her feet and stretched. "You want to sit in? I'm sure the boss won't mind," she asked Lex, then looked to her grandmother for confirmation.

Lex shook her head. "Actually, I need to make a few phone calls, if you don't mind me borrowing your office."

"My office?" Amanda was confused for a moment. "Oh, yeah. Sure. I'll be back in a little while." After kissing Lex on top of the head, she entangled her arm with Anna Leigh's. "C'mon, Gramma. Let's go harass the help."

Chapter
Four

AMANDA SAT THROUGH the endless congratulations with a smile on her face, but even her normally good nature began to slip as the boundary to her personal space continued to shrink. *If one more person pats me on the head, I swear I'll bark.* The actual meeting and announcement only lasted about ten minutes, but the group of employees had circled their new office manager and showed no signs of leaving, even though it was almost an hour later.

Anna Leigh heard her granddaughter sigh for the third time in the past five minutes. *I think it's time to save Mandy from our well-wishing friends.* She stood up and cleared her throat, getting everyone's attention immediately. "Everyone, I realize how excited we all are, but let's give your new boss a break." Accepting the grateful smile from the young woman, she continued. "With all that has happened in the past week, I'm still going to insist that my granddaughter take another week or two off to get some things settled. I know I can count on you all to continue on without her for a little longer." Agreeing murmurs were heard, and the happy employees began to file out of the room.

Amanda stood and stretched, then stepped over to Anna Leigh and wrapped her arms around the older woman. "Thank you. I know they meant well, but the walls were beginning to close in on me." She pulled back to look her grandmother in the eye. "Are you sure you want me to take more time off? I don't really need to."

"Yes, I'm sure. Honey, you've been through more in the past week than some folks handle in years, and I think you need an extended vacation to sort through it all." Anna Leigh kissed Amanda's forehead and pulled her into another hug. "You have a lot of issues to work through, even if you don't realize it."

Amanda's thoughts went back to the phone call with her mother, and she felt her elation sink. "Yeah, I know. I guess the first thing I need to do is go back to LA, pack up all my stuff, and get it shipped here."

"What's the rush?" Anna Leigh kept an arm looped around Amanda's waist. "It's been there for over six months. What difference would a little longer make?"

Amanda allowed her grandmother to escort her out of the conference room and back to her new office. *My office. That's going to take some getting used to.* "Well, after my last couple of conversations with Mother and Father, I wouldn't put it past them to either throw it all away, or give it to charity. They're pretty upset with me."

They were at the open office door when Anna Leigh asked, "So, when are you leaving for Los Angeles?"

"Probably next week." Amanda didn't see the stricken look on Lex's face as she stood up from the desk. "Lex, did you get your phone calls taken care of? I'm sorry we took so long, but I thought we'd never get out of that meeting."

"Yeah." Lex gazed around uncomfortably. "Umm, I've got a couple of errands to run." She ran a shaky hand through her hair. "Do you want to stay here for a little while and get settled?"

Amanda looked at her quizzically. Her lover appeared pale and shaky. *What's up with her?* She stepped a little closer and put her hand on Lex's arm, causing Lex to jump slightly. "Okay. But when you get back, I have something to talk to you about." When she felt the arm under her hand tense, Amanda looked up into Lex's face. "Are you okay? You're not looking too well."

Taking a breath to speak, Lex shook her head. *She's right. I heard the tail end of the conversation and panicked.* "Sorry." She stared down at the floor unable to meet either woman's eyes. "Did I hear right? You're going back to California?"

Amanda mentally slapped her forehead. *Idiot! She's already shook up, and then she hears that?* Getting inside Lex's guard, Amanda snuggled up to her. "Yes. That's what I wanted to talk to you about. Do you feel up to taking a trip with me sometime next week? I want to go get the rest of my stuff packed up and shipped back here before my parents throw it out." When she felt the body she was holding relax, Amanda knew she had said the right thing.

Unsure, Lex asked, "You want me to go to your parents' house with you? Do you really think that's such a good idea?"

When she heard the office door close quietly, Amanda smiled to herself. *Gramma always seems to know.* She leaned back slightly and then threaded her hands through Lex's hair, so she could pull her head down. "I want them to meet you, so that they can see why I love you." As she brushed Lex's lips with her own, Amanda felt her lover tremble. Enjoying the moment, she deepened the kiss until a warmth spread throughout her own body.

Strong hands wrapped around her waist slowly migrated downward, pulling Amanda nearer. Groaning into Lex's mouth,

Amanda squeezed closer, until their bodies melded almost into one.

Breaking off the kiss to breathe, Lex nuzzled Amanda's ear. "You'd better stop now, or your new office is going to get more of a christening than you can imagine." She felt the body she held shake with laughter.

"Oh, God, Lex. I think that would be a little hard to explain, don't you?" Small chills ran down her spine as Lex nibbled on her earlobe. "Uhhh...L...Lex...ah....you'd better stop, or you're gonna....mmmm...end up on my...ah...desk."

Kissing the tip of Amanda's nose, Lex grinned, then backed off. "Don't tempt me." She took a deep breath, pleased to note that her ribs didn't seem to have been damaged in the earlier scuffle, and the wound the doctor had cleaned had settled down to a dull ache. "So, when are we leaving?" she asked, seeing a smile cover her companion's face.

"Really? You'll go?" Amanda wrapped her arms back around Lex's body exuberantly. Hearing the sharp intake of breath, she let go quickly. "Oh, no, Lex. Your ribs! I'm so sorry—"

"Ssh, they're fine. Just a little tender." Lex brought Amanda close again. "And of course I'll go. Do you actually think I could stand to be without you for what...three, four days? Nope. You're stuck with me, sweetheart." She lightly kissed the top of Amanda's head.

"Cool. I think I can handle that." Amanda was about to say more when a knock on the door interrupted her. She gave Lex one final quick kiss on the lips before backing away a step. "Come in."

Anna Leigh poked her head into the office. "Sorry to disturb you, Mandy, but Elizabeth is on the phone asking for you." The older woman gave her granddaughter a somewhat disgusted look. "Sounds like your mother is in another one of her little 'moods.'"

"I'm sorry, Gramma. You might as well send her on through." Amanda went over and sat down behind the large desk as Anna Leigh left the room again.

"I'll give you some privacy." Lex started for the door.

"No," Amanda almost shouted. "Please stay? For moral support?" she begged, as the phone buzzed. She waited until Lex was seated in the chair across from her before she picked up the handset. "This is Amanda. Hello, Mother."

"Amanda Lorraine Cauble! I've been calling all over town looking for you," Elizabeth's pinched voice whined.

"I'm fine, thank you for asking." Annoyed with her mother's attitude, Amanda decided to get right to the point. "Is there something I can do for you, Mother?"

"Don't take that tone with me, young lady. I'm still your

mother, even though you never bother to call me anymore," Elizabeth berated. "When are you coming home? I fail to see how you can be happy in that horribly small town. They don't even have a proper museum."

Amanda rolled her eyes. *Well, we do have the Texas Oak Tree Museum, but I guess she's probably not interested in that.* "Mother, believe it or not, the world does not revolve around museums and the cultural arts."

Elizabeth gasped. "Dear Lord! Don't say things like that. I do believe that living with your grandparents has completely ruined you. They've never appreciated the finer things. I have no idea how your father turned out the way he did."

"I've often wondered that myself," Amanda muttered under her breath. "Is there a reason you called, other than to belittle Gramma and Grandpa?"

"See? You made me so upset I almost forgot the reason I was looking for you. It's very important that you come home next week. We are having our annual Fall Dinner for your father's business associates, and he would like for you to be here."

"Mother, I have a job and responsibilities here. I can't just drop everything to fly halfway across the country for a dinner party!" Even though she was planning on going back next week, Amanda did not want to give her mother the satisfaction. Needing some comfort, she crooked a finger at Lex.

Lex raised an eyebrow, but rose and walked behind the desk. Amanda stood, then pushed the lanky form of her lover into the chair, sliding into Lex's lap. Being wrapped in Lex's arms calmed her, and Amanda was able to listen to her mother's ranting without getting upset.

"I think we've been too lenient with you, Amanda. You didn't used to act this way with us." Her mother's tone was harsh. "I told your father that it was not a good idea for you to spend so much time down there."

Amanda tensed. "Why? Because I'm actually thinking for myself?" Lex gave her a squeeze, and her anger dissipated, replaced by an aching sadness. "I'm sorry I'm such a disappointment to you, Mother."

"Amanda dear, it's not that you're a disappointment, you've just gotten so headstrong. What happened to my little girl?"

She's still in Los Angeles, working in the gallery. Jeannie was always her little girl. I was always her disappointment. "I guess I grew up."

"Thank God," Lex whispered in her ear. She was so close to Amanda that she could hear what Elizabeth said, and it took all she had not to take the phone and give the woman a piece of her mind.

"I'm sorry, what was that, Mother?"

"I said, it would mean a lot to your father and me if you could make it back for this dinner." Elizabeth paused, then added, "You can even bring your new friend if you want to. We'd really like to see you, dear."

Lex's voice tickled Amanda's ear again. "Oooh, an invitation. I guess I'd better starch my jeans."

Amanda slapped the hands resting on her stomach. "Actually Mother, that would work just fine. I need to come and pack up the rest of my stuff anyway." She leaned back as soft lips nibbled lightly on her neck. "What night is the dinner?"

Elizabeth breathed a sigh of relief. "Next Friday. Could you come a day or two early? Jeannie and Frank will be staying at the house next week, and I know they would love to see you."

Turning slightly, Amanda sent a questioning glance Lex's way, and was rewarded with a nod. She gave Lex a light peck on the lips. "Mother? We can fly out early Wednesday, but I have to be back here on Sunday, all right?"

"Four days? Well, I suppose that it's better than nothing. Call us Tuesday with your itinerary, and we'll have the driver pick you up."

"No, that won't be necessary. We'll just rent a car." Amanda hated the limousine and all that it stood for. Her parents each had their own vehicles, but whenever they went someplace where they might be seen, they always took the limousine for appearance sake.

"Fine. I won't bother to do anything for you." Elizabeth muttered. "Your father would feel better if you acted more to your upbringing. We worked very hard to get where we are, and I really don't want you to embarrass him by acting so *lower class*. At least rent a decent car, not like that old junker you drive now."

Oh yeah, they worked terribly hard—waiting until certain family members died to get at their inheritance. "Yes, Mother." It was hard to stay angry with Elizabeth while Lex kissed the back of her neck. "I'll see you on Wednesday." She hung up the phone before any further complaints came her way. "Dammit, she's so infuriating!"

Lex squeezed her tighter, and then kissed her on top of the head. "Mmm. Just think of it this way. You'll get your revenge when you show up with me."

"What's that supposed to mean?" Amanda turned so they were looking into each other's eyes.

"Well, I don't think I'll fit in too well. But don't worry. I'll try not to spit on the floors or anything."

Amanda ran her fingertips along Lex's jaw. "Do you actually think I would be ashamed or embarrassed by you?"

"No, I don't think *you* would feel that way, but I can't help but feel a little 'common' around folks like that." Lex hated admitting something so personal, and decided to try and change the subject. "I guess this means I'll have an occasion to wear my new boots."

"Honey, people probably could call you a lot of things, but common certainly isn't one of them. Gorgeous, sweet, funny, wonderful—"

Lex covered Amanda's mouth with her hand. "Hush. I get your point; but I don't have anything to wear to something like that. I'd do anything for you, you know. It's just that," she lowered her gaze, and a slight blush covered her face, "I hope I don't have to wear one of those slinky-looking numbers. I haven't worn a dress since I was four years old."

Amanda waited until Lex looked back up into her face. "Sweetheart, I would never ask you to be something you're not. You can wear cutoffs and an old dirty tee shirt, and I'd still be proud to walk in with you."

Lex laughed. "Now that would be a picture." She gave Amanda a light kiss. "But I think I should probably find better clothes to wear. I really don't have anything but jeans. Would you mind going with me to pick something out?"

"Oh, yeah. I'd love to. Shopping is my favorite hobby. Gramma and I go for hours, looking and trying on clothes, but rarely buying anything." Amanda gave Lex a sexy grin. "Well, it *was* my favorite hobby, until recently. We'll pick up a new outfit when we get to L.A. There are some great places to shop." She climbed off Lex's lap and offered her a hand up. "Let's go eat. All this talking has made me hungry."

"Me, too." Lex knew the matter wasn't completely closed, but she trusted Amanda. She just hoped she'd be able at least to be civil to her girlfriend's parents, when all she wanted to do was slam their heads together and see what kind of sound it made. *Probably like a couple of hollow logs. I'm so not looking forward to this trip.*

AFTER TELLING ANNA LEIGH goodbye and not to wait dinner for them, Amanda and Lex found themselves sitting at a secluded table in a nearby restaurant. Tinny Mexican music floated through the air from unseen speakers, while brightly colored serapes and piñatas decorated the walls and ceilings, respectively.

Amanda attacked the chips and salsa with gusto. "This is great," she mumbled between mouthfuls. She noticed Lex staring at her with an amused look on her face. "What?"

"Amazing."

"What?" Amanda stopped chewing long enough to speak. "Do

I have something on my face?"

Lex unsuccessfully tried to lose the silly smile she knew she must be wearing. She loved how Amanda enjoyed life to the fullest. No matter how mundane something was, even if it was just eating at an inexpensive restaurant, the woman across from her took pleasure from it. "No." She took a sip of her ice tea, then cleared her throat. "I can't help it. You're just too damned cute."

Amanda blushed, then ducked her head. "Thanks." Her eyes grew large as a waiter brought a sizzling platter of fajitas to their table. "Ooh."

"Hey, I just realized something."

Amanda looked up from assembling her fajita. "What's that?" She added a dollop of guacamole, then folded the tortilla over in triumph. "Perfect."

"This is the first time we've gone out to eat together. Kind of like a first date, huh?"

Chewing then quickly swallowing, Amanda nodded. "You know, you're right. Want to do the entire cliched first-date thing? How about a movie after dinner? We could make an evening out of it."

"Sure. But do I have to get you home early? How late is your curfew?" Lex lifted a forkful of Spanish rice to her mouth. *This place is good. We'll have to come here more often.*

"Nothing to worry about there. My grandparents trust me. I've never had a curfew with them." Amanda took a sip of her tea, then batted her eyes at her "date." "Of course, I've never had such a good incentive to stay out late before, either." Watching Lex flush, she giggled.

Lex, finished building her own fajita, tried to will the redness from her face. "Then I guess it's probably a good thing we didn't meet any sooner. I might have corrupted your tender sensibilities. Although, I believe it would have been fun to try."

Amanda wiped her face with her napkin, then returned it to her lap. "You can say that again."

After flirting shamelessly with Amanda throughout the meal, Lex dropped her napkin to the table with a heavy sigh. "It's actually a pretty nice evening and not too cool. Could I interest you in a walk through the park instead of a movie? I need to work off this dinner, somehow." *I really need some fresh air. All of this indoor activity is starting to make me a little stir-crazy.*

"Do you feel well enough to go on a walk? How's your side?"

Lex leaned back away from the table. "I feel fine. Stuffed, but fine." She waved at the waiter for the check. "Are you about done?"

Amanda placed her napkin on the table and groaned. "Mmm. I think a walk is a great idea since I won't be able to eat another bite for a least a week. As a matter of fact, there's a nice little park a few blocks from the house, and it has a small lake and path to walk on." She grabbed the check as soon as it hit the table. "My treat. I asked you to dinner, remember?"

Lex conceded with a nod. "Okay, next one's on me." Seeing the smirk on Amanda's face, accompanied by a lecherous waggling of the eyebrows, she shook her head. "Uh-uh. Don't you even *think* about going there."

Amanda struggled to keep an innocent look on her face. "Who, me?" She left money on the table with the check and then stood up. "Let's go see what kind of trouble we can cause at the park. I'll get my dessert later." With a wink, Amanda strolled happily out of the restaurant, leaving her companion to pick up her jaw and scramble after her.

Chapter
Five

THE LAST OF the sun's rays reflected brightly off the pond in Schicksal Park. There were no other cars in the lot when Lex parked the dark truck in a nearby space. "It looks pretty deserted around here." After she got out of the truck, Lex pulled on her old, faded denim jacket, closed the door, and crossed to the other side of the vehicle.

Amanda climbed down out of the truck then slipped on the coat she had brought—the old leather jacket Lex had worn in high school that she had appropriated from her lover. "Yeah, but you should see this place in the spring and summer. You can rarely find a parking space then." She shivered, and buttoned the coat closed. "Brr. That wind is getting pretty chilly." Amanda led Lex to a paved path. "Let's get moving, so I'll warm up."

The quiet of the lake was something Lex needed, although she hadn't realized it until they were there. She watched as Amanda's face relaxed as well, then asked, "Do you come here often?" When the arm linked with hers tightened, other cares fell back into the distance.

"Yeah. This is my thinking place," Amanda said. "I usually bring old bread along and feed the ducks for hours at a time." The paved path was easy to walk, and the leisurely pace they set kept them from getting around the pond too quickly. "When I was in school, I always spent my summers here in Texas. Mother never understood why I wanted to." They continued their trek slowly around the tranquil water, keeping off the path for a while. "She and Dad would go to Europe, and Jeannie traveled with them, or spent her time at one type of camp or another. I always begged to come here to visit Gramma and Grandpa. I suppose I craved the quiet, normal summers that a small town allowed, instead of traipsing all over the world."

Lex pulled her close. "I don't really remember much about any of my grandparents," she said quietly. "Dad's folks died when he was just a kid, leaving him the ranch, so I never knew them. I vaguely remember my mother's father. He was tall and handsome and a really nice guy. But after Mom died, I never saw him or my grandmother again." She straightened a little, then smiled. "They didn't care much for Dad. He's kind of rough around the edges."

Feeling her heart break at the wistfulness in her partner's voice, Amanda put her arm around Lex. "I'm sorry."

"Don't be. I'm not. Martha and the guys at the ranch more than made up for it, believe me. I had more attention from all of them than most kids ever get from two sets of grandparents." Lex leaned down and kissed the top of Amanda's head. As much as she hated baring part of her inner self to anyone, it just seemed right to be speaking of these things to the woman beside her. Her heart swelled with the love she felt.

"Really?"

"Oh, yeah. Of course, most of the hands usually helped me get into trouble. Poor Martha spent most of her time chasing me with a spoon and hollering, 'Get your filthy butt out of my kitchen and get into the tub!'" Lex paused, and a thoughtful look crossed her face. "Come to think about it, she still does that."

"I bet you were a real handful growing up."

"I didn't think so, but I'm sure Martha's opinion would differ."

Amanda reached for Lex's hand. The area was deserted; even so, she wouldn't have cared if anyone saw them. "Let's not use the path. Do you mind if we just walked along the shoreline?" She held the hand in hers tightly as they continued their walk.

They were on their second circuit around the water when Lex's cell phone rang. Jumping slightly, she stopped and pulled the device from her coat pocket. "Hello? Martha, what's wrong?"

"Lexie, I'm really sorry to bother you like this." The usually unflappable housekeeper seemed very upset.

"Don't worry, we were just taking a walk. Now tell me what's the matter." Lex forced herself to stay calm. *Martha hardly ever calls me...I can't remember the last time I heard this damned phone ring.* "Go on, tell me."

"It's your brother. He called the house a few minutes ago looking for you."

"Okay. Did you tell him I was in town?" Since Martha would usually wait until she got home before giving her this type of message, Lex didn't like where this conversation was going.

"No, not at first. I didn't figure it was any of his business. I told him you weren't available. That really upset him."

Lex laughed. "I'll bet. Then what?"

"He told me it was very important that he talk to you immediately. I told him again you couldn't come to the phone. That's when he really started getting angry."

Dammit. Lex felt a headache fast approaching. "What did he say to you, Martha?"

"Oh, well, he yelled and whined quite a bit, then he said, 'Forget it. I'll just come out there myself,' and hung up."

"He's on his way to the ranch?" Lex ran her hand through her hair. "Shit." She glanced at Amanda, who was watching her with a worried expression. "How long ago did you talk to him?" Lex was already pulling Amanda down the path, on their way to the parking lot.

"I just hung up with him right before I called you."

"Good. I'm on my way. Just lock all of the doors in case he gets there before I do. Don't let him in for any reason." They were back at the truck, and Lex held the passenger's door open for her companion to get in. Still holding the phone to her ear, she closed the door, then quickly jogged around to the other side and climbed in.

"Why? Are you expecting him to cause trouble?" The tone of Martha's voice changed, from amusement of Hubert's usual antics, to one of concern. "What's going on, Lexie?"

Holding the phone with her shoulder, Lex put the truck in reverse and backed out of the parking space quickly. "I don't know what to expect. We found out that he's the one who's been taking money from the ranch account." She turned and asked Amanda with her eyes what she wanted to do. Even though it would take more time, Lex wouldn't mind dropping her friend off at the Cauble's if that's what Amanda preferred.

Amanda understood the unspoken question. Nothing was more important to her at the moment than being by her lover's side. She said, "Tell Martha to sit tight. *We're* on our way."

Lex smiled at her companion and turned the truck south, on the road out of town. "Amanda says to hold tight—"

"She's there?" Martha cut in. "Let me talk to her." She could hear the roar of the truck engine on the phone. "You shouldn't be talking on the phone while you're trying to drive anyway, it's not safe."

"Yes, ma'am." Lex handed the phone over. "She wants to talk to you."

"Hi Martha. It's great to hear from you, although I'm sorry about the circumstances." Amanda genuinely missed the older woman, even though it had only been a couple of days since she had last spoken to her.

"I know what you mean, Amanda. I loved meeting you, but I just wish it hadn't been due to being dumped into our creek. How are you doing?"

"Great! I've really got a lot to tell you when I see you again. So much has happened."

"Really? Well, I can't wait. Were you able to get Lexie to see the doctor? I swear, that woman argues with me sometimes just for sport."

"Yesterday morning, as a matter of fact. Her side was terribly infected, but Dr. Anderson took care of that." Amanda reached over and caressed her lover's leg, causing a slight smile on Lex's face and removing the serious look that had been there.

"Blast it! I knew that would happen. But you say she's okay? She never takes care of herself," Martha muttered, more to herself than to Amanda.

"She's fine. Lex got a couple of stitches, and Dr. Anderson made her promise to keep her ribs wrapped for another week. He thinks it'll help keep the bandage in place for the gunshot wound. There was one thing. He says she's gotten too thin." This tidbit of news got her a glare from the subject in question. She glared right back at Lex and said, "Don't give me that look. And keep your eyes on the road." Then she turned her attention back to Martha's voice.

"Well, if I could get her to sit still long enough to eat, she wouldn't look like she's about to blow away. But, I think that Lexie's eaten more in the last week or so than the entire last month combined. And I have you to thank for that. She's happier now than I can ever remember seeing her. So thank you, Amanda, for giving my little girl back her heart."

Lex turned to glance at Amanda, who had stilled suddenly. Even in the fading sunlight, she could see a deep blush on Amanda's face. Trying to keep one eye on the road and one on her passenger, she reached with one hand and touched her lover's shoulder. "Hey, are you all right?"

"Yep." The heartfelt words from Martha meant a lot to her, and it took Amanda a moment to get herself back together. She finally was able to speak into the phone again. "Martha, I think I got the best end of the deal."

"I think you both did. How far out are you now?"

The truck turned off the main road, and Amanda could see the old bridge up ahead. "We're almost to the bridge, so we should be at the house in about ten minutes or so."

"Great. I just started a fresh pot of coffee. I have a feeling we're gonna be needing it." Martha stopped. "Hold on a minute, Amanda. I think I hear a car pulling up out front."

"Wait! Martha? Are you there?" Amanda heard the sound of the handset being placed on a table, or countertop. After what Lex had said about Hubert, she was worried about Martha's safety.

"What?" Lex struggled to keep her eyes on the road as they started across the bridge.

Amanda listened intently to the phone, trying to hear any unusual noises. "She thought she heard a car drive up and put the phone down to go look."

"Dammit!" Lex sped up the truck, practically flying across the old wooden structure.

"Lex, Slow down! We're not going to be any help to Martha if you kill us!" Suddenly more afraid of Lex's driving than what could happen to Martha, Amanda used one of her hands to brace herself against the dash.

Almost against her will, Lex slowed the truck down. "Has she come back to the phone yet?" She had a death grip on the steering wheel, and the dash lights cast an eerie glow on her tense face.

"No, not—wait, I think I hear something."

"Amanda?" Martha sounded breathless. "Are you still there?"

"God, Martha, don't scare me like that. Are you okay? We're almost to the house."

"Oh heavens, yes. But I'm afraid Hubert is going to hurt himself trying to get in. It sounds like he's working his way around the house, banging on windows and doors as he goes."

The truck skidded to a stop in the long driveway, right beside a grossly expensive BMW convertible. Lex turned to Amanda. "Do you want to wait here, or—"

"Do you really want me to?" Amanda was hurt by Lex's question. She unbuckled her seatbelt, hoping she wouldn't be forced to stay behind when she was just as concerned about Martha as Lex was.

"No, I'd rather you stay with me. I'm less likely to strangle Hubert if there are witnesses." Lex gave her a wry grin before unclipping her own buckle and opening the door. "Come on, let's go get this over with."

They were almost to the front door when they heard a man's voice yelling from somewhere behind the house. "Dammit, old woman, I know you're in there. Open this fucking door before I kick it in!"

Lex unlocked the front door and ushered Amanda inside, then closed and locked the door behind them. "Martha, we're here."

Martha stepped out of the den, causing Amanda to yelp in alarm. "I'm sorry, Amanda. I didn't mean to startle you." A loud banging on the front door interrupted anything else she might have wanted to say.

"Goddammit, unlock this door you old bitch, or I'll knock it down!" Hubert kicked the door ineffectually.

Lex swung the door open. "What the hell is your problem?" She stood in the doorway, daring him to try and get by her. "And watch what you say about Martha."

"Get the hell outta my way, Lex." He tried to push past her, but was stopped when Lex put her hand in the middle of his chest. Hubert was only an inch or two taller than his younger sister, but he outweighed her by at least thirty pounds. The extra weight didn't seem to help him though, and he sputtered when his progress was halted.

"Why?" Lex pushed her brother back a step. "What business do you have in this house?" She stepped out on the front porch with him. "I believe we settled that when I gave you the house in town. You didn't want anything to do with this 'old, dirty ranch,' or so you said then."

Hubert stood quietly, remembering. He'd always hated the ranch, even as a child. Illogically, he felt that this place killed his mother, since she had gone into labor here at the house, and it took longer than it should have to get her to the hospital in town. Then, of course, his father bypassed him and taught his younger sister how to run it. It continued to hurt, all these years later. Looking at Lex now, he realized just how much he missed his mother. *She looks so much like her.* Shaking his head slightly, Hubert glared at his sister. "I don't want anything to do with this shithole. But I seem to be having some trouble accessing the bank records, and I thought I may have left some papers here last time I did the books."

"I should hope you're having trouble getting into the account. I changed it." Lex leaned back against the doorframe and stuck her hands in her jeans pockets. She seemed completely unconcerned about her brother, and the thought rankled him.

"What?" Hubert grabbed the front of his sister's denim jacket with both hands, and pulled her close. "You can't do that!"

Lex grabbed his wrists and squeezed them. "Let go of me," she muttered quietly, "or I'll break 'em. Then we'll let the sheriff deal with you." She enjoyed seeing the fear of comprehension flicker across Hubert's angry features.

Hubert pushed her away as he released her. "Bitch." He took a couple of steps and then ran his hand through his dark, slicked-back hair. "Why didn't you call the law when you found out?"

"Because, no matter what else I think of you, you're family," Lex answered wearily. "Why did you do it? Couldn't you have just asked?"

The big man let out a derisive snort. "Yeah, right, so you could lord that over me like you have everything else?" He shook his head. "You're so damn high and mighty, and you're always acting like you're better than everyone else. I don't have to explain anything to you. Besides, you can't prove a thing."

"What do you want from me, Hubert?" Lex dropped down gracelessly onto the porch swing. Bracing her elbows on her knees, she sighed. "I'm not going to press charges, but I think it would be a good idea if you stayed away from the ranch for a while."

A movement in the doorway caught his eye. "Oh, you'd like that, wouldn't you?" As was his normal habit, he eyed the woman walking up to Lex and then straightened his shirt. "Is this your latest plaything? I'll have to hand it to you, she's...urk!"

Lex had jumped up and pinned her brother against a nearby support post, her forearm against his throat. "Say what you want about me, you asshole, but, never let me hear you talk about Amanda that way again." She enjoyed the look of fear on Hubert's face as she held him against the post, his face getting redder by the moment. A gentle touch on her back brought her to her senses.

"Lex? Let him go, will you?"

The soft request calmed her, at least a little. Lex let go and flexed her arm, which caused Hubert to stand up on his toes and gasp for air. "I've had it with you, asshole. I didn't ask for this ranch, but by God, I'm going to work it with everything that I am, and no two-bit bean counter is going to change that." She felt Amanda's hand on her shoulder. "Especially not the likes of you." Shifting slightly, Lex shoved her brother down the stairs and off the porch.

Hubert stumbled to the driveway while holding his throat and wheezing. "This...isn't over, Lex." He backed his way clumsily to his car. "I can promise you that."

"Go home, Hubert." Lex braced her hands on the railing of the porch and watched as her brother got into his car and drove away. Bowing her head, she closed her eyes against the exhaustion that was left behind as her rage dissipated.

"God, Lex," Amanda whispered.

Lex felt the words as if they were physical blows. Afraid to turn around, she took a deep breath. "Yeah. I completely lost it." She felt Amanda duck under her arm and snuggle close.

"Was he always such a jerk?" Amanda asked, turning to look up into the anguished face above her.

It took a moment for the words to register. "Huh?" Finally Lex realized that she hadn't frightened off her lover with her temper. She wrapped her arms around Amanda in reflex.

Amanda smiled at the gesture. "Good grief. How you've kept from killing him until now is a complete mystery to me."

"Ahem."

Both women turned around to see Martha standing in the doorway with her hands on her hips. "Are you two gonna stand out there all evening mooning over each other, or are you coming inside for coffee?"

Lex laughed. "Well, how can we resist such a gracious

invitation?" Allowing Amanda to enter the house before her, she stopped in front of the smirking housekeeper.

"What?" Lex placed a kiss on the top of Martha's head, which pleasantly surprised the housekeeper. Although their relationship had always been loving, it wasn't often her charge would initiate any sort of contact.

"Thanks." The words were uttered so softly, they were barely audible.

Her own emotions were close to the surface, and Martha feared she would burst into tears at any moment. "For what, honey?"

"Everything," Lex murmured, then followed Amanda into the house.

Martha watched them go, then wiped a tear from her eye with the corner of her apron. "Rotten kid," she grumbled. "Just when I think I have her figured out, she says something like that." She sighed heavily as she re-entered the house and closed the door behind her.

THE THREE WOMEN spent the next several hours in the kitchen while Amanda caught Martha up on the happenings of the last couple of days. She tried to gloss over her involvement in the incident with Rick, but Lex wouldn't let her.

"Back up, Amanda." Lex stopped her lover's narrative, then turned her attention to Martha. "She's not telling you the best part. Rick was going for Mrs. Cauble, so I stepped in behind him to try and get his attention. He elbowed me in the ribs—" Lex cleared her throat, "and I dropped like a rock."

"Gracious." Martha reached across the table and placed her hand on Lex's arm. "Are you all right?"

"Yeah, it just kind of took my breath away for a few minutes." The look Lex gave Amanda warned her not to contradict her. She was fine now and didn't want to worry Martha more than necessary. "Anyway, there I was, on my knees trying to catch my breath, when I see Rick on his way to hurt Mrs. Cauble. He only got about two steps when his head popped back, and he fell over in a dead faint."

Martha glanced between the two women. "How?" She hated waiting, and now she was practically on the edge of her seat.

"Amanda did some sort of kung fu, or something."

Embarrassed, Amanda looked down at the table. "Karate, actually. I only studied it for one summer, years ago, and was much better with my legs than my hands. It's amazing what you remember when you need it." Her partner was making a bigger deal out of it then it was, she was sure.

The housekeeper's mouth dropped open. "You kicked him?"

"Nailed him right on the chin," Lex supplied helpfully. "Guess Ol' Rick's got a glass jaw." Amanda poked her on the shoulder. "What?"

Amanda shook her head slowly. "I know I shouldn't have, but I just reacted. He was really mad at Gramma, and I was afraid he would hurt her or Lex. I guess I'm no better than him." What really bothered her was the rage she felt when she saw Rick hurt Lex. Part of her wanted to do more than just kick him under the chin, and Amanda knew it would be a long while before she reconciled that part of herself.

Martha stood up. "Don't feel bad, honey. I think it's great that you can defend yourself, or someone you care about." She patted Amanda's arm. "It's been a long day, and there's no sense in your driving back to town this late, so I think it would be best if you two stayed the night."

Amanda looked at Lex, who shrugged her shoulders. "That sounds like a great idea. Just let me give my grandparents a call so that they won't worry." She stood up. "I'll just use the phone upstairs, if that's okay."

"Sure," Lex said. "I'll be up in a minute." Totally smitten, the rancher's eyes followed Amanda as she left the room. She couldn't help but enjoy the way her lover walked and remember how that body felt next to hers.

Not too surprised, Martha snapped her fingers to get Lex's attention. "Lexie? Earth to Lexington. Hello?"

"Hmm?" Lex continued to daydream about the things she wanted to do to Amanda. Whipped cream and cherries figured prominently in her thoughts. "Oh! Umm, sorry about that." She straightened in her chair. "What's up?"

Martha moved until she stood next to Lex. Running one hand through the dark hair, she murmured, "I was so proud of you this evening, Lexie."

The rancher leaned into the contact. "Really? I thought you would be disappointed. I almost strangled my brother on the front porch, Martha." She released a heavy sigh and wearily closed her eyes. "Dad was right."

"About what?"

"He said my temper would cause nothing but trouble, and he was right. First Lou, and now Hubert." She fought back the reemerging pain when she thought about her youngest brother.

"How can you say that?" Martha sat in the chair next to the anguished woman. "Louis was killed in a boating accident. You weren't even there."

Lex fought to keep her composure. "And if I hadn't lost my

temper with him, he would have never gone in the first place." It was right before her father had left her in charge of the ranch, and the Texas summer was one of the hottest on record. Lex had been stuck in the office when she would much rather have been down at the creek, swimming with her younger brother and their friends. She was both sister and mother to the teenager, and between fighting with Hubert and trying to run the ranch while her father was away for a few weeks, her nerves were frayed.

Louis had come into the office, telling his sister about a group of friends going to Lake Somerville, and asking her if she wanted to go. She couldn't because of her duties at the ranch, and when she found out that the oldest boy in the group was only sixteen, she forbade Louis to go. He yelled at her that she wasn't his mother and went anyway.

Several hours later, Lex received a phone call from one of the rangers at the lake. The boat the group had been riding in capsized when another boat broadsided it, and Louis had been killed. The police came to her home to take her to identify her brother's remains, just as her father was returning from his trip. The patriarch never got over it. With his wife and youngest son both dead, and his two older children having reached adulthood, Rawson Walters departed for good, leaving the ranch to Lex, which left her to the mercy of her vengeful brother, Hubert.

Looking back, Lex realized that the day Louis died was the day she started shutting herself down. She only went through the motions of day-to-day living, until Hubert brought Linda home. For a short while, Lex allowed herself to feel, until Linda handed her heart back to her in pieces. Then it became easier to hide inside a bottle than to face the loneliness. After she sobered up, Lex decided just to quit caring. You couldn't get hurt if you didn't care. She never really mourned the death of Louis, choosing instead to shut off all of her emotions, until a certain beautiful realtor splashed into her life.

Martha leaned over and pulled Lex into her arms. "Sweetheart, blaming yourself for that does no good. It was an accident, plain and simple. No one was to blame, especially you. Let it go." She kissed the top of Lex's head and held her close as Lex sobbed, finally releasing some of the grief she had held in for so many years.

Amanda stood quietly in the doorway, feeling guilty for witnessing such a private scene. *I vaguely remember that summer, except that it was really hot. And I had no idea who that boy was who had been killed. Poor Lex.* Amanda wasn't very fond of the water, so she and her grandparents rarely went to the lake when she visited for the summers. But she remembered hearing them speak of the tragedy right after it happened. Sparing one final glance in the kitchen, she turned and walked silently up the stairs, tears of compassion in her eyes.

Lex pulled away and wiped her eyes with the back of her hand. "I'm sorry, Martha. I don't know what came over me. Hell, it's been almost ten years. Why did I fall apart now?"

"Honey, it was easier for you to hate yourself all these years than to give in to your grief." Martha nodded toward the stairs Amanda had just ascended. "I think you finally feel safe enough to give in to your feelings, safe enough to grieve." *No sense in telling her how afraid I've been, wondering what would happen if she ever did open up. My poor child.* Even though Lex was a grown woman, in Martha's heart she'd always be her little girl. She picked up a napkin from the table and wiped Lex's face with it like she used to do when the rancher was a youngster. "Now you go upstairs and get a good night's sleep."

Lex took a deep breath and gave Martha a shaky smile. "You're right, as usual. I'm pretty worn out." She leaned over and kissed Martha on the cheek. "Thanks."

"No need to thank me, child. That's what I'm here for." Martha stood, embarrassed. She could handle just about anything, except seeing the woman she raised from a small child fall apart.

Smiling to herself, Lex got to her feet as well, then enveloped Martha in a hug. "Well, thanks anyway." She felt the embrace returned. "I love you, you know," Lex whispered, just before she released the older woman.

"I love you, too." Martha stepped back and turned Lex to the doorway. "Now go on upstairs before Amanda thinks you've run off." Feeling back to normal, she swatted Lex on the rear.

"Yes, ma'am." Not having to be told twice, Lex left the room and hurried up the stairs, her thoughts returning to whipped cream and cherries.

Taking and releasing a deep breath, Lex stood in the darkened doorway of the master bedroom, the only light in the room coming from the low burning fireplace.

"Amanda?" she called out quietly, unable to see if her lover was asleep on the bed. A movement near the fireplace caught her eye.

"Over here." Amanda sat up from her curled position in one of the stuffed chairs.

Lex crossed the room quickly and dropped to her knees at Amanda's feet. "Are you okay?" she asked, placing her hands on her friend's legs.

Even in the dim light, Amanda could see the red and puffy eyes. Reaching out with a gentle hand, she brushed the unruly hair from Lex's face, then continued to stroke her face. "I'm fine. But you're looking a little rough around the edges. What say we take a quick shower and go to bed?"

"Mmm." Lex closed her eyes and absorbed the loving touch. "That's the best offer I've had all day." She gathered her wits about her and stood. "Come on, I'll scrub your back." She helped Amanda to her feet and wrapped both arms around her lover's torso.

Amanda enjoyed the warm security of the strong arms she found herself in. Closing her eyes, she was content to stand and absorb the love emanating from Lex. "I could stay here forever," she murmured, not realizing she had spoken out loud until she felt Lex squeeze her a little tighter.

"I hope so," Lex whispered in her ear, "because I have no intention of ever letting you go." She pulled her head back slightly so that she could look into Amanda's eyes. "I love you." Leaning down, Lex covered Amanda's mouth with her own, placing a soft, re-affirming kiss on slightly parted lips.

Amanda turned into the kiss, accepting the almost hesitant touch from Lex. Finally breaking off the kiss in order to breathe, she rested her cheek against the rancher's heaving chest. "Let's go get that shower." Amanda led her dazed lover in the direction of the bathroom, "If you're real good, I'll practice my massage techniques on you." She swatted Lex on the rear and closed the bathroom door.

Chapter
Six

THE NEXT MORNING, the sun had barely peeked over the horizon when Lex opened her eyes. Snuggled behind Amanda, her nose was tucked in the sweet, fragrant hair. Since the day would go on without her and she had a lot of things to do, Lex reluctantly lifted her head and began disentangling herself. She climbed out of bed and tucked the comforter back around her lover's body. She felt wonderful, unsure if it was due to the release of long-held in emotion or the full body massage she had received from Amanda's talented hands the prior evening. Dressing quickly, Lex left a short note on the pillow next to the sleeping woman and then crept quietly out of the room.

Bounding down the stairs, Lex was on her way to the office when she saw a light coming from the kitchen, so she made a slight detour. When she saw Martha at the counter humming to herself as she rolled out biscuits, Lex crept up behind the unsuspecting woman with an evil smile on her face.

"Good morning, sunshine," she bellowed, scooping up the shocked housekeeper and spinning her around the room.

Martha screamed, then reflexively grabbed Lex's head, coating her dark hair with flour and bits of dough. "Put me down, you crazy brat," she huffed. "I'm getting airsick!"

Lex stopped spinning the older woman around, allowing her feet to touch the ground. Remembering what Martha had been doing, she cringed when she saw the housekeeper remove her hands from where they had been clinched in her thick hair. "Ugh. So, I'm guessing I look pretty good in white hair?" Trying to keep an innocent look on her face, Lex reached behind her back and rubbed her palms across the flour-covered countertop.

"I'm sorry about that, Lexie. It's just that you startled me." Seeing the look on Lex's face, she shook her head and pointed a finger. "Now, wait just a minute." Martha backed up several steps, with Lex closing in on her.

"What's the matter, Martha?" Lex continued her pursuit, with her hands remaining behind her back.

The older woman put her hands in front of herself defensively. "Don't be doing anything that you might regret—"

"Me? Never." Closing in on Martha, Lex cornered her against the stove. Just as she was about to raise her hands and rub flour in Martha's hair, she felt two arms wrap around her from behind, trapping her hands to her sides.

A soft voice whispered in her ear. "I can't leave you alone for a minute, can I?"

Martha laughed and then wiped another blob of flour onto Lex's nose. "Thanks, Amanda." She edged past the two women and went back to her biscuit making.

Lex twisted, then picked Amanda up and dangled her in her arms. "Good morning, traitor."

Amanda looked into the sparkling eyes, then noticed the flour and dough in Lex's hair. "Umm, good morning?" She used one hand to brush the flour away. "Are you trying to help Martha cook breakfast again?"

Lex rolled her eyes, then shot a look at the housekeeper's back. "No. This was completely unprovoked. All I did was come in and tell Martha good morning." To make her case, Lex's lower lip poked out in a slight pout.

Martha felt the need to defend herself. "Don't believe a word of it. The brat sneaked up on me and started spinning me around the room."

Amanda's eyes narrowed. "You didn't."

"Well—" Embarrassed, Lex gave up and continued to look deeply into Amanda's eyes. The tiny smile on her face never wavered, nor did her attention.

The look of total love on Lex's face made Amanda feel complete. They stood there, motionless, until Amanda worried that she might be too heavy for Lex to continue to hold in her arms. "Ah, Lex?"

"Mmm?"

"Do you want to let me down now?"

"Not really," Lex admitted. "I could do this for the rest of my life," she said quietly. "And I hope to." The last words were spoke even more softly, as Lex was afraid of sharing too much of herself, too soon.

The quiet admission took Amanda's breath away. "Me too. I can't think of any place I'd rather be."

Martha had watched the two women in the middle of the room for a while, and then decided things were getting a little too serious. "How am I supposed to cook with you two giving each other puppy-dog eyes in the middle of my kitchen? Either sit at the table, or go somewhere else to moon." That got the intended response, as both Lex and Amanda blushed furiously.

Lex let Amanda down so that she could stand on her own feet. "Sorry about that. I kind of forgot what I was doing."

Amanda gave her a gentle pat on her good side. "Don't be. I enjoyed it." She saw that Martha was diligently working on the biscuits with her back turned to the couple. Amanda pulled her lover's head down. "Let me give you a proper good morning." She gave Lex a long, passionate kiss, ending only when Martha cleared her throat.

"Excuse me, wouldn't you two be more comfortable upstairs?" the housekeeper asked.

"Oops." Amanda looked directly at Martha, not uncomfortable in the least. "Probably. But I'm so hungry I could even eat some of Lex's pancakes."

Lex scowled while the other two women enjoyed the joke. "Remind me to bring you breakfast in bed one morning. That'll teach you to tease me." She patted Amanda on the rear and then sat down at the table. "Need any help, Martha?"

"As a matter of fact, you could be a big help and go find something else to do for about twenty or thirty minutes," Martha hinted, trying to keep Lex out from under her feet. For someone capable enough to run a ranch, her Lexie had a knack for getting in the way whenever Martha tried to do anything.

Amanda walked over and pulled Lex out of her chair. "Come on, let's go for a walk." She led Lex from the room, while Martha's laughter floated after them. Instead of going out the back door, Amanda led her partner down the long hallway and then pulled her into the darkened den. She pushed Lex onto the couch, then moved over to the entertainment center nearby.

"I thought we were going for a walk?"

"I changed my mind. It looks chilly outside this morning, so I thought we could just sit in here and enjoy your wonderful stereo system." Amanda placed a CD into the stereo and pushed play, then turned the volume down until it became background sound. The lights from the stereo cast a soft glow in the room allowing her to see the smile on Lex's face.

Lex patted her lap. "Chilly, huh? Why don't you come over here, and I'll see about warming you up?"

Amanda walked slowly across the room to climb onto her lover's lap, straddling her legs. She wrapped her arms around Lex's neck and whispered, "You're right. This is much more comfortable." Amanda placed a light kiss on Lex's lips and then snuggled close until her head was under her partner's chin.

"Happy to be of service, ma'am." Closing her eyes, Lex was able to completely relax, somewhat shocked that she was able to sit still for such a long length of time without the urge to be up and doing something. She enjoyed the feel of the woman in her arms and felt at peace. *You're a bad influence on me, Amanda, but I wouldn't want it any other way.*

HALF AN HOUR later, after hearing the sounds of The Corrs floating down the hallway, Martha peeked into the den. Seeing the two women curled up on the sofa, she couldn't help but smile. *They look so darn cute, all snuggled up together like that.* She crept quietly into the room, trying not to startle them. "Lexie?"

Lex slowly opened her eyes. "Hey, Martha." She spoke quietly, trying to keep from disturbing her sleeping companion. "I take it that breakfast is ready?"

"It sure is. Do you think you can tear yourself away?"

"Well, if I have to, I guess." Lex gave the older woman a wry smile. "Of course, after breakfast I'm gonna need to wash my hair for some strange reason."

Martha put her hands on her hips. "It's not my fault. You shouldn't sneak up on an old woman like that."

"You're not an old woman," Lex snorted, causing the bundle in her arms to moan and then snuggle closer. But the comment made her pause for a moment. Lex studied Martha seriously, seeing for the first time the wrinkles on the once-smooth skin, and the hair that was becoming more gray than brown. *When did that happen? Have I been so self-absorbed that I never noticed?*

Martha noticed the far away look in Lex's eyes. "Is everything okay?"

"Damn, Martha. It's been twenty-five years, hasn't it?" Lex asked. "I can't believe that much time has passed."

Martha perched on the other end of the sofa. "It is hard to believe, isn't it? I told you I was getting old."

"No, not old, but you've spent half of your life babysitting me. A little more than you bargained for, I'll bet."

"And well worth every single minute of it," the housekeeper replied. "Although, I could do with less excitement, if you don't mind. This past week or so has been a little bit too much, even for you." Martha stood. "Now why don't you wake up Sleeping Beauty there, and come and get some breakfast?" She hummed to herself as she left the room, once again quite proud of herself for getting the last word in.

After watching Martha leave, Lex promised herself she'd do something for the housekeeper to let her know how much she meant to her. She decided to ask for Amanda's help in figuring out what that was. Thinking of Amanda, she bent to whisper in the sleeping woman's ear. "Amanda?"

"Mmm. No." Amanda buried her face deeper into Lex's chest.

Although she enjoyed the contact, Lex didn't want to disappoint Martha who had probably gone to a lot of trouble with the meal, and she would like to start in on it before it got cold. She kissed the top of Amanda's head. "Sweetheart, you need to wake up."

"Don't want to."

"Breakfast is ready."

Amanda opened her eyes and her head lifted away from Lex's body. "Do we have to? I'm comfortable right where I am."

Laughing, Lex pulled her lover closer to her. "You are absolutely priceless, Amanda."

"What's that supposed to mean?"

"That means," Lex placed a kiss on Amanda's lips, "I don't know," another kiss, "what I would do," a longer, more passionate kiss, "without you."

"Mmm." Amanda curled up against Lex. She was about to continue when she heard Lex's stomach growl. Ignoring the loud rumble, she threaded her hands through Lex's hair and forced her companion further into the sofa.

Lex sat back and enjoyed the gentle assault, until her stomach rumbled again. Seeing that her lover had no intention of stopping, Lex decided to take matters into her own hands, in a manner of speaking. She dropped her hands from Amanda's shoulders and then them down slowly until they came to rest on her hips. Moving forward slightly, Lex stood, taking Amanda with her.

"Whoa! The couch is moving," Amanda exclaimed as she looked around. Without realizing it, she had wrapped her legs around Lex's waist. She glanced down at their entangled bodies with a flush of embarrassment. "Umm, I guess I should let you go, huh?"

"Well, I could just carry you into the kitchen like this, if you want. Or, I could carry you up the stairs, and give you a different kind of breakfast, although I would leave it to you to explain that one to Martha."

As Amanda unwrapped her legs, she said, "As much as I would love to go back upstairs with you, I don't think either one of us wants to face Martha's wrath if we don't have breakfast." She appeared to give the matter some thought. "But, we may need some way to work off such a wonderful feast, don't you agree?"

"SO, WHAT KIND of mischief are you girls going to stir up today?" Martha asked. The three women sat around the kitchen table after breakfast, each enjoying a cup of coffee.

Lex traded looks with Amanda, who shrugged. "Well, I thought we'd spend today and tonight here, then I have to go back to my grandparents' home to get packed for our trip next week."

"A trip? Where are you going?"

Amanda finished the last sip of her coffee, then placed her mug back on the table. "That's right, we haven't had a chance to tell you yet." She nodded her thanks as Lex refilled both hers and Martha's cups with the professionalism of a seasoned waitress. "My parents are having this big dinner party next week in Los Angeles, and I've convinced Lex to go with me. Besides, I'm going to need some help packing up my stuff and sending it here to my grandparents' house, since I've decided to move to Somerville for good."

"That's wonderful news, Amanda." Martha laid a hand on Amanda's forearm and then turned her attention to Lex. "How are you planning on getting there?"

"Fly, of course. Why do you ask?" Amanda followed Martha's gaze, where Lex had paled suddenly.

Oh, shit! I didn't even think about how we were going to get there. "Yeah, Martha. You didn't think we'd walk, did you?" Lex tried to keep her tone light.

"Ri-i-ight. I guess it was a pretty silly question, wasn't it?" Martha spared a glance at Amanda, who was looking at Lex with concern.

Lex said, "No, it wasn't silly. I hadn't really thought about having to fly." Seeing the worry on her lover's face, she gave Amanda an embarrassed smile. "I, uh, have a little trouble, on airplanes."

"What kind of trouble?" Amanda took Lex's hands in hers. "Do you get airsick?"

Martha chuckled. "We should be so lucky." She then quieted after Lex
glowered at her.

"No, it's not that." Feeling the gentle pressure on her hand, Lex continued, "I get a little anxious on airplanes."

"I'd say more than 'a little anxious,' Lexie." Martha turned back to Amanda. "We had to practically knock her out with tranquilizers the last time. Not the best experience, let me tell you."

Amanda found it hard to believe that someone as in control as Lex would be anxious over something that she herself thought of as trivial. "What is it about flying that bothers you so much?"

Lex looked down at the table, unable to meet Amanda's eyes. "I'm not sure. It could be one of several things, I guess. The enclosed space, the fact that we're thousands of feet up in the air with nothing holding us up, or maybe it's just the sickeningly perky flight attendants. I don't know."

"Maybe you just need something else to occupy your mind."

"Such as?" Lex couldn't help the sultry grin that crossed her face.

Amanda blushed. "Umm, let's try another tact." She cleared her throat. "Maybe your anxiety is due to something that happened before. Have you had any bad experiences on an airplane?"

"Hmm. You mean other than the food?" she teased, receiving the expected slap on the arm for that remark. "No, nothing that I can think of. I've only flown three times, and each time was more of a disaster than the last."

"Four, actually," Martha added. "Once when you were about eleven or so. But that was with your father, and it wasn't very far. I doubt if that had anything to do with it."

"And yet you're willing to put yourself through all of that again?" Amanda was shocked. She didn't know if she'd be so quick to face her fears, no matter what the reason. *Keep spiders and other crawly things away from me, or I'll go running into the night, screaming.* She mentally shook her head. *Nope. I couldn't do it.*

Lex shrugged her shoulders. "Yeah. I figure it's about time to face my fears. Right, Martha?" She looked at the housekeeper, who had a perplexed look on her face.

She's certainly got it bad, if she's willing to do that, again. "If you say so, Lexie. I know you've really been bothered by this for a long time." Martha looked at Amanda. "She swore after the last time that she'd never fly again."

"Why? What happened the last time?"

Lex rolled her eyes, while Martha laughed. "They say," Lex looked pointedly at the older woman, "that I hit a flight attendant, but I don't remember it. The medication I had been given to help me with my jitters was really something else."

Martha interrupted. "You did. The tranquilizers made Lexie really woozy, and she stood up to grab something from one of the overhead compartments. They said she started to tumble back, and the flight attendant caught her. You kept hollering that he..." she was laughing so hard that she had to stop and catch her breath "...grabbed your hind end. I heard it took three security guards to get you off the plane." Martha noticed that she wasn't the only one losing the battle with her laughter. Amanda had one hand over her mouth, trying to stifle her own giggles.

Amanda lost it, and began to pound the table with one hand while she laughed. "Oh, God, that poor man."

Lex gave her an indignant look. "Hey, it was my ass he was

groping."

The housekeeper wiped the tears of mirth from her face and eyes. "And for that you broke his nose? I met the poor man later. Believe me, you weren't his type. I'm just thankful he was so understanding and didn't press charges against you."

"I've always wondered what you told him to keep me out of jail," Lex mumbled. To her amazement, Martha blushed.

"I, uh, appealed to his kind and generous nature," Martha stammered, somewhat embarrassed at the length she went to in order to protect Lex.

Lex put her elbow up on the table, and propped her chin on her open hand. "Oh, this I gotta hear." She waved her other hand regally. "Please, continue."

"Brat." Martha took a deep breath. "Okay, well, we got you settled in the car." She winked at Amanda. "And she slept like a baby for almost two days, too. Anyway, the poor man was in the airline security office, screaming about lawyers, court, and brutish psycho women who should be locked away for the good of society."

Now Amanda was curious as well. "So, how did you calm him down?"

"Well, for starters, I cried. Then, I told him how Lexie had been taking care of me in my declining years." Martha rolled her eyes at her audience. "And that she was all I had left in this world after her daddy up and left us. After all, it really wasn't a lie now, was it?"

Shaking her head at the story, Lex couldn't help but marvel at Martha's ingenuity. "Martha, only you could make a man feel bad for getting beat up on an airplane."

"Yes, well, after I also explained to him that she was heavily tranquilized and had no idea what she was doing, he understood." Then she looked at Lex with undisguised glee. "He told me his little poodle was the same way when they had to sedate her for long trips." Amanda cracked up, as her mind suddenly filled with the picture of Lex sporting a poodle cut.

Lex sat there blushing furiously and gazing at the two near-hysterical women. Once they calmed down, she gave Amanda a serious stare. "Woof." The single word set both women off again. Standing up, she tried to preserve as much dignity as possible. "I'm going upstairs for a shower, if you two ladies don't mind." She got to the doorway and turned back toward them. "Try to stay out of trouble, if you can."

Amanda and Martha looked at each other, paused, then burst into laughter again.

THE NEXT FEW days were a whirlwind of activity for both women. They spent two days at the ranch, so that Lex could finish up any business she needed to, not to mention trying to get Lex packed for the upcoming trip. When they were upstairs, the rancher was almost embarrassed to open her closet.

"Uh, Amanda?" Lex was ashamed of her wardrobe or, more to the point, the lack thereof. "Maybe we should just buy some clothes when we get there."

Amanda stopped at the closet door, her hand on the knob. "Why? Have you suddenly outgrown all of your clothes?"

Lex snorted. "Not yet, although I'm sure I will soon if Martha and your grandparents keep stuffing me three times a day." With a resigned sigh, she moved past Amanda to open the closet door, which caused the light inside to come on.

"Whoa." Amanda was impressed at the way the area was set up. The closet itself was only ten feet deep and six feet wide, but it had two wooden poles on each side that went the length of the closet. The rear wall was covered with large oak shelves, which had folded shirts and sweaters in individual cubbyholes. But what surprised her most was how empty it was. Only the right side of the closet had any clothes hanging in it, and even those didn't fill the space all the way to the end. Shirts hung from the top pole, with jeans and a few pair of khaki slacks on the bottom pole.

Placing her hand on Amanda's shoulder, Lex sighed again. "Yeah. I told you I don't have many clothes. No sense in it, really. Who's going to see me, anyway?"

"Honey, I have yet to see you dressed badly. You've got to be the best-dressed rancher around. Besides, I don't think Martha would let you out of the house if you weren't all clean and pressed."

Her fears dissipated, Lex pulled Amanda into a one-armed hug. "Oh, yeah. We've argued about that for years. She keeps insisting on ironing my jeans and denim shirts. I keep telling her that the cattle don't care what I look like." She followed Amanda into the closet. "And just how many ranchers have you seen?"

"Well, to be honest, you're the first one I've ever really met. But," Amanda turned to face her lover, "I've watched a lot of TV, and you are most certainly the best looking cowhand I've ever laid eyes on." Amanda stood on her tiptoes and wrapped her arms around Lex's neck.

Lex put her arms around Amanda and bent her head to meet her halfway. "Why, thank you kindly, ma'am," she drawled, lowering her lips to Amanda's.

Amanda leaned into the embrace. "Mmm." She felt Lex's hands slide down her sides to tuck themselves into the back pockets of her jeans. Breaking off the kiss to breathe, Amanda leaned her forehead into Lex's heaving chest. "Much better." After giving one last squeeze to the lanky body in her embrace, Amanda stepped back a pace. "Whew. Okay. Let's see about getting you packed." She looked at the row of neatly pressed pants. "Most of these jeans look brand-new. Have you been shopping lately?"

"Not exactly." Lex looked at her feet. After a moment of silence, she glanced back up into the questioning eyes before her. "I keep wearing the same couple of pair because they're comfortable. It drives Martha crazy."

"You're so bad." Amanda stepped back and pulled several pairs of jeans off the pole, as well as one pair of khakis. "Here, hold these." She shuffled through the hanging shirts, then stopped. "Hey, where did you get this?" she asked, running her hand across the soft material. "Doesn't look like something you'd wear chasing cattle."

Lex touched the fabric with tentative fingertips. "Oh. I forgot I had that shirt."

"This is perfect. It'll go great with these." Amanda pulled a pair of pants from the rack, and handed them to Lex. She wandered to the back of the closet to grab a pair of shiny boots, and as an afterthought snatched a pair of scuffed Nike's from a nearby shelf, holding the sneakers in the air. "I didn't know you owned anything like these."

"Smartass." Lex scowled at her. She held the items in her hands aloft, and asked, "Are all of these clothes really necessary? We're gonna be there what, four or five days at the most?"

"Absolutely. And you should consider yourself lucky that I'm really packing light." Amanda stepped past Lex and back into the bedroom. "Do you have a bathing suit?"

Lex grabbed a suitcase from one of the high shelves in the closet. "Yeah, somewhere. But I haven't worn it since high school. Why?"

Amanda helped Lex carry the clothes and suitcase over to the bed. "My folks have a really nice hot tub. I thought it might be fun to try it out with you."

"A hot tub, eh?" Lex stepped up behind her lover, until her body was in complete contact with Amanda's. Moving Amanda's hair to one side, Lex started placing small kisses on her neck. "I don't think your family would approve of what I could do with you in a hot tub." She felt the woman in front of her tremble slightly.

Amanda's knees weakened. "I really don't, care...mmm..." She raised an arm behind her head, taking a handful of thick dark hair in her fist and enjoying the sensation of lips nibbling on her throat. "...what my family thinks. Ahh..." When Lex's hands worked their way underneath the front of her shirt, all her other thoughts faded.

"Ahem." Martha stood at the doorway, with her hands on her hips and an almost stern expression on her face. "You two are never going to get packed at this rate."

Lex turned around and pulled Amanda in front of her. "And this would be a bad thing?"

"Don't get sassy with me, Lexie. I can still take you over my knee." Martha stepped into the room, and moved toward the couple.

"Watch it, lady, or I'll sic my bodyguard on you," Lex threatened, right before she ducked behind a blushing Amanda.

"Hey, don't get me involved here."

Martha gestured at the way Lex had her arms wrapped around Amanda. "Looks to me like you're already pretty much involved, Amanda."

"She's got you there," Lex murmured in Amanda's ear while she tickled her on the stomach.

Amanda slapped her hands. One more touch from her lover, and she'd toss Lex on the bed, whether Martha was there or not. "Stop that."

With her libido in almost as bad shape as her lover's, Lex decided enough was enough. She propped her chin on Amanda's shoulder. "Is there something we can do for you, Martha?"

"Actually, I came up here to tell you Dr. Anderson called in your prescription of tranquilizers for your flight. He said you can pick them up in the morning on your way to the airport."

"Thanks, Martha, but I'm going to try and do without them."

Martha was uncertain as to whether that was such a good idea. "Are you certain you want to do that?"

Lex released her hold on Amanda and sat on the bed, then ran a hand through her hair in a nervous gesture. "Yeah. I don't want to be drugged out when I meet Amanda's family."

"Honey," Amanda sat down next to her and grasped her hand. "I don't want you to put yourself through hell just because of them." She stroked Lex's arm with her free hand. "Believe me, they're really not worth it."

Martha sat down on the other side of Lex. "Okay, what about this?" She ran one hand across Lex's back. "Why don't you take the medication with you and then you'll have it, just in case?"

Lex opened her mouth to argue.

"Shh, she's right." Amanda stopped her. "And," she linked her arm with Lex's. "We both might need sedatives around my family. They tend to be a little high strung."

"Oh, so that's where you get it, huh?" Lex teased. "Ow!" She rubbed her shoulder where Amanda poked her.

"Serves you right, Lexie." Martha stood up. "You girls going to be ready for lunch soon?"

Lex scowled. "Lunch? We just had breakfast. Just how much do you plan on making us eat?" Lex mumbled, then found herself pushed back onto the bed. "What?" she asked the two retreating figures.

AFTER LUNCH, LEX packed up the truck and then she and Amanda prepared to leave the ranch. Standing on the front porch, Martha tearfully hugged each woman.

"Now you girls try and stay out of trouble." She had just embraced Amanda, and stepped back to look into the shining eyes of the younger woman. "Take care of her."

Amanda pulled the housekeeper into another hug. "I will, I promise," she whispered into the Martha's ear, then kissed her on the cheek.

Lex rolled her eyes at how the other two were carrying on. "It's not for that long. I'll call you as soon as our plane lands, don't worry." Seeing the tears on Martha's face, she pulled the older woman into a fierce embrace of her own. "Are you gonna be okay out here by yourself while I'm gone?"

"Heavens, yes. I thought I'd get those new curtains made for my house while you are away." She stepped back and gave them both a shy look. "And I thought it would be nice to have Charlie out for dinner a few nights this week. I know he must get tired of the food at the boarding house."

Lex winked at Amanda, then gave Martha a no-nonsense stare. "Maybe I should stop by the boarding house later tonight and find out what his intentions are."

"You wouldn't dare," Martha yelped, not seeing Amanda quickly cover her mouth to hide a grin. "Lexington Marie! How could you even think about—" The housekeeper paused, hearing the slight giggle behind her. Seeing Amanda trying to control her laughter, she turned back in time to catch Lex grinning widely. "Oh, you!"

Laughing, Lex brought Martha back into another hug. "Sorry, Martha. I just couldn't resist." She left a kiss on the older woman's forehead. "Charlie is like a second father to me. I hope you two will have some wonderful dinners while I'm gone." She leaned down and whispered into Martha's ear. "I love you, you know. Try and behave yourself until I get back." She left another kiss, this one on a wrinkled cheek, and then stood up straight. "This isn't getting us any closer to town. I'll also carry the cell phone, so just call me if you need anything."

Martha practically pushed her off the porch. "Stop worrying. I'm a grown woman, Lexie. Now go on, and have a good time."

Amanda followed Lex down the steps. "Well, I can't guarantee fun, but I know for a fact it won't be boring."

Lex opened the passenger's side door for Amanda, then helped her into the truck. "Guess I'll have to invest in one of those little steps for the truck," she teased her friend, before closing the door. "See you in a few days, Martha." Lex waved at the housekeeper as she crossed to the driver's side of the vehicle. Through the rearview mirror, she watched Martha wave at them until they were out of sight of the house. Releasing a heavy sigh, she turned her attention back to the road.

"Lex?" Amanda placed a hand on her arm. "Are you okay?"

Blinking, Lex turned back to her companion. "Yeah, I'm all right."

Not to be deterred, Amanda let her hand drift down the forearm until she was able to intertwine their fingers. "Sure you are. Now tell me what's bothering you."

Lex pulled their joined hands to her lips, and kissed Amanda's knuckles. "I don't like the idea of Martha staying out at the ranch for so long all alone. Especially with Hubert acting like such an ass."

"From what I've seen, I don't think she'll be alone, sweetheart."

"You think so?" Lex turned slightly, and gave Amanda a more genuine smile. "I sure hope so. He's been trying to get her to marry him for almost as long as I can remember." Turning her eyes back to the road, she sobered. "I know she loves him, but she seems determined to stay with me."

"Why don't we call Charlie tonight and talk to him? Maybe he'll keep an eye on things while you're gone." Amanda was concerned at the look on Lex's face. *She's going to make herself sick worrying about all of this.* "I think she's just worried about you being alone there at the ranch." She gave the hand in hers a squeeze. "Although I don't think that's going to be a problem anymore."

"Yeah?"

"Oh, yeah. Most definitely," Amanda replied, love shining in her eyes.

Chapter
Seven

Once the truck had made it safely back into town, Lex turned to Amanda, hoping that the request she was about to voice would be considered reasonable. "Would you mind too terribly much if we went straight over to the boarding house? I can't concentrate on anything else until I know Martha has been taken care of. I promise it won't take too long."

Amanda squeezed the hand she had been holding throughout the entire drive. "Good idea. I'd feel a lot better too."

Ten minutes later, they pulled onto a quiet residential street in one of the older sections of town. Large, two-storied, wood-framed homes populated the block, several of them sporting historical landmark signs in their front yards. Lex pulled the truck up to a house in the middle of the block which had a sheriff's department car sitting in the driveway.

"Wow." Amanda looked around as Lex helped her from the truck. "It's beautiful!" She followed the rancher up the stone walkway to the front porch. "Charlie lives here?"

Lex stopped on the porch. "Yep. He lives here with Mrs. Wade and her son, David." Seeing the unasked question in Amanda's eyes, she continued. "Mr. Wade passed away about ten years ago, and Mrs. Wade needed a boarder to help make ends meet and to take care of things around the house. Charlie was living in a tiny efficiency apartment on the other side of town, away from the Sheriff's Department. He'd been good friends with the Wades forever, so he jumped at the chance for a nice room and home-cooked meals." Her short story finished, Lex knocked on the door.

Soon the door opened and a tall man about twenty-five opened the door. "Lex," he bellowed, swinging the door inward and stepping out onto the porch. "It's been way too long." He scooped her up in a bear hug, swinging the poor rancher around in a circle.

"Dammit, Dave, put me down," Lex yelled, wriggling unsuccessfully to get out of his grasp.

Placing Lex back on her feet, David grinned, his white teeth shining against his ebony skin. When he saw Amanda, his smile faded a little. "Uh-oh. I didn't realize we had company."

Lex stood off to the side, watching as Amanda's eyes sparkled with amusement. "Sorry about that, Dave." She motioned Amanda forward with a wave of her hand. "This is Amanda Cauble. Amanda, this brute is David Wade." She almost laughed at the chagrined look on his face.

"Oh, shi...uh, I mean, hello, Amanda. It's nice to meet you." He held out a large hand tentatively.

Amanda grasped his hand firmly. "It's nice to meet you too, David. Have you known Lex very long?"

"Over half of my life, I think. And please call me Dave." He ushered the two women into the house and into a spacious living room. "Have a seat, ladies. Can I get you something to drink?"

Lex waited until Amanda sat on one end of a navy blue loveseat, then positioned herself beside her. "Nah. We were hoping to chat with Charlie for a few minutes. Is he around?"

Dave leaned against the nearby sofa. "Yeah, I think he's upstairs getting cleaned up. He should be down in a few minutes." He was about to continue when an older, very petite woman walked into the room.

"Lexie Walters. I thought my old ears heard your voice. Get yourself over here right now," she demanded, opening her arms.

Lex dutifully rose from the loveseat and crossed the room, bending low to embrace the older woman. "Mama Wade, you just keep looking younger and prettier every time I see you."

Mrs. Wade slapped Lex on the arm. "Don't be spreading your bull around me, Lexie. I've had to hear it for too many years to be believing it."

Kissing the wrinkled cheek, Lex escorted the lady of the house to a wooden rocking chair. "I'm sorry it's been so long, but it's been pretty hectic at the ranch."

Mrs. Wade slapped at her again. "You better quit treating me like some sort of senile invalid. I can still whip your fanny, young lady." She noticed Amanda sitting quietly on the loveseat and pointed. "Is that your latest catch?"

"What?" Lex spun around in the middle of the room, stopped before she could finish walking back to her seat.

"Charlie told us how you fished a young lady out of the creek. We figured this must be her." Dave explained, enjoying seeing Lex turn several shades of red.

"Where are your manners, girl?" the Mrs. Wade asked. "Or should I just refer to her as 'the catch of the day'?"

Where's a good rock to crawl under when you need one? Lex swore to herself that the old woman got more full of herself every time she saw her. "I'm sorry. Mama Wade, allow me to introduce you to Amanda Cauble. Amanda, this is Dave's mother, Mrs. Ida Wade."

Amanda stood and walked over to the chair. "Pleasure to meet you, Mrs. Wade." She held out her hand.

"Goodness," Ida scoffed, standing up. "Come here." She embraced a surprised Amanda in a hug, which was enthusiastically returned. "Call me Mama, honey. Everyone else does."

She's got to be one of the few adults I've ever found who is actually shorter than I am. "All right. Thanks, Mama Wade. Dave tells me you've known Lex for a long time?" Amanda hoped Mrs. Wade could tell her some interesting stories of her lover's earlier life, since Lex rarely shared any information about that time.

"Goodness, yes. Ever since little Davey brought her home after school. Must have been fifteen years ago. Have a seat, and I'll tell you all about it."

Lex stood. "C'mon, Dave. I think that's our cue to leave. Want to show me how that work in the garage is coming along?" She pulled the poor man out of the room before he could respond.

Ida waited until the two left, then leaned back into her chair. "So, you want to know about the time your Lexie met my David? Let me see if I can remember it all." She paused for a moment to gather her thoughts. "When Davey was ten, he came home from school with blood all over his face. There were some older boys who took a liking to his backpack and tried to beat him up for it."

"That's horrible!"

"Isn't it? Kids can be so mean. Anyway, he kept crying about helping someone who was hurt. It took me a bit to calm him down enough to understand what he was talking about." She rocked in her chair, her eyes glazing over slightly as she remembered that earlier time. "We went several blocks, and he showed me this young girl who was lying under a tree. She must have been twelve or so, and she was unconscious."

Amanda's eyes widened. "Lex?"

"Yes, although we didn't know her from Adam, at the time. She saw the boys stalking Davey and missed her bus so she could see what they were up to. When they attacked him, Lexie took them all on, getting a black eye and a pretty nasty gash on the back of her head for her trouble. We took her home and called the sheriff."

"Charlie, right?" Amanda joined in. "I bet he was upset." As protective as he was of Lex now, she could just imagine his reaction to seeing a younger Lex in pain.

"Upset would be putting it mildly. I thought the poor man was going to cry. When Lexie woke up, she started crying and asking us not to tell Martha. She just knew she'd be in trouble when she got home."

The thought of Lex being so young and scared upset Amanda, too. "Why would she be in trouble?"

"For fighting, of course. According to Charlie, that happened quite often." Ida stood up and stretched. "But, she seems to have grown up all right. I think she's a fine young woman."

"So do I," Amanda agreed, feeling even more proud of her lover than ever.

The look on Amanda's face drew a smile from Ida. "After that, Lexie walked Davey home from school, then Charlie took her back to the ranch after his shift. Although I think the fresh-baked cookies had as much to do with it as anything else. She even made sure my David went to college, helped him get a scholarship and everything. Now he's got a business degree and runs his own shop," she finished proudly.

Dave and Lex stepped back into the room. "Aw, Mama," he grumbled.

Lex moved across the room to sit next to Amanda. "Mama Wade been telling her tall tales again?" She couldn't help but smile at the look of outrage on the older woman's face.

"Hrumpph! I'll give you tall tales, young lady." Before Ida could continue her tirade, Charlie walked into the room.

"Well, well. Isn't this a pleasant surprise?" The lawman took the chair nearest Ida. "Good evening, Ida. These kids giving you a hard time?"

Dave couldn't let that comment pass. "She gives as good as she gets, you know that." He bent down and kissed her gray head. "I'd love to stay and visit, but I'm expecting a late delivery at the store." He gave a wave to the two women sitting on the loveseat. "Amanda, it was great meeting you. Don't be a stranger around here. And Lex, you'd better start showing up over here a little more often—or else."

Amanda pointedly ignored the glare coming from her companion. "Thanks, Dave. I'll get her over here more, I promise."

Ida stood. "I'll walk you out, honey." She wrapped an arm around her son's waist as they left the room.

Charlie was surprised to see Lex. She rarely took time just to visit, and he hoped there wasn't anything wrong. "Everything okay out at the ranch?"

Lex stood and walked over to the fireplace. Leaning on the hearth, she turned back to face Charlie. "Yeah, pretty much. I do have a favor to ask of you, though."

Charlie could barely keep his jaw from dropping. *She's asking for help? Now that's a change.* "Sure, Lex, name it."

"Amanda and I are flying to California tomorrow to pack up

her stuff, and I'd appreciate it if you would stay out at the ranch while we're gone."

The lawman watched as Amanda stood and joined Lex by the fireplace, then gave her a gentle rub on her back.

"Why? Not that I mind, but Martha has stayed out there by herself before." He looked at the undisguised sadness in Lex's eyes. "What is it?"

"Hubert is up to his usual tricks, although I really don't think he has the balls to do anything. But he was pretty pissed when I chased him away from the ranch the other day, so I'm not sure what he may do." Lex ran a hand through her dark hair nervously.

Uh-oh, they're at it again. Charlie remembered breaking up several altercations between the siblings when they were growing up. "Umm, was there a particular reason you ran him off? He's not going to try and press charges against you again, is he?"

Lex laughed. "Ah, no." She shook her head. "I don't think he'll come running to you this time, but I'd appreciate it if you'd stay out there, just in case."

"Well, it'll be a hardship, but I guess I can do it. How long are you planning on being gone?" The teasing tone in Charlie's voice belied his words. He was just glad that Lex didn't have a problem with him seeing Martha, which would be near impossible to get around.

Amanda guided Lex back to the loveseat. "We fly out tomorrow morning, and will be coming back Sunday afternoon. I've got to be back in the office on Monday."

"Have you picked up the sedatives yet?" Charlie teased. "Or do you just need to borrow some handcuffs for the flight?"

Lex's eyes narrowed. "Charlie—"

He laughed and winked at Amanda. "Or I should get someone from Animal Control to dart her before she boards?"

Lex stood up, glaring. "Charlie, I'd hate to make Martha a widow before you could talk her into being a bride."

Looking surprised, the lawman blushed. "What makes you think, she's never, ah, hell." He stared down at the floor.

Teach him to pick on me. "Come on, Charlie, would it really be so bad to live at the ranch?"

His head lifted, and his eyes met hers. "You wouldn't mind?"

"Mind? Why the hell would I mind?" Lex stared at him in disbelief. "Martha is a grown woman, and I certainly have no hold on her."

"Well, yeah. I know, but, I mean, she's—"

Lex stood and crossed the room quickly, then knelt at Charlie's feet. "You know, growing up, I had this ongoing dream. A fantasy, I guess." She waited until the flustered man's eyes met hers. "In my head, and I guess in my heart too, Martha was my mom. My real mom, and you were my dad." The shocked happiness on his face let Lex know she was on the right track. "Hell, Charlie, you two practically raised me anyway. My own dad never really gave a damn about what I was doing. I just wish Martha would quit worrying so much about me and take care of her own happiness."

Charlie cleared his throat, and there was a trace of tears in his gray eyes. "Honey," he glanced at Amanda, "I don't think she has a thing to worry about anymore." He leaned forward and kissed her forehead. "Now I guess I'd better go on upstairs and pack a bag, since I'll be out of town on vacation for a few days." He winked at Lex, then stood. "And if I had ever had a daughter, I would hope she'd be like you." He enveloped Lex in a loving hug. "Have a safe trip, Lex." Charlie kissed the top of her head again and turned to leave the room. "Take care of our girl, Amanda."

Lex sniffed, wiped her eyes, and then looked over at Amanda. "Come on, let's go. We still have to get you packed."

WANDERING AROUND THE Caubles' house, Lex felt a little lost. Amanda was upstairs packing, and she found herself in the kitchen, watching as Anna Leigh stirred something on the stove.

"You look a little distracted, dear. Is something wrong?" Anna Leigh studied the quiet form leaning against the counter.

At the concerned tone, Lex looked up and saw only gentle understanding in Anna's face. "Umm, actually, could I ask you a question? I'd really like your opinion on something." She dropped her eyes back to the floor.

Sensing Lex's discomfort, Anna Leigh led her over to the table, guiding Lex into a chair. "Of course, dearest. What is it?"

"Well—" Unsure, Lex paused, until she felt Anna Leigh squeeze her hands. "I would ask Amanda, but I don't want to upset her. She's got enough on her mind right now." She looked down at their connected hands, startled at just how dainty Anna Leigh's looked in hers.

"Lexington, look at me. Please." Anna Leigh waited patiently until the shadowed eyes locked with hers. "There's nothing you could ask of me that you should be embarrassed about."

The rancher took a deep breath, momentarily closing her eyes. "I feel like such a hick." She opened her eyes and gave Anna Leigh a shaky smile. "I don't want to worry Amanda, but I'm a little concerned about this damned dinner party we're supposed to attend."

Anna Leigh looked at Lex in confusion. "Concerned? Why should you be concerned, Lexington? It's just a dinner, not a costume or fashion ball."

"Oh God, that would be a real nightmare, wouldn't it? Although I'm gonna feel like I'm in some sort of costume anyway." She looked into the beautiful eyes that reminded her so much of Amanda's. "You know I love your granddaughter, right?" At Anna Leigh's nod, she continued, "And that I'd do anything for her?"

"Of that, I have no doubt, dear." Anna Leigh squeezed the suddenly cold hands that were laced with hers. "But?"

Lex looked down again. "I want to be there to support her, but I really don't have anything good enough to wear to this sort of thing. And, I'm gonna be real uncomfortable in anything we buy, and then they'll know what a bumpkin their daughter is hooked up with." She gave the older woman an intense look. "I don't care what they think about me. But I'll be damned if I'm the cause for even one second of embarrassment for Amanda." She released Anna Leigh's hands and stood abruptly. "What am I going to do, Mrs, uh, I mean, Anna Leigh?" Lex paced back and forth across the bright kitchen like a skittish animal. "I'd die before hurting her."

"Lexington, I don't think that's going to be necessary." Anna Leigh stood and put her hand on the disturbed woman's arm. "Don't worry, we'll figure something out." She rubbed the tense arm soothingly. "Now, why don't you go on upstairs and drag my granddaughter down for dinner? It should be ready in about ten minutes."

"Thanks for listening, Anna Leigh. Now I know where Amanda got her heart." Lex left the older woman standing in the kitchen before she could reply.

AMANDA SAT IN the den watching the fire crackle in the fireplace. They had finished dinner over thirty minutes ago and Lex apologetically left the house shortly thereafter, after having received a mysterious phone call. *She was so cute about leaving and worried that I'd be upset.*

Anna Leigh's voice echoed down the empty hallway. "Mandy? Where are you, dear?"

"In here, Gramma." Amanda turned around on the sofa as her grandmother stepped into the room. "Hi."

The older woman came in and sat down beside Amanda. "Is everything all right, dear? Lexington certainly left in a hurry. You two didn't—" *Have a fight or argument,* she finished to herself, worried.

Amanda patted her grandmother's leg. She heard the unasked question. "Oh, no, nothing like that. Lex just got a phone call and left to take care of something. She said she would be home in an hour or so."

Anna Leigh relaxed against the sofa. "Thank goodness. I was afraid that you two had an argument about this trip."

"What would we have to disagree about? Lex seems really excited about going." Amanda turned sideways, so she could get a better look at her grandmother's face. "Has she said anything to you?"

"Earlier while you were upstairs, Lexington came into the kitchen, asking if I needed any help. I could tell that something was bothering her, so I asked." Anna Leigh chewed on her lower lip for a moment, thinking. When her granddaughter opened her mouth to interrupt, she held up her hand. "Shh. Wait, let me try and explain." The shocked look on Amanda's face made her words rush out. "Well, she did mention she's a little afraid of embarrassing you."

Amanda felt tears well up in her eyes. "I thought she was just nervous about flying." *My poor Lex. What am I going to do with you?*

Anna Leigh caught Amanda's hand. "Honey, I didn't mean to upset you. I just thought that you should know. Lexington was embarrassed about the whole dinner thing."

"I can't believe she didn't tell me how much this whole thing was bothering her," Amanda muttered, an errant tear making its way down her face.

"Oh, Mandy." Anna Leigh brushed the tear from Amanda's cheek. "It's not what you're thinking. Lexington was afraid of upsetting you. She knows how worried you already are about this trip, and she didn't want to add to your anxiety."

"That goofy cow-chaser. When is she going to figure out that she's a whole lot more important to me than any stupid dinner party?" Amanda whispered, more to herself than to her grandmother. Wiping her eyes with the back of one hand, she sniffled. "That's it. I'm calling Mother right now and canceling. I refuse to make Lex feel this way." She started to stand, but found her progress halted by a strong grip on her arm.

Anna Leigh pulled her granddaughter back down. "Wait. I really don't think that's a good idea." She waited until she had Amanda's complete attention. "How do you think it will make Lexington feel if you cancel out now?" When her granddaughter gave her a questioning look, she continued, "She'd probably feel that she was right, and that you're embarrassed because she's not used to being in that type of environment."

Amanda opened her mouth to disagree, and then realized that what her grandmother said was true. "She would, wouldn't she?" She already knew that her brooding lover, for all her kiss-my-butt attitude, was emotionally very insecure. "But what can I do? I can't hurt her that way. But I don't want her to feel belittled or not good enough for my family, either." Then a devious smile broke out on her face. "Oooh. I think I've got an idea."

Elizabeth had better watch out. Mandy's got that 'take no prisoners' look on her face. "You're not going to do anything you might regret later, are you?"

Amanda laughed. "Of course not. I just have to plan my wardrobe, that's all." She leaned over and wrapped her arms around Anna Leigh's neck. "Thanks, Gramma, you're the best." Amanda kissed the older woman's cheek then stood. "If you don't mind, I'm going to go upstairs and finish packing."

Anna Leigh rose as well. "No, not at all. Do you need a ride to the airport in the morning?" The nearest airport was an hour and a half away, and she didn't know if Lex and Amanda wanted to leave a car there for the entire week.

"No, Lex said she just wanted to leave her truck at the airport, so no one would have to make a three hour round trip drive to take us and then pick us up." Amanda stopped at the doorway. "But I really appreciate the offer, and I know Lex would too. I'll see you and Grandpa in the morning, right?"

"Of course. Do you think we'd miss seeing you two off? Your grandfather would never forgive himself otherwise." She crossed the room to meet Amanda at the door. "Try and get some rest tonight, dearest. The next few days will run you ragged, otherwise." Anna Leigh pulled her granddaughter into an embrace.

"I will, I promise." Amanda returned the squeeze, and felt a light kiss on the side of her head. "I love you."

"I love you, too, Mandy. Goodnight." Anna Leigh watched as the beautiful young woman walked down the hall and then practically skipped up the stairs. *She's up to something, and I can't wait to see what it is.*

LEX PULLED THE truck up to the Juvenile Detention Center and looked at her watch. *I really should have told Amanda where I was going, but then she would have insisted on coming with me. I know she wants to spend as much time as possible with her grandparents before we leave.* Lex walked through the doors of the two-story brick structure, the white walls almost brown with the passage of time. The foyer was brightly lit, with several heavy doors around and a Plexiglas service window off to the left of the entry doors. The rancher blinked a couple of times to adjust her eyes to the glare, then stepped up to the open window.

A middle-aged woman in a sheriff's department uniform smiled up at Lex from the desk stationed behind the bulletproof service window. "You must be Lexington Walters. Do you have any weapons to check?" At Lex's negative shake of her head, she continued, "Come on inside, Sergeant Roland is waiting for you in his office." She pointed to the heavy door to the right of the window, "Go on, I'll buzz you in."

Lex walked over to the door, embarrassed by the loud sound her boots made on the tile floor. She put her hand on the doorknob and waited until she heard the tinny, buzzing of the lock release, then opened it. Letting the steel door close behind her, the rancher got a slight chill down her back when she heard the audible click, knowing she was locked in until someone let her out. *Damn. I really hate this feeling.* She shook her head, trying to dispel the growing unease she felt. She waited in the sally port until the other door buzzed, then stepped through into a hallway.

A deep voiced jarred her from her thoughts, as a short heavy-set man in his mid-fifties stepped out of a nearby office. "Ms. Walters, thank you for getting here so quickly. Please, come in and have a seat." The smiling man escorted Lex into his office, pointing her to a chair in front of a severely cluttered desk. "I'm Sergeant Roland, by the way. I'm in charge of this facility." He shook her hand before sitting down.

Lex leaned back slightly in her chair. "Is this in reference to that boy who was with the cattle thieves we caught on my property?" She rushed to the point, wanting to get out of the 'facility' and back to Amanda. *Oh, I've got it bad, all right. I can't even be out of her sight for more than a few minutes. Totally disgusting.*

"Yes ma'am, as a matter of fact, it is." He spent a few moments digging through the multiple piles of paperwork on the desk. "Ah. Here we go." He opened up a plain brown folder and shuffled through the papers in it. "Sheriff Bristol said you were interested in putting the boy to work at the Rocking W, is that correct?"

"That's right. But only if he's interested. I have no desire to force the kid to work for me if he doesn't want to." Lex ran a hand through her hair. "And," she leaned forward in her chair, "I don't think anyone should be judged or punished for something that someone else in their family has done."

Having heard the town gossip about the Walters' family, the lawman could only nod his head. *Having that skunk Hubert for kin certainly is proof of that theory.* He read a page from the file, then closed it. "Well, it looks like Ronnie is an average student. Says here that he's quiet and has never been in any type of trouble before. Would you like to talk to him before you make your decision? If you both agree, we'll have to get him assigned as your ward, so that you both would be legally covered."

"I'd be appointed as his legal guardian?" Lex questioned,

unsure of her feelings. *I didn't do a very good job with the last boy in my care.*

"Yep." Sergeant Roland stood up. "Why don't we go talk to Ronnie, and then we can discuss all the boring legalities." He escorted a silent Lex out of the room, guiding her down the eerie hallway until they reached another steel door. "Do you have any weapons that need to be checked?" Although he knew they asked the same question at the front window, he learned a long time ago not to take anything for granted in his line of work.

Making a show of patting her pockets, Lex quipped. "Hmm. I seemed to have left my bow and arrows in my other pants."

Sergeant Roland shook his head. "Charlie warned me about you, and he told to give him a call if you caused too much trouble." Using a key, he opened the door. "Follow me, please."

Lex followed the chuckling man into another hallway, suppressing a shudder as the door clicked behind them. *Good thing I never went in for a life of crime. I'd never survive being locked away like this.*

Understanding what was keeping his guest quiet, the good sergeant decided to play tour guide. "Most of the boys we have stay in what we refer to as the Clubhouse. It's an open bunk area that can hold up to twenty kids at once. Right now we only have seven." He smiled proudly. "And they're all pretty good boys, mostly just got in with the wrong crowd, or their families didn't have time for them, sort of like Ronnie." He opened a door on the left side, a few steps before the end of the hallway. "Here's one of the visitation rooms. Make yourself comfortable, and I'll go fetch the boy."

Lex was pleased that this door didn't automatically lock when it closed. *Yeah, like it matters. Where in the hell can you go from here?* She wandered around the small room, which had a table, two wooden chairs, and an old loveseat that hugged one wall. The walls were unadorned, but she was able to look out a double-glassed, wire meshed window, seeing the dark, empty street outside.

She was still staring out the window when the door opened. Turning slightly, she studied the young man who stepped in ahead of Sergeant Roland. *He's not much bigger than Amanda is.* Slight of frame, his sandy blonde hair was much shorter than she remembered, only coming down to the top of his collar. He wore what appeared to be new jeans and a clean white, button-down shirt.

Lifting his head, Ronnie finally gathered enough courage to look the unknown woman in the eye. *Whoa. She's a lot taller than I am.* The thought intimidated him somewhat. He felt the sergeant's hand on his shoulder as he was guided to a chair.

"Why don't we all have a seat and get acquainted?" the heavy lawman said, waiting until Lex took the other chair at the table before sitting down on the loveseat. "Ronnie, this is Ms. Walters."

The young man, who had been looking at the table silently ever since he had sat down, glanced up again as the woman stood and offered her hand to him.

"Ronnie?" She gave him a firm handshake, treating him like an adult. Her eyes, which looked almost violet in the odd light caught his attention immediately. *Wow, she's got beautiful eyes.* Embarrassed, Ronnie blushed and swallowed.

Lex looked into the young man's light brown eyes, which conveyed sadness and more than a little fear. *Poor kid looks scared to death,* she thought sadly. *I wonder if it's me, or the circumstances?*

"You're the lady from the house, aren't you?" His eyes widened, as he scooted back in his chair. "D...don't b...b...be mad at m...m...me. Matt made me g...g...go." He covered his face with his hands and began to cry softly.

Guess that answers that question, doesn't it? Lex moved away from the table, a hurt look on her face. She glanced over at the sergeant, who shook his head sadly.

Roland rose and stepped over to the table, placing his hand lightly on the boy's back. "Shh. It's okay, son. She's not here to hurt you." He looked up at the rancher helplessly.

Lex sat down across from the sniffling young man. "Ronnie, look at me," she commanded in a low voice. Waiting until he complied, she looked directly into his tear-filled eyes "Yes, that was my house you were in. But I'm not mad at you, okay?" She gave him a kind smile. "I don't blame you for anything your brother did, do you understand?" Pausing to let her words soak in, she added, "I know how you feel, because I have an older brother, too." She watched as the boy wiped his eyes on his sleeve, and gathered his wits about him. "Do you like it here, Ronnie?"

Ronnie cocked his head to the side, confused by the question. Looking over at the sergeant, who had resumed his place on the loveseat, he replied, "Uh, well, it's not that bad. I have guys my own age to talk to, and they gave me these nice clothes. I miss going to school, though. We have classes here, but it's just not the same."

Lex stood and walked over to the window. Turning around, she crossed her arms over her chest and leaned against the cold glass. "What do you want out of life, Ronnie?"

The young man seriously considered her question for several moments before speaking. "I want to finish school, then I hope to go to college." He gave her a shy smile. "No one else in my family has ever graduated from high school. I'd kind of like to be the first."

Lex moved back to the table and sat on its edge. "How hard are you willing to work for your goals?" She purposely sat close, so that he would have to look up at her.

"I really want to finish school. I'll work as hard as I need to." Ronnie's light eyes sparkled with a strong resolution. "I'm not going to be like my brother."

Barely suppressing a grin, Lex looked him straight in the eye. "Are you willing to come and work on the ranch for me? You'd stay in the bunkhouse with the other hands, and ride the bus to school, then work on the weekends."

"You're kidding, right?" Ronnie asked, shifting his gaze between the two adults. "I'd be working on a ranch?" Disbelief colored his tone.

"Yep. And you'll get paid for the work you do. All you have to do is keep your grades up. I'll make sure that you have clean clothes, food, and a roof over your head. What do you say?"

"Really? I can go to school *and* get paid?" he marveled, a smile lighting up his youthful face.

"That's right, you sure can." Lex stood and held out her hand. "Deal?"

Ronnie flinched when he saw her hand coming at him. Old habits died hard. "Sorry." He slowly stood and returned her grip. "When do I start?"

Sergeant Roland cleared his throat. "Well, it'll take a few days for the paperwork to go through." He waited for the rancher to nod her head in confirmation, then turned to Ronnie. "Do you think you can handle it in here until next week?"

"Sure. I'm supposed to go and visit Matt tomorrow anyway. Can I tell him?"

Lex pulled a card out of her coat pocket. "It's okay with me, Ronnie. Here's my home number and my cell phone number. I've got to go out of town for a few days, but call me if you need anything, day or night, okay?"

"Thanks, Ms. Walters." The young man beamed up at her. "I won't let you down, I promise."

Placing a hand on his slight shoulder, Lex felt proud for her decision. "I have complete faith in you, Ronnie. And you can call me Lex, since you'll be working for me."

"Yes, ma'am." He grinned at her, then turned serious, holding out his hand again. "Thank you for giving me this chance. I won't forget it."

Lex returned his handshake. "You're welcome. I can always use another good hand at the ranch." She tried to downplay the reason for helping him, since she wasn't completely certain why herself.

"Well, come on, Ronnie. Let's get you back to the Clubhouse." Sergeant Roland put one arm across the young man's thin shoulders. He winked at Lex as he led the boy out.

Oh, God, what have I done? Lex sat down on the loveseat and placed her head in her hands. *What right do I have to take care of that boy? Am I doing the right thing? What if—*

Her thoughts were halted when Sergeant Roland opened the door. "You want to get those papers signed now so you can get out of here, Ms. Walters?"

Lex stood and followed him back down the long hallway. "Call me Lex, Sergeant."

AMANDA LOOKED AT the mantle clock for the third time in as many minutes. *Twelve-thirty.* She had finished her packing, put her bags in the front hall, taken a shower, and played cards with her grandparents during the course of the evening. *Where on earth is she?* Amanda paced back and forth in the darkened den. The crackling of the logs in the fireplace was the only sound in the room, except for her occasional mutterings as she moved around.

Jacob and Anna Leigh went to bed hours before, trying to get their granddaughter to do the same. When she refused, they good-naturedly teased her about 'letting her wayward child stay out too late' and then wished her a good night. *I know she's a grown woman. I know she can take care of herself. I know there's a perfectly good explanation for her not being here with me right now,* she thought to herself, dropping her now exhausted body onto the sofa. "Lex, where are you?" she asked out loud.

"Right here," a voice from behind her uttered quietly.

Amanda squealed, then vaulted over the couch, practically jumping into Lex's arms. "I'm glad you're okay." She wrapped her legs around Lex's waist. "I thought...when you didn't—"

Lex carried the mumbling bundle to the sofa and sat down. "Shh, everything's okay." She rocked Amanda back and forth gently.

Amanda finally calmed down and then pulled away slightly to look up into Lex's shadowed face. "I'm sorry. I guess I'm just really tired. And I'm a little nervous about tomorrow, because I'm afraid of how my family is going to treat you."

"Don't worry about me. I'm a big girl." Lex gave her a tender smile, while she wiped the tears from her lover's face. "I'm sorry it took me so long tonight. I had a lot of paperwork to sign." She kissed Amanda lightly on the nose. "I tried calling a couple of times, but the line was busy. Is everything okay here?"

"Uh, yeah. Everything is just fine." Amanda hid her face in her friend's chest, embarrassed by her earlier emotional outburst.

"Amanda? Sweetheart?" Lex waited until she had Amanda's attention before she spoke. "I'm really sorry I caused you to get so upset. Aren't you even curious where I went?"

Amanda chewed her lip thoughtfully. "Well, I figured if it was any of my business, you'd tell me when you got ready to."

Uh-oh. Time to soothe some ruffled feathers, I think. "It was stupid of me not to tell you earlier, but I thought that if you knew, you'd force yourself to go." Lex looked deeply into eyes a breath away, almost drowning in their depths. "And, I knew how much you wanted to spend time with your grandparents before we left." She cupped the beautiful face in her hands. "You have me so tightly wrapped around your little finger, I can't tell you no. One look into your eyes, and I've fallen. One touch of your hand, and my heart beats wildly. I can deny you nothing, but would gladly forsake everything to see your smile."

Amanda opened her mouth, closed it, and then shook her head in disbelief. "You know, for being the strong, silent type," she ran her hand lovingly across Lex's jaw, "you can bring me to my knees with just a few words." She looked down, smiling at the proof of her statement. She was on her knees, straddled across Lex's legs. She stood and brought her lover up beside her. Bringing Lex's head down for a kiss, Amanda murmured, "Let's go to bed. We can talk tomorrow." And she led a willing Lex down the dark hallway and up the stairs.

Chapter
Eight

Lex was understandably nervous as she and Amanda walked through the terminal. *Were they just trying to be funny when they named it a terminal? I'm feeling pretty terminal myself right now.* She followed her lover down the crowded walkway, feeling her stomach cramp with every step. *I don't know if I can do this.* Lex looked around frantically for the nearest restroom as she felt her breakfast begin to rebel.

"This way, Lex." Amanda tossed the words over her shoulder, not bothering to look back. By unspoken agreement, she led the way, since she was more familiar with the airport. "We've still got to pick up our boarding passes. According to the monitor, our flight leaves in a little over an hour."

Lex was torn between following her heart and emptying her stomach, and then another painful cramp made her gasp and almost drop to her knees, which made the decision for her. "Amanda," she moaned, trying to get her companion's attention. *Aw, hell.* Lex made a mad dash for the ladies' room, dropping the bags inside the door to the lavatory.

Amanda turned to point out something to her partner and saw that she was nowhere to be seen. "Lex?" She stopped and looked around slowly. *Now where is she?*

An elderly man sitting on a nearby bench waved to her, beckoning Amanda over. "Miss? Are you looking for that rather tall young lady who was behind you?" he asked kindly, patting the empty spot beside him.

"Yes, the one with the dark hair. Did you happen to see where she went?" Amanda sat down next to him.

"Oh, yes." He patted her hand. "Poor thing. She doesn't fly much, does she?"

Amanda tried to control her anxiety. "No, I'm afraid she doesn't. You said you saw her?" She kept scanning the people milling around them, hoping to spot Lex.

He scratched his stubbled chin. "I could tell, you know. She looked like a fish out of water, that one did. I like to try and figure out where people are from, and where they're going. Why, just the other day—"

"I don't mean to sound rude, sir," Amanda butted in gently, "but I'm a little concerned about my friend. Where did you see her go?" *She wouldn't change her mind and leave, would she? No, not without telling me.*

Realizing that he was going to lose his audience no matter whether he told or not, the old man pointed in the direction of the ladies' room across the walkway. "I figured she was feeling a mite ill, 'cause she grabbed her stomach, turned about three shades of pale, and high-tailed it over there." He was about to tell the pretty young woman more, but she absently thanked him, patted his shoulder and took off running across the concourse.

"Excuse me...sorry..." Amanda carefully battled her way through a large group of people who had just disembarked from an arriving flight. Once inside the restroom, she dropped her bags next to Lex's and shouldered through several women who were standing next to the sinks, complaining about the airline food. "Lex?" she called out, trying to find out which stall held her friend.

"Over here," a weak voice muttered, from the sink on the end. Lex was frighteningly pale, leaning up against the wall with a wet paper towel over her eyes.

Amanda's heart ached at the sight. *I really wasn't taking her fear of flying seriously,* she berated herself, noticing how the hand holding the paper towel trembled. She stood beside the slumped form and placed a hand on Lex's arm. "Oh, Lex."

"Sorry." Lex took a deep breath and removed the damp towel from her eyes. When she saw the sympathetic look on her lover's face, she forced a smile to her lips. "I didn't mean to take off on you like that."

Fighting the urge to pull Lex into her arms, Amanda settled for squeezing the arm her hand rested upon. "Are you going to be okay?"

Lex swallowed several times. The dry, cotton feeling probably wouldn't go away until she was on the ground in California, so she knew it was no use in complaining about it. "Yeah, I'll be fine." She pushed away from the wall and made her way to the door, picking up her bags before going outside. "Let's go." The ladies' room was getting more and more crowded by the moment, which wasn't helping her queasiness any. *Where in the hell did all these damn people come from, anyway?*

Once they were safely out of the restroom, Lex was tempted to turn back around and hide in one of the stalls. Two flights had just unloaded their passengers, and the roaring throng of people was nearly more than she could stand. *Now I know why I hide away on a ranch.* She leaned up against the wall, trying to gather up what was left of her nerves. *I can do this.* When she felt a light touch on her side, Lex looked down into the concerned eyes of her partner. "Lead the way, my friend. I'll be right behind you."

Amanda started to say something, then stopped. *Maybe it'll be less crowded by our gate. We can get our passes and she can sit and let her stomach settle.* She slid the strap of her carryon over her shoulder. "Okay. Stick close, and give my bag a tug if you need to make another side trip." She almost reached up to caress Lex's unusually pale cheek, but quickly reminded herself where they were.

Lex gave Amanda's bag a test pull. "Gotcha."

Politely maneuvering them through the crowd, Amanda turned back every few steps to check on the condition of her companion. Over halfway to their gate, she noticed a fine sheen of perspiration covering Lex's brow. Stopping in the middle of the concourse, she asked, "Are you going to make it? We can stop for a moment, if you need to."

"No, I'm okay," Lex assured her, although her legs were shaking from the strain. "We're almost there."

Not able to stand it any longer, Amanda took a firm grip on Lex's arm. "You don't look okay." She looked around for someplace to sit. Amanda pulled her lover over to a group of chairs by the window, and saw Lex collapse gracelessly onto the nearest one. "Let's take a little break. Why don't you sit here with our bags, and I'll go get our boarding passes?" When the pale woman tried to argue, Amanda dropped to her knees beside Lex. "I think my shoulder is about to fall off from dragging this darn bag around. Humor me, please?"

Lex lifted her hand to touch Amanda's cheek. "You are so transparent, sweetheart." The smile on her face took the sting out of her words. "Okay, you win. I'll wait for you right here."

"All right." Amanda gave the thigh under her hand a squeeze. "I'll be back in a few minutes." She winked at Lex and then stood, hoisting her purse to her shoulder as she hurried away.

She watched Amanda's form move through the crowd with ease, until she finally disappeared from sight. Lex closed her eyes for a moment, only to have them pop back open when the plane parked next to her window started its engines. *Shit. Just what I need. Come on, Lexington, don't be such a damn baby.* Her stomach spasms became more painful. Lex moved to stand, but dropped back to her chair as another cramp hit her. *I am not going to throw up again,* she thought to herself angrily. Inhaling through her nose to combat her nausea, Lex wrapped her arms around her waist, bent over, and laid her head on her knees. *Maybe I should have taken a tranquilizer,* she thought as she fought to ease her rebellious stomach.

Calm. I need to stay calm, focus on something else. Breathing deeply, Lex let her thoughts drift to her gentle lover. In her mind, she pictured the hazel eyes, the small perfect nose, and the petite, but well-built body. She imagined holding Amanda in her arms and burying her face in her silky, shoulder length hair. *I can almost smell her perfume. This self-hypnosis stuff really works.*

"Lex?" A light touch to the top of her head brought Lex out of her musings.

"Hmm?" She raised her head slowly and focused on the eyes she had just been thinking of. "Hi."

Amanda sat down next to the perspiring woman. "Honey, you're really pale." She wiped the damp hair out of Lex's eyes. "Is there anything I can do for you?" Ignoring the disgusted stare from the woman sitting two chairs away from Lex, Amanda pushed her lover back in the chair and twined their fingers together.

"Nah. I think I'll live. And you're doing more by just being here than any medication can do." She brought their linked hands to her lips, and kissed Amanda's knuckles. "Thanks."

"Hrumpph. Disgusting!" The middle-aged woman nearby glared at them, gathered her collection of shopping bags and luggage, and then stormed off.

Lex loved Amanda's sudden blush. "Maybe I should have pulled you onto my lap and kissed you senseless. That would have given the old bat something to stare at."

Amanda glanced around them. The other chairs in the waiting area were occupied by people who were focused on their on families and flights, or were biding their time by reading or napping. The irritated woman seemed to be the only person paying any attention to them. "Lex," she gently chided her partner, "you're so bad."

"I thought that's what you liked about me."

"As a matter of fact, it's one of your better qualities." Amanda squeezed Lex's hand. "You must be feeling better. The color is coming back to your face."

"Yeah. I'm sorry. I really didn't think it would be so bad. Were you able to get our passes?"

"Actually, I got them and something extra. I explained our situation to the lady at the gate, and we're going to get to board early, before the plane gets crowded." Hoping to make Lex feel even better, Amanda pointed to a nearby cart. "And I also procured transportation for our fine luggage." With her foot, she nudged the duffel bag resting beside her. *I really didn't see any need to pack much. I have plenty of clothes in Los Angeles. Besides, Mother will have little green kittens when I show up without matching luggage. I might as well take my points where I can.* "We still have to check this stuff."

Standing up, Lex offered her hand to Amanda, who was still seated. "Right, boss. Well, let's get this over with." She pulled Amanda up, then grabbed several bags and loaded up the cart.

AMANDA GRINNED, QUITE pleased with herself. She had managed to sweet talk an older couple into exchanging seats with them so Lex would have easier access to the lavatory, just in case. Sneaking a sideways glance at her silent partner, Amanda was gratified to see that Lex appeared to be doing okay, other than the death-grip she had on Amanda's hand. *Whatever works. I'd sit on her lap if I thought it would help.* Unable to help herself, she giggled softly, *Face it, Mandy. You'd sit on her lap even if it didn't help. Oh, I've got it bad, all right.*

"What's so funny?" Lex asked, turning her head to face her friend. She took a deep breath when the plane lurched slightly.

"Umm, nothing, really." Amanda gave Lex's hand a comforting squeeze. "Just thinking."

Lex gave her a look that said she didn't believe it was *just nothing.* "About what?"

Amanda leaned over and placed her lips very close to Lex's ear. "I was wondering if these seats would comfortably fit two. I'm seriously considering crawling into your lap and—" Her last few words were spoken almost too softly to hear, and were punctuated by a light nibble on a tasty earlobe.

But Lex understood, and the words, coupled with the feel of Amanda's teeth on her skin caused her face to flush. "Ahem." She cleared her throat in an attempt to control the surge of desire rushing through her. "I think that would certainly help me keep my mind off flying. Airplanes, anyway. You have a delightfully wicked mind, my love."

"You don't know the half of it."

Oh, boy. Lex felt another shiver of excitement travel down her spine. *I don't know what has gotten into Amanda, but I think I like it.*

A friendly voice over the intercom interrupted their banter. "Attention, ladies and gentlemen, this is your captain speaking. We will be landing in approximately twenty minutes. It's a beautiful seventy-eight degrees in Los Angeles—"

"I can't believe we're already about to land. You're the best medicine I've ever had, Amanda," Lex said over the captain's rambling voice. She pulled their linked hands up and kissed her partner's fingertips. "Guess now you'll have to fly with me all the time."

"Such a terrible price to pay." She placed her free hand on her forehead, palm out. "Oh, dear me, I guess I'll just have to suffer." Then she gave the rancher an impish look, "Like I would ever let you out of my sight long enough to take a flight alone."

The look that crossed Lex's face was a serious one. "I don't know how I ever survived anything before you." Her words were spoken from the heart, as were the quieter words after them. "I love you, Amanda." Not realizing or caring where they were, she leaned forward and kissed Amanda.

They pulled apart slowly, each content to sit and enjoy the strong feelings coursing between them.

Lex had one more anxious moment as the plane touched down, but Amanda held her hand tightly and leaned close, whispering soothing words of comfort to the visibly shaken woman.

"Focus on my voice, Lex. Close your eyes and breathe deeply. That's it." Using her free hand, Amanda caressed the arm she held, feeling it begin to relax. "I'm here with you, love. We're okay. I love you, Lex. Concentrate on me..." She continued to speak in a soothing tone.

So absorbed was she in Amanda's quiet words, Lex never felt the plane land or come to a stop. Hearing excited voices around her, she opened her eyes to see people gathering their personal items and crowding the aisles, eager to exit the plane. Turning her head, a surprised Lex was captured by smiling eyes at very close range. "We're here?"

"Yep. And in one piece, too. How are you doing?"

Lex paused to give the question some thought. "Great. My stomach doesn't even hurt anymore." She took a cleansing breath and gave her lover a heartfelt smile. "Thanks for being my security blanket."

"Hmm. Do I get the usual perks?"

"Perks? What kind of perks are we talking about here?"

"Well," Amanda ran a teasing finger up Lex's arm, "normally, security blankets get to be taken everywhere, snuggled, cuddled, and held tightly all night."

Lex laughed. "I think something could be arranged." She looked around the plane. They had played and joked until almost everyone had disembarked. "Ready?" Standing up and stretching her arms over her head until her fingertips touched the top of the cabin, Lex almost laughed again as Amanda took the opportunity to tickle her ribs. "Be careful what you start, lil' bit."

"Oh, yeah? You really don't want to start a name-calling contest with a realtor. We can be very creative, Snookums."

Lex nearly dropped the bag she was pulling from the overhead compartment. "What?" Letting the bag fall into her seat, she put her hands on her hips. "Where in the hell did *that* come from?" She leaned menacingly over her lover, who was getting more enjoyment out of the word play than she should have. "Snookums?"

"How about, Sugar Lips?" Amanda kept the bag between her and the now beet-red rancher.

"Amanda." Lex took the bag away from her partner, leaving nothing between them. "I'll show you 'Sugar Lips'." She flipped the bag onto her shoulder and stepped closer.

Reaching for her own bag, Amanda batted her innocent eyes at her would-be assailant. "Umm, have I told you lately how much I love you?"

Those words did the trick. The word game forgotten, Lex stepped into the aisle to allow her lover to get in front of her. "I love you, too."

"Sugar Lips!" Amanda chortled, then rushed down the aisle with her lover hot on her heels.

"IS IT ALWAYS this, ah, hazy?" Lex asked, looking up at the sky. They were on the road out of the airport in a shiny red Mustang convertible.

Amanda looked above them. After so many months in a small town, she had forgotten how bad the pollution could be. "Actually, it's pretty nice today. You can breathe without choking." Sparing a glance at her companion, Amanda came close to laughing out loud. Lex was fighting a losing battle with her hair, trying to keep it out of her mouth and eyes. "Problem?"

"I knew I should have worn my hat." Grimacing, Lex wiped another strand of dark silk away from her mouth. Although she wanted to make a good impression with Amanda's parents, she had been wearing her western hat when they had left earlier in the morning, much to Martha's consternation. The housekeeper took away the dilapidated headwear and promised to care for it properly until they returned. No amount of pleading or bribing could sway her, and Lex was still perturbed about the losing the argument.

"Do you want me to put the top up?"

"No!" Lex turned to look sheepishly at her friend. "I'm really enjoying the semi-fresh air." At the airport, they had nearly driven the poor car rental agent crazy. He tried to talk them into a luxury car or import. Lex wanted something big with lots of headroom, and Amanda wanted something sporty. So they compromised on a convertible, with Lex only agreeing to the smaller car on the condition that they could drive with the top down.

Having tied her own hair back before leaving the airport,

Amanda used one hand to dig through her purse. "Here." She handed Lex an elastic hair tie. "I always have a ton of these in the bottom of my purse."

Taking the offering thankfully, Lex quickly pulled her wind whipped hair into a ponytail. "Thanks. I was about ready to cut it all off with a rusty pocketknife."

"You'd better not! I love your hair." Amanda turned sideways to glare at her partner.

Lex noticed the cars stopped ahead of them, and pointed. "Amanda? Do you want to keep your eyes on the road, please?"

Amanda hit the brake, then quickly glanced up into the rearview mirror, hoping no one was directly behind them before she slammed her foot down harder. "Damn!" *Whew.* She bit her lip and gave Lex an embarrassed look. "I'm sorry about that."

With one hand braced against the dash and the other gripping the door's armrest, Lex tightly closed her eyes and silently prayed they'd make it to where they were going in one piece. She had never seen so much traffic in her life, not even when she'd traveled to Dallas or Austin. "No problem—" she croaked. Finally, she opened her eyes and relaxed back into her seat. "There aren't any bridges on the way to your parent's house, are there?"

"None that I can think of, why?" Amanda answered automatically, before finally realizing what Lex was asking. "Now wait just a damned minute. That wasn't my fault."

"Of course not. Just because that bridge had been standing for as long as I could remember without mishap, then suddenly collapsed the first time you drove across it, I don't see any connection whatsoever."

Amanda snorted and waived her arm dramatically. "Oh yeah. I had to time it just right, too. Getting that tree to hit at just the right moment was a pure stroke of genius on my part. But—" She reached over and grabbed Lex's hand, "—the best part of my plan was making you jump into the creek after me, and then getting you to take me home with you."

"I like the way you think." Lex pulled Amanda's hand up and kissed it.

Amanda's family's house was nestled snugly in the hills surrounding Los Angeles, off a tree-lined road. She brought the car up to a large iron security gate and pressed a code into the keypad next to an intercom. As the gate creaked open, she looked over at her companion, who had a thoughtful look on her face.

"Seems kinda sad to live like that," Lex observed.

"Like what?" *Had she noticed the homeless people we passed on the street on the way out here? She didn't say anything at the time.*

"Spending all that money for a big expensive house, then

having to lock yourself away." Lex shook her head. "Why live like that?"

Navigating the rental car down the winding road that eventually led up to the house, Amanda sighed. *Why, indeed?* "I guess that's why I spent so much time in Somerville," she said quietly. "This place has never felt like home, more like an expensive hotel."

Lex turned sideways in her seat, and took her lover's hand in hers. "I'm sorry, I didn't—"

"No," Amanda reassured her, "it's all right. I was always sent to the best schools, had everything a child could want, but it wasn't until the summer that I actually *lived*. I had a really great childhood with my grandparents. And if I hadn't spent so much time with them, I may never have met you."

"Well, then. Maybe I should thank your parents for letting you come to Texas," Lex drawled. When the house came into view she was struck speechless. Three stories of light-colored brick gave it an almost marble-like quality. The six marble pillars in the front helped with the illusion. Huge trees covered the landscape, and a wide brick walkway completed the picture. "Damn."

"Yeah. Ostentatious, isn't it? I still get lost in there sometimes." Amanda pulled the car up into the circular drive and parked in front of the walk. She took a final look at the house, before she climbed out of the car. "Come on, let's get this started."

"Oh, boy." Lex walked up the brick steps next to Amanda, who stopped at the door and rang the bell. Before Lex could question that action, the massive oak doors opened inward, and a slender woman in a maid's uniform opened the doors.

"Miss Amanda? Welcome back!" she exclaimed.

Amanda stepped forward and wrapped her arms around the woman in an exuberant hug. "Beverly, you look fantastic." Amanda stepped back to study the woman. "Good grief! You must have lost fifty pounds."

Beverly laughed at her. "Fifty-four, to be exact." She then turned to the open doorway, where Lex stood watching the interaction silently. "Oh, my."

"Sorry about that." Amanda grabbed Lex by the arm and pulled her into the gleaming marble foyer. "Beverly, this is Lexington Walters. Lex, this is Beverly, who actually runs the house."

Lex moved forward and held out her hand. "It's a pleasure to meet you, ma'am." She saw the maid look at her strangely before accepting her hand.

"It's really nice to meet you, Ms. Walters." *Nice woman, but I hope Mr. and Mrs. Cauble don't catch her being this friendly with the household staff. They'll just make her stay here miserable.*

"Call me Lex," the rancher requested. "Ms. Walters sounds like a school teacher."

"Miss Lex." Beverly turned her attention back to Amanda. "Miss Amanda, your father is in the library. He's expecting you."

Amanda rolled her eyes. "Thanks, Beverly. What kind of mood is he in?"

The maid shook her head as she closed the front doors. "He's been upset all day. Mr. Cauble spoke to his father this morning and has been in the library ever since."

Lex looked up at both women, torn between wanting to stay, and wanting to protect her lover. *I bet I have a pretty good idea what the argument was about.* She let out a sigh. "Maybe I should just bring your bags in, then go get a hotel room." She started for the door. "I don't want to cause any more trouble for you with your family."

Amanda grabbed the back of her friend's belt. "Oh, no you don't." She pulled hard. "You're not going anywhere."

Beverly took the opportunity to leave, stepping quietly into the next room. She had been trained to allow the family their privacy, although all she wanted to do was see who won the battle of wills in the entryway.

Lex turned around slowly. "Amanda, you know I'd do anything in the world for you. I just don't want you to be forced to choose between your family and us. That's not fair to you." She stepped closer and gently cradled Amanda's face in her hands, not really caring where they stood.

"There would be no decision to make. I'd choose us every time." Amanda looked down at the expensive floor, then put her hands on Lex's waist. "You'd make me face them alone? Are you ashamed of me? Of us?"

"Of course not. Never!" Lex used her thumb to wipe a fallen tear from Amanda's cheek. "I just, I was trying to, aw, hell." Lex leaned down and kissed Amanda. "I'll stand beside you for as long as you want me." She pulled her into a firm embrace. "I'll never leave you, I swear." Lex waited until both their hearts stopped pounding before she pulled back. "But would you rather visit with your father alone at first? I could wait outside the door for you."

Amanda inhaled, trying to pull Lex's soapy clean scent deeply into her lungs. "I don't *want* to see him alone." She looked up into Lex's concerned eyes. "But I guess it would be the decent thing to do, huh?"

Lex noted the fear and sadness in the younger woman's face. *She looks scared half to death. We've never really talked about her folks. I just thought her father would be like Jacob, not someone she'd be afraid of.*

How can I ask— "Amanda? Are you afraid of him?" She felt Amanda snuggle closer. "Are you afraid he's going to hurt you?" *If she says yes, I won't let her out of my sight for an instant.*

"No. He's never hurt me." When she looked up and saw the angry set to Lex's face, Amanda knew she had to do a little damage control. "Really. He just gets a little loud sometimes, and it makes my ears hurt." When the look didn't fade, she patted Lex's stomach gently. "Are you okay?"

"Hmm?" Lex answered, somewhat distracted. "Yeah, I'm fine." *Damn. To be that afraid of your own father. Dad and I didn't always get along, but I was never afraid.* She grimaced inwardly, remembering. *But I think he was, a time or two.* "How about you? Is there anything I can do?"

Amanda placed a quick kiss on Lex's lips, then stepped back. "You already have." She grabbed Lex's hand and pulled her first across the foyer, then into an elegant corridor. "I want to introduce you to my father."

Lex allowed herself to be led down the well-furnished passageway. *Their hall has more furniture than my entire house.* She also saw the ease in which Amanda moved through the expensive home, and suddenly realized just how vastly different their lifestyles were. *Stop it. Just because their house is fancier, that doesn't make them any better than you.* Her mental chastising halted when Amanda stopped in front of a pair of closed French doors.

"Well, here we are." Amanda turned and looked back at the woman she had dragged all over the house. "I've changed my mind. Would you come in with me, please?"

Running a hand lightly down Amanda's face, Lex felt her own nervousness dissipate. "Sure. Just give me a sign if you want me to leave. Otherwise, I'm your shadow."

Amanda leaned gratefully into the touch. "Thanks." Taking a deep breath, she knocked on the door.

"Enter," a deep voice commanded from inside.

Pushing one of the doors partially open, Amanda poked her head tentatively inside. "Daddy?"

"Amanda," the voice boomed. "It's about time you arrived. Get in here."

Starting forward, Amanda reached behind her back and gathered a handful of Lex's shirt, tugging hard. "Hi, Daddy."

Sitting behind a massive cherry desk, Michael Cauble was dressed as if he were in a business meeting. He was in his mid forties with reddish brown hair showing very little gray. His hazel eyes hidden behind expensive glasses studied the two young women carefully as they stepped into the room. Making no move to stand, he waved at two chairs strategically placed in front of the desk. "Have a seat."

Lex was barely able to control her anger. *The sorry bastard hasn't seen his daughter for over six months, and he treats her like a business appointment?* She waited until Amanda sat down, then took the other chair.

Michael leaned back and steepled his fingers together in front of his chest. "Did you have a good flight?" he asked, more as a matter of form than any real concern.

Amanda sat up stiffly in her chair with her hands clasped in her lap. She nodded. "Yes, sir. Very smooth."

She looks like she's in the principal's office, waiting to be chewed out, Lex thought indignantly. She was about to say something when Michael turned his cold gaze on her.

"You must be Lexington Walters." He gave her a smile that didn't quite reach his eyes. "You're the one who pulled my daughter from the creek." It was a statement, not a question.

"That's right," Lex answered, her own smile somewhat forced. Standing up, she held her outstretched hand across the desk. "Nice to meet you, Mr. Cauble."

Michael stood and accepted her hand, looking surprised at the strength of her grip. "Yes, well," he said. He released her hand quickly and returned to his seat. "I suppose you're here to collect some type of reward for your efforts?" He looked her over as though assessing her value, and Lex knew what he saw: clean, slightly faded jeans, worn cowboy boots, and a denim shirt, all of which were neatly pressed. In a ruthless, almost challenging voice, he asked, "How much do you want?"

Amanda moved to jump up, but Lex's hand on her arm stopped her. "Actually, Mr. Cauble, I've already gotten my reward." Lex stood and slipped behind Amanda's chair, resting her hands casually on the back. "I met your daughter."

Amanda saw her father redden, which was usually a sign his explosive temper was on the verge of erupting. A warmth flowed through her, knowing Lex was purposely diverting his attention to her instead. *I shouldn't let her do this, but it feels so good to have someone stand up for me.*

Michael rose, his ire obviously growing. "What are you trying to say?" He looked like he wanted to reach across the desk and slap the smug look off Lex's face. "Amanda!" He turned to address his daughter. "Leave us for a few minutes. Your *friend* and I have some business to discuss."

Before Amanda could say anything, Lex placed her hands gently on her shoulders. "Mr. Cauble, as far as I'm concerned, there's nothing you have to discuss with me that Amanda can't hear."

He stepped around to the front of the desk, leaning casually against one edge. "Very well. I was just trying to save you some embarrassment, Ms. Walters." He matched stares with Lex, pointedly ignoring his daughter's sputtering. "Now," he pulled up one knee and put both hands around it, trying to appear casual. "You look like you could use money." Michael held up his hand to forestall Amanda's argument. "Amanda, be quiet or I'll ask you to leave." Turning his attention to Lex, he went on. "I hear you work on a ranch. And from what I've read lately, you certainly can't make any money doing that these days."

Lex could feel the waves of anger rolling off Amanda through the hands she still had on her lover's shoulders. "Well, the recent rains haven't helped much, but we're doing okay." She struggled to keep the happy smile from her face when she felt Amanda's hands cover her own.

Michael knew of his daughter's "life's choice," but seeing her blatantly rub his nose in it, caused him to see red. "Look. Let's cut to the chase, Walters. We have money. Quite a bit of it. How much do I have to give you to leave my daughter alone?"

Lex stalked around the chair and stepped right up into Michael's face. "Do you think so little of you daughter that I have to be after her money?" She looked him straight in the eye. "All the gold in Fort Knox couldn't replace Amanda in my heart. I love her, and no amount of money can run me off." She stepped back and quietly added, "Only her word could do that." She heard the rustle of fabric as Amanda got up and stepped behind her, and felt a calming touch on her back. "I know I don't look like much, but you gotta believe that I would do anything for Amanda. I'll sign any damn papers you want to disclaim any designs on your precious money." Lex let out a tired breath and sat down, and Amanda moved back to perch on the arm of her own chair.

Appearing shocked by her speech, Michael said, "Ms. Walters..." He said the words as though speaking to someone far beneath his station. "You must understand my position. I love my daughter. And I would do whatever it takes to protect her from people willing to take advantage of her for her money."

Livid at how her father jumped to conclusions without even speaking to her, Amanda stood up. "Hello? I'm sitting right here, *Father*. I'm a grown woman, and I'm more than capable of making my own choices about my life. Why can't you see that?" She rose and stepped up in front of her father to place a hand on his arm. "Do you honestly still think of me as this young girl with absolutely no clue about what's going on?" In hopes of swaying him, she lowered her voice. "Daddy, I know we don't see eye to eye very much any more, but can't you trust my judgment on something this important? Please?" She turned to the woman beside her. "Lex?"

Lex nodded and then stood. "I'll just go get our bags out of the car." She held out her hand for the keys. "See you in a bit." Lex looked at Michael and nodded once. "Mr. Cauble." She turned and left the room.

Amanda watched Lex leave, noticing her slow movements. *I don't think she's quite recovered from the past couple of weeks. Maybe I'd better give her a thorough "checkup" later tonight.* She felt her father's eyes upon her, and turned to face him.

He said, "She's not just some fling you brought to toss in our faces, is she?"

"No, Daddy, she's not. And I can guarantee that she's not after *your* money. Just ask Gramma or Grandpa Jake."

"That's what Dad told me this morning on the phone. They seem quite taken with your farmer."

"She's a rancher. And she's not some dumb cowpuncher who doesn't have any feelings." Taking a deep breath, she walked over to a side table, picking up a paperweight to study it. "I know you don't approve of what I've done with my life."

Michael walked toward her, unsure. "Amanda, it's not that. Your mother and I just think you could do so much more than sell real estate in a backwards little town in Texas." He looked like he was afraid of being rebuffed, but to his credit, he put a hand on her shoulder. "You were always the smart one, and Lord knows you're certainly headstrong enough to accomplish whatever you put your mind to." He lightly stroked her hair. "I just don't want you to waste your talents. You've got such a good head for business. I was hoping you'd come to work for me."

Amanda spun around. She had waited most of her life to hear those words from him. "What?" She looked up into her father's face in an attempt to see if he was telling the truth or not. "Why the sudden change? You didn't want to have anything to do with me after I graduated from college."

And that had hurt. She had studied every waking moment during her college years, taking more than a full load to graduate over a year early. She majored in business, foolishly thinking her father would finally take notice of her and welcome his youngest daughter into his consulting firm. But when she proudly showed him her diploma, Michael had patted Amanda condescendingly on the shoulder and told her to take a year or two off to "travel, enjoy life, find a good man, and settle down." The ache and disbelief she'd felt back then at her father's words even now freshly wounded her.

"Amanda, please." Michael guided her over to a chair to sit, then took the chair next to her. "To tell you the truth, I really didn't expect you would want to work after you got out of school. Your sister only used college as a place to keep up with her friends, and I just assumed you were doing the same."

Doing her best to fight her anger, Amanda willed herself not to cry. "Is that why you thought I took such a full load of classes? So that I could party with all of my friends?"

He looked away. "Uh, well, I really didn't notice your class load. I just assumed you were doing a lot of extracurricular activities."

Amanda stood up and threw her hands in the air. She paced away from the desk, too upset to even look at her father. "I can't believe this!" She spun around, finally looking Michael in the eye. "And now you want me to come and work for you?" Walking back over and sitting down, she asked, "Why now?"

AFTER A SHORT argument with Beverly and the chauffeur, whose name was Paul, Lex was finally allowed to carry their bags into the house.

"At least let Paul help you, Miss Lex. Mrs. Cauble will throw a fit if she finds out we let a guest carry their own luggage." The maid stood in front of the denim-clad woman, wringing her hands nervously.

Even though she hadn't met the formidable Mrs. Cauble, Lex had a pretty good idea what the maid was talking about. In order to keep the peace, she handed Paul half of the bags. "This better?"

"Thanks, Miss Lex." Relief showed on Paul's face. Short and burly, even he was a little afraid of the woman of the house.

Lex gave him a disgusted look. "Could you please drop the 'Miss'? At least when the bosses aren't around?"

Paul looked around carefully, then gave her a shy smile. "Uh, sure, Lex."

Beverly slapped him on the shoulder. "Paul, quit flirting and show...Lex," she gave their guest a wry look, "the guest room across from Miss Amanda's."

Lex hefted her suitcase, while the chauffeur gathered up the rest of the luggage. "Lead on, Paul. Thanks again, Beverly." She gave the slender maid a friendly salute as she followed Paul up the large staircase. Shaking her head as they moved down the opulent corridor, Lex noticed an antique settee. "Hell, I could sleep comfortably out here."

"I know what you mean," Paul said. "My garage apartment doesn't have as much furniture as one of these hallways. But you get used to it, I guess." He stopped in front of a door. "Here's Miss

Amanda's room." Then he pointed to the door Lex was standing next to. "And you're welcome to use that guestroom. I think Beverly likes you."

Setting her bag down, Lex opened the door a bit and peeked inside. "Good God Almighty," she muttered, then turned her attention back to the chauffeur. "Why do you think Beverly likes me?"

Paul opened Amanda's door and took the rest of the luggage inside, then placed them next to the bed. "Well, she normally assigns one of the guestrooms down the way. But that's the biggest one, and the sun won't wake you in the mornings."

Glancing around Amanda's room, Lex found it hard to believe her vivacious lover had ever lived here. *It looks so..so impersonal.*

The large room was furnished with only the essentials: a bed, desk, dresser, and two high-backed armchairs. The room was professionally decorated with a flowery bright bedspread and matching curtains. If Lex didn't know any better, she would have sworn this was a room at an expensive hotel, not the room a young woman lived in.

Lex shook her head and made her way back across the hallway, opening the guestroom door and stepping inside.

Similarly furnished, this room had darker furniture set off with navy blue and maroon plaid covering the bed and adorning the windows. *Damn room is almost as big as the entire upstairs at home.* Opening a door on the near side of the bed, she was pleasantly surprised to find a huge walk-in closet, complete with oak hangers. *Better than the Holiday Inn, I suppose.* Closing the door, Lex noticed another door on the other side of the bed. "Well, what do we have here?" The door opened into a nice sized bathroom, with a large platform bathtub taking up an entire corner. "Oh yeah. That'll hit the spot." She closed the door, walked over to the bed, and then opened up a suitcase. *Think I'll get cleaned up. Might as well try out that tub.*

Chapter
Nine

Trudging up the stairs, Amanda replayed her conversation with her father over and over in her mind. *Why now, Daddy? Why do you suddenly want me to come to work for you?* Michael had deftly skirted around that very question, until she finally decided to give up and go find Lex. *Would I be happy working for him? At one time, I would have sold my soul to do that.* She bit her lip as she thought seriously about the repercussions of that action. *And isn't that what I would be doing now? Giving up my soul?* Amanda knew that even if Lex would leave the ranch to live in Los Angeles, the move would slowly kill her emotionally. *It would be like trying to cage a mountain lion. She would die in "captivity." She needs her freedom.*

Once upstairs, Amanda opened her bedroom door. When she saw that it was empty except for the bags that were by the bed, she momentarily panicked. "Lex?" she called out quietly, looking around. The room, once decorated according to her personal tastes, was now as sterile as a hotel room. *Mother strikes again.* All of her personal possessions were gone. The pictures of friends and family that once adorned her walls were missing, along with all the small knickknacks she had collected over the years. *They were probably packed away the day I called her.* The bookcase and dresser her grandfather had built for her were also nowhere to be seen.

Beverly, who had heard Amanda's footsteps on the stairs, came up to check on her. She stood in the doorway and saw the dejected set to the other woman's shoulders. "Are you all right, Miss Amanda?" *I should have warned her that Mrs. Cauble had her room packed up and put everything away into storage.* "Is there anything I can get for you?"

"I guess Mother couldn't wait to get rid of me, huh?"

"Actually, she said that since you wouldn't be here for very long, she didn't want you to spend all of your time packing when you should be visiting your family." She walked over and placed a hand on Amanda's arm. "If it helps, I supervised the packing, not your mother."

Amanda let out a relieved breath. *The thought of Mother digging through all of my personal things makes me sick. I could just imagine the comments she would have made.* "You have no idea how much that helps." Now that the mystery of her room was solved, she had other things to think about. "Have you seen Lex? I just finished talking to my father, and I thought she'd be up here."

"We put her in the guestroom across from you. Paul said Lex nearly fainted when she saw the size of the room."

"I'll bet." Amanda raised an eyebrow at the maid's familiarity with her lover. *Lex, huh? She must really like her. That's the nicest room on this floor.* "I think I'll go over and check on her. She's had a pretty rough day." Amanda gave the older woman a hug. "Thanks for everything, Beverly. I'm really going to miss you." Even though she hadn't given her father an answer to his "offer", she had no intentions of ever living in this house again.

"You've certainly been missed around here, Miss Amanda. But I think you'll be much happier in Texas." The maid pulled back. The house had been a lot more quiet, and less interesting, without the youngest member of the Cauble family around. She knew that she'd continue to miss her more than she wanted to let on. "Now, I'm going to leave you alone so you can rest up from your trip. Dinner will be in a few hours. I'll send Sophia up to get you when it's ready."

Once Beverly left the room, Amanda counted to ten, then peeked out into the hallway. She looked both ways and saw that the coast was clear. Feeling like a teenager again, she sneaked over and knocked lightly on the door. When there was no answer, she knocked more firmly.

Maybe she's asleep. Not wanting to disturb Lex if she was actually getting some rest, Amanda slowly opened the door. "Lex?" she whispered, stepping into the room. Looking over to the bed, she saw that it was empty except for a set of clean clothes laid out neatly at the foot.

The bathroom door was closed, but Amanda could see a sliver of light leaking out from under the door. Knocking softly, she called out to her partner. "Lex?" When there wasn't a sound, she opened the door slowly, and poked her head into the steamy room. A quick glance around brought her upon the woman she had been looking for. *Aw, she looks so cute.*

Lex was sound asleep in the bathtub, with a damp washcloth covering her eyes.

Amanda closed the door and then locked it behind her. "Lex?" She moved forward carefully, so as not to startle the sleeping woman.

"Mmm." Lex rolled her head to one side, still not awake. She slipped a little lower in the water, until it came almost to her chin.

Kneeling down next to the tub, Amanda removed the washcloth from Lex's face. "Lex? Honey?" She pushed the damp bangs away from the still woman's face. "Hey."

Sleepy eyes partially opened. "Hmm?" Lex moaned, then blinked. "Amanda?" She struggled to sit up a little. "Wha...damn." She pulled one hand out of the water and rubbed her face. "Sorry. I must have dozed off there."

"Do you always fall asleep in the tub?" It seemed like every time she saw Lex in the bath, the poor woman was out like a light. She ran her hand down Lex's face. "Who woke you before I came along?"

"That's why I normally don't take baths. They take up too much time. But Martha would usually—" Her words were stopped by insistent lips. "Mmm." Arms worked their way around her neck, and Lex lifted both of her arms out of the water and wrapped them snugly around the sturdy body next to the tub.

"Ah, Lex." Amanda broke the kiss long enough to breathe. "You're getting my shirt, ummm," a warm mouth attached itself to her throat. "Lex. My shirt," she moaned. "Aaaack!" Amanda soon found herself in Lex's lap. In the tub. Fully clothed. "I can't believe," she began, until her lips were again captured by her now heavily breathing lover. Shaking hands began to unbutton her shirt, and Amanda gasped as the cool air hit her wet, bare skin. Giving up the battle that she didn't seem to be all that interested in fighting, she kicked off her shoes as those roaming hands unsnapped her jeans. "Guess a bath couldn't hurt."

Lex helped Amanda slip out of the rest of her clothes and then pulled her farther into the tub. "You got that right."

"SO, HOW ARE we supposed to dress for dinner?" Lex was sprawled out on the bed, still wrapped in a towel.

Amanda stepped out of the bathroom. She had just finished drying her hair, and was now brushing it until it shined. She noticed the relaxed form on the bed, and her libido tapped her on the shoulder. Again. "In clothes, preferably." She was clad only in her bra and underwear, after sneaking across the hallway to grab dry clothes while wearing only a towel.

Lex suddenly appeared behind her, handing Amanda her towel. "Smartass." She kissed the back of her lover's neck. "I thought I'd just go like I am. What do you think?"

"I think that if you don't get something on, we may never make it downstairs for dinner." Amanda turned around and placed a kiss on Lex's throat. "Thankfully, my parents don't insist on anything formal for dinner, so it's really not that big a deal." She gave Lex's belly a light pat. "Come on, let's get dressed. Sophia will probably be coming for us soon."

"Who's Sophia?" Lex rummaged through her suitcase. She hated traveling anywhere because it was always a pain trying to find what she needed. "Where did you put my—oh, here they are." She grabbed her socks and underwear and then tossed them on the bed.

Amanda finished donning a multi-patterned casual skirt with a pale cotton top. "Sophia is the maid for this floor. Beverly said she'd come for us when dinner is ready."

Lex turned around, her neatly pressed jeans on, but unbuttoned. "Should I wear a tee shirt, or one of my button downs?" She walked over to the closet to find a suitable shirt. "Just how casual is dinner in this place? Will I have to wade through ten different types of forks before I find the right one?" She grabbed a light blue oxford shirt and held it up to her body. "How's this?"

Walking over to obviously nervous friend, Amanda took the shirt from her and removed it from the hanger. "It's perfect." She draped the fabric over Lex's shoulders, helping her put it on. "Don't worry so much. It's just a simple dinner. You *have* eaten in public before, haven't you?" She hoped that her attempt at humor would get Lex to calm down.

Lex watched Amanda's hands button the shirt for her. "Yeah, of course I have. It's just that, well, they're...I just want to make a good impression, that's all." She took a deep breath and sighed. "I don't want your family to think I'm some sort of backwoods hick who eats with her hands."

"Honey, they're not going to think that. Just because you own a ranch, that doesn't mean you don't have any manners. Martha raised you much better than that." Amanda wrapped her arms around Lex's waist and pulled her close. "And if for some reason their little snooty brains think that way, no matter how wrong it is, I don't give a damn. I love you, so they'll just have to love you, too."

"Oh, yeah?"

Amanda nodded into Lex's chest. "Damn right."

A knock at the door interrupted them, and a soft, lightly accented Spanish accent interrupted their play. "Miss Amanda, are you there?"

"Come in, Sophia." Amanda only took one step away from Lex, who finished tucking in her shirt and buttoned her jeans closed.

Not looking them in the eye, the short, heavyset woman spoke softly. "I'm sorry to be disturbing you, Miss Amanda, but Mrs.

Cauble asked that you and your guest join them in the drawing room before dinner."

"Thank you, Sophia. Let me introduce you. This is Lexington Walters. Lex, this is Sophia, who spent a lot of time chasing me up and down these halls when I was a child." Her words brought a smile to the maid's face, and the woman finally lifted her head and smiled.

Lex stepped forward and held out her hand. "Nice to meet you, Sophia. You can call me Lex."

The maid was somewhat at a loss, looking up into the friendly face. She wasn't used to being treated as an equal, except by Amanda. "Thank you, Miss Lex. It's a real pleasure to meet you." She released Lex's hand. Still nervous from the encounter, Sophia curtsied to them both, and started to leave the room. "I'll let Mrs. Cauble know you'll be down soon."

Amanda stared at the quickly closed door. "You seem to have enchanted our entire household staff." She turned and looked at Lex, who was now sitting on the bed slipping on her socks.

"Oh yeah. I think I'm more of an oddity. They act like they've never seen someone wearing scruffy boots before." She pulled on one of the talked about pieces of footwear.

"That's not it at all, honey." Amanda sat down beside her, wrapping an arm around her friend's shoulders. "It's because they're not used to houseguests treating them like people. I don't think my mother knows anyone's name except Beverly's, and she only knows hers because Beverly is in charge of the staff."

Lex leaned her head over until it touched Amanda's. "That's a real shame. They're all really nice folks." She stood up, and then held her arms out away from her body. "Do I look okay?"

Amanda scratched her chin, apparently deep in thought. "Hmm." She pursed her lips. "No, you don't look okay." When her comment brought an upset look to Lex's face, she hurriedly continued, "You look much better than okay, you look great." Amanda stood up and grabbed her partner's hand. "Now that we're both presentable, let's go face the inquisition."

It wasn't long before they were outside the closed doors to the sitting room. Amanda attempted to gather her courage, then she glanced at her companion. Her own worry was beginning to affect Lex, so she mentally shook head and pasted a smile onto her face. "Ready?"

"As I'll ever be."

Conversation stopped and all heads in the room turned to face the door as Amanda and Lex entered. An auburn-haired young woman, who looked like a slightly older version of Amanda, stepped forward. "Mandy, it's so good to see you again." She hugged her sister, then pulled back and tugged on the end of Amanda's hair. "What did you do to your hair?"

"I cut it to make it easier to take care of." She unconsciously brushed the shoulder-length strands away from her face. "Between taking care of Grandpa and working at the office, I just didn't have time to mess with long hair." When she lived in California, Amanda bowed to her mother's wishes and kept her dishwater blonde hair longer than she wanted. But, once away from home, Amanda felt more comfortable doing what she really wanted to do.

"It makes you look older," her mother commented. She was enthroned on an expensive Queen Anne chair and wasn't about to stand, especially for her wayward daughter. Her own hair was fashioned in a shorter style, impeccably bleached a light blonde, with a few soft strands strategically framing her thin face. In deference to her commanding presence, not one hair dared shift out of place. She lifted a hand in the air. "Are you going to stand there all evening, or are you going to come tell me hello?"

Amanda traded looks with her sister. They had been holding court with their mother for as long as they could remember. Although, as of late, her demands were getting more and more bizarre, and they joked that one day, she'd be wearing a crown and brandishing a scepter. "Hello, Mother. You're looking well."

Elizabeth Cauble stood and placed her hands on Amanda's shoulders, then leaned forward to place a light kiss on her daughter's cheek. "Thank you, dear." She stepped back and patted her short hair with one hand. "I had Antoine make it a little lighter this time. I keep telling you that you'd seem so much better light, instead of the natural dingy color you insist on wearing." She glanced over her youngest daughter carefully. "You do appear a little washed out, dear. Showing strange people dirty houses all day is not something a lady should be doing." She said the words as if work were a disease. "Have you been working too hard?"

"No, I haven't. Actually, I've been on vacation for the past couple of weeks, and it's been raining too much to get any sun." *Not to mention that most of my "activities" lately, have been indoors.* "And I really don't want to have another argument about my job right now." Tired of fighting with her mother, Amanda turned back to the doorway, where Lex quietly stood. "Lex, could you come over here, please?" She waited until her partner stood beside her, then took Lex's hand. "Mother, this is Lexington Walters. She's the woman I told you about over the phone. Lex, this is my mother, Elizabeth Cauble."

Lex held out her free hand to the older woman, who took it with slight disdain. "It's a pleasure to meet you, Mrs. Cauble."

"Yes, I'm sure." Elizabeth removed her hand quickly, wiping it not so discreetly with a handkerchief and giving the woman an icy glare.

Amanda missed the look her mother gave Lex as she grabbed the rancher's arm and directed her over to where her sister and a tall, handsome man stood. "Jeannie, Frank, this is Lex, the love of my life." She turned back in time to see Lex's face flush slightly. "Lex, this is my sister Jeannie, and my best friend Frank Rivers, who just happens to be married to her."

Frank shook Lex's hand with enthusiasm. His dark hair was cute short, and his deep brown eyes sparkled with merriment. "So, you're the mysterious rancher our Mandy has been raving about." He pulled her into a hug, and whispered into her ear. "Welcome to the family, Lex. Just don't let the old battle-ax get to you." Frank released the somewhat flustered woman, who gave him a shaky smile.

"Thanks, Frank. It's really good to meet you." Lex cut her eyes over to Amanda. "Although Amanda hasn't told me much about her family, I'm looking forward to getting to know all of you before we leave. I'm sure you have some interesting stories to tell." Then she turned to Jeannie and held out her hand. "Nice to meet you, Jeannie."

Amanda's sister took her hand cautiously. "Lex. It seems that we owe you our thanks for saving my sister's life." She didn't really understand Amanda's lifestyle, but knew from listening to her mother's ravings that this woman was her 'girlfriend'. *Well, I'll give my little sister one thing, she certainly has great taste. This woman is gorgeous and doesn't look like the money-hungry demon Mother described, either.*

Lex gave Jeannie an embarrassed look. "I just happened to be in the right place at the right time, that's all." She was saved from any further comments by a clear voice from the doorway.

Beverly gave Elizabeth a slight curtsy. "Excuse me, but dinner is ready, Mrs. Cauble."

Elizabeth held out her hand for Michael to take. "Very well. Shall we all continue our conversations in the dining room?" she asked the others, as she and her husband took the lead and stepped from the room.

Frank winked at Lex and Amanda. "Guess that's our cue to follow." He allowed Jeannie to take his arm, then followed the older couple out of the sitting room.

Lex waited until the others left, then turned and bowed to Amanda, holding out her arm. "Shall we, my dear?"

Amanda swatted the offered arm and then wrapped her arms around Lex tightly. "God, I love you," she murmured into the taller woman's chest. "Do you think they'd miss us if we just stayed right here, like this?"

"Uh, yeah, I'm afraid they would." Lex looked over Amanda's head and saw Elizabeth's angry glare from the doorway, before the older woman turned on her heel and fled the scene. "Come on, sweetheart. Let's go impress your family with my table manners. I promise to use my fork instead of my fingers."

"Don't even joke about that. But it would be fun to see my mother's face if you did." Amanda lifted her head up and gave Lex a quick kiss. "Now, let's go watch my mother display her queenly abilities at the dining room table." She pulled Lex out of the sitting room and down the hall.

They stepped into a lavish dining room with a heavy cherry table that could easily seat twenty people. Michael Cauble sat at the head of the table, with his wife to the right of him, and his eldest daughter to the left. Frank stood next to Jeannie's chair, waiting for the other women to take their seats. There was a place setting next to Elizabeth, and another on the other side of Frank. Before Amanda could complain about the seating arrangements, Lex nudged her toward the chair next to her mother, while the rancher took her place next to Frank.

He pulled Lex's chair out for her, getting an upraised eyebrow in response. "Thanks."

"Now that we're all finally seated," Elizabeth gave Lex an annoyed look, "you may have dinner brought in, Beverly."

Everyone was completely silent as the servers brought in the meal, waiting until they left the room to begin speaking. Michael was bound and determined to show how unworldly Amanda's choice in suitors was. In a smug voice, he said, "So, Lex. Is this the first time you've ever been to Los Angeles?"

"Yes it is, Mr. Cauble. I don't usually take the time to travel from the ranch, but since Amanda decided she needed to come with her, wild horses couldn't keep me away." Lex gave her lover a smile across the table.

Frank decided that Lex could use an ally. "What exactly do you raise on your ranch? Cattle, horses—"

"Cattle, mostly. But I'm trying to turn it into more of a horse ranch. What is it that you do, Frank?"

The big man cleared his throat. "I played professional football for a couple of years, until I blew out my knee. Now I'm in the public relations business."

"You're *that* Frank Rivers?" Lex exclaimed. "I used to curse you when the Cowboys would play the Rams. You were one of the best defensive backs I've ever seen play the game."

"Such a barbaric game, grown men trying to hurt each other." Elizabeth daintily wiped her lips with her napkin, then returned it to her lap. "But I suppose you'd be interested in that sort of thing, wouldn't you, Ms. Walters?"

Amanda hated where the conversation was going and didn't want to see her lover attacked by her family. "I don't think—"

Lex, even though she appreciated Amanda's attempt at protecting her, felt she could hold her own with the society matron. "I enjoy watching the game, but I'd just as soon be out riding than sitting in front of a television or stuck inside with a desk job."

The matriarch fussed with her napkin. "Most desk jobs, as you put it, are very good ways of making a living. At least it's steady income."

"I agree, Mrs. Cauble. I just can't ever see myself locked in that sort of position. But folks that do have my complete respect." Lex noticed the red flush rising on the older woman's face, and inwardly grinned. *Not going to get me to lose my temper over something that trivial, lady.*

Since the only person losing control of their temper seemed to be his normally calm wife, Michael changed the subject. "Amanda, have you thought any more about my offer? You could have the office right down the hall from me, and of course you'd be making ten times what you could at that puny real estate office." The look of shock on the rancher's face brought him a note of satisfaction.

Amanda looked across the table to Lex, whose face had turned quite pale. She turned to her father. "Um, I thought we were going to discuss this tomorrow?"

Elizabeth beamed and then placed a hand on her younger daughter's arm. "You are? Amanda, dear, that would be wonderful. You've always wanted to work with your father. We could have all of your things brought back out of storage in the morning." She gave the quiet woman across the table a triumphant look.

Lex felt her whole world collapse. She dropped her fork to her barely touched plate and swallowed the lump in her throat. "If you'd please excuse me, I need to make a few phone calls." She promptly stood up and left the room.

Michael watched her leave, and a satisfied smirk crossed his face. "Well, Amanda, I guess we should talk about your salary."

Elizabeth cut in before her younger daughter could speak. "Michael, you know we don't discuss money or politics while we are eating. It's bad for the digestion." She turned to Amanda. "We really must do something about your wardrobe, dear. I think you've spent too much time in the company of that woman. You look like a migrant worker or something equally distasteful."

Amanda tossed her napkin on the table in disgust. "These are the same damn clothes I wore when I lived here." She rose and was about to leave, but Elizabeth's grip on her shirt stopped her.

Michael stood up, his face an ugly shade of red. "Watch your language, young lady. Apologize to your mother this instant." He pushed his chair out of the way, prepared to go around the table to get to his youngest daughter.

"Daddy, let's all calm down, here." Jeannie reached for her father's arm, and pulled it to her. "It's been a really long day, and we're all tired." She gave a nervous smile as Michael sat back in his chair. Turning to her sister, she asked, "Amanda? Come on, why don't you sit back down and we can finish dinner like civilized adults?"

"I'm really not that hungry. If you will all excuse me, I'm going to check on my friend. Amanda pushed her chair back to the table and left the room.

Waiting until the young woman closed the door behind her, Michael faced his wife. "Dammit, Elizabeth. You just had to start on her clothes." He pointed to his oldest daughter. "And I don't want to hear anything out of you."

"Okay, sure." Jeannie shrugged her shoulders. *Poor Mandy, they're just not going to let this go.*

"Please, Michael. Calm yourself. I can't help it if our daughter has begun dressing like a...a...field hand. Did you see that outfit? The skirt was at least a year old, and not even pressed," she tsked.

"I think she looks great. And I love her hair." Jeannie turned to her husband. "What do you think? Should I get mine trimmed, too?"

"Whatever makes you happy, sweetheart. You'd look great without any hair at all." Frank enjoyed the look of shock on her face.

Jeannie grimaced, then stuck her tongue out at her husband. They both continued to tease each other, much to the consternation of the older couple at the table.

AMANDA WALKED OUT of the dining room, closed the door quietly behind her, and started down the long hallway on the way to the sitting room. "Lex?" She peeked inside, only to find the large room empty. *Okay, if I were an upset rancher in a strange house, where would I go?* Turning around, she almost screamed out loud when she came face to face with Beverly.

"Goodness. I'm terribly sorry to give you such a scare. Are you alright, Miss Amanda?"

"I'm fine. You wouldn't happen to have seen Lex in the past few minutes, would you?" Amanda leaned up against the doorframe, releasing a heavy breath.

"As a matter of fact, I have. She told me she needed some fresh air, so I showed her how to get to the back gardens." Beverly noticed the lines of tension on the younger woman's face. "Is it true that you'll be staying? Mr. Cauble called me earlier and told me to have your things pulled from storage tomorrow, but I wanted to check with you first."

"I'm afraid that's just wishful thinking on his part, Beverly. At the rate things are going, I'm not sure if we'll even be here through tomorrow." Amanda spared a wistful glance toward the rear entrance to the house. "I've got a moving truck and crew scheduled to show up tomorrow. Would you—"

The maid patted her on the shoulder. "I'll send them over with Paul to the storage facility. He'll make sure that they get everything." She saw how Amanda kept looking down the hall, fidgeting. "Why don't you go and check on Lex? I'll tell everyone that you retired for the evening."

A relieved smile crossed Amanda's face. "Thanks, Beverly. I owe you one." She forced herself to walk away slowly, when all she really wanted to do was race to the gardens as fast as her feet would carry her.

SITTING ON A slight hill under an Eucalyptus tree, Lex looked down at the massive "garden". The sound of a beautiful fountain, surrounded by a ten-foot hedge on three sides, soothed the rancher's frazzled nerves. Rows upon rows of colorful flowers peppered the area, and multi-colored leafed botanicals were everywhere. Propping her chin on an upraised knee, Lex stared at the gurgling pool, mesmerized by the play of lights and the sinking sun on the spraying water.

Come on, Lexington, pull yourself together. This was just the sort of thing you were afraid of, wasn't it? That she'd come back here and pick up where she left off? All of her friends are here, and her family. She angrily brushed away a tear from her face. "Look at this place. What in the hell could I possibly have to offer her to compare with this?"

"Your love," a gentle voice whispered from behind. "Your heart." The owner of the voice, whose soft hair was framed by the setting sun, suddenly blocked Lex's view. "Mind some company?" Amanda asked, touching Lex's knee with her hand.

"Uh, sure." Lex shifted so Amanda could sit in front of her, framed by her legs. She wiped at her eyes, disguising the motion by using the same hand to comb her hair out of her face. "I'm sorry about running out on you like that, but the walls were starting to close in on me." Lex wrapped her arms around Amanda and pulled her close.

Leaning back into the embrace, Amanda sighed, then bent her

head to kiss one of the arms holding her. "Don't apologize. I'm just really sorry that my father said what he did."

"Was it true? Are you considering staying here, and going to work for him?" Taking a deep breath, Lex continued, "If that's what you want…I'll…support your decision. I love you, and I want you to be happy." The heartfelt speech took more out of her than she expected, and Lex laid her head on her lover's shoulder.

Amanda tangled her fingers into the thick hair spilling over her shoulder. "What about us? Do you think I could just walk away from this? From you?" She felt the body behind her take in a shaky breath.

"No, I don't think that. But I'm also not stupid enough to disregard what a great opportunity this is for you." Lex raised her head slightly to place a kiss just below Amanda's ear. "I could, um, give you some time to get settled, then come back out here, if you want." Lex found herself torn between her heart, which was screaming not to go, and her mind, which knew that this was the best thing for Amanda. *Oh, God, what am I going to do?*

Amanda turned around slightly, so that she could see Lex's face. "What about your ranch?" She put a hand up to touch her friend's tense jaw.

"I'll sell it, or hire somebody to run it. I don't care about the damn ranch." *How did this happen so fast?* She didn't know, and, if she were truthful to herself, she didn't care. Lex closed her eyes and leaned into Amanda's loving touch. She felt a fingertip brush away another tear from her face. "I care about you. Nothing else matters to me."

Fighting back tears of her own, Amanda brushed the dark bangs from her lover's face. "You'd give up your ranch for me?"

"In a heartbeat." Lex opened her eyes. "Hey, don't cry." She lifted a shaky hand to Amanda's face to brush the tears away. "What's wrong?"

"No one's ever offered to do something like that for me before." Amanda looked deeply into Lex's eyes. "Oh, Lex."

Lex pulled Amanda closer, kissing the top of her head. "Shh." She began to rock the sobbing woman. "Please don't cry, sweetheart. I love you. Do you really think I'd let you stay here alone?"

Amanda let herself calm down before continuing. "No. I know you wouldn't leave me, but you don't have to worry. I would never ask you to give up something that means so much to you."

"What are you saying?" Lex felt a jolt of fear shoot through her. "Do you…don't you…you don't want me to stay?" she finished in a quiet voice.

"No, I don't want you to stay. I would get really lonesome in

Texas without you." Amanda looked up into Lex's eyes. "The movers are going to pick up everything that's in storage tomorrow. Do you still want to stay? We can leave whenever you get ready."

"But what about Friday? Won't your father be upset with you?" Lex was so happy, she almost laughed out loud. *She's not staying. She's going home with me!*

Amanda wrapped her arms around Lex and squeezed. "He's already upset. And to quote a good friend of mine, 'you're more important' than some stupid dinner party."

"Thanks." The idea that Amanda would put everything and everyone secondary to them touched Lex deeply inside, but she didn't want to be the cause of a feud between her lover and her family. "But we're already here, so we might as well stick it out." She leaned down to give Amanda a kiss, which was eagerly returned.

After breaking off to catch her breath, Amanda tucked her head into the warm spot underneath Lex's head. "You know, this is one of my favorite places. I was hoping I would find you here."

"Really?" Lex murmured, rubbing her cheek on the soft blonde hair. "It just seemed so peaceful and secluded. Kind of reminds me of home." She thought about that for a moment. "Without the fancy fountain, of course."

"Yeah. It would probably scare the horses half to death, not to mention the fuss Martha would make over it." Amanda raised up a little and kissed the skin on Lex's throat. "I used to sit out here for hours, reading...dreaming."

"What did you dream about?" Lex was enthralled at this peek into Amanda's early life.

"When I was really young, I'd dream about the usual things. Who I would marry, what I was going to do when I grew up. You know, that sort of stuff." She felt the arms tighten around her. "For as long as I can remember, I wanted to go to work for my father. Of course, I alternated that idea with working for Gramma, or even helping Grandpa Jake. I had a hard time deciding. But mostly, I wanted to follow in my father's footsteps."

Understanding where the conversation was headed, Lex felt her heart constrict. "Oh, sweetheart."

"No, wait. I went to college and took a lot of extra classes so I could graduate early. You know, because I wanted to make my dad proud. But he really didn't take me seriously, just sort of brushed me off and told me to travel for a couple of years, like my mother had. So, in my fit of rebellion, I used my degree to join a small accounting office here in Los Angeles." Seeing the sad look on Lex's face, Amanda touched her cheek gently. "And I thank God every day that it all happened that way." She leaned forward, and the kiss she started soon heated up, as she allowed her passion to take over. "Because," she punctuated her point with a smaller kiss. "You are," another, slightly longer kiss. "My greatest dream come true." This time, she met Lex's lips halfway, pulling her lover's head down, with one hand tangled in Lex's dark hair.

Lex returned Amanda's passion with her own, then gasped as she felt a hand unbuttoning her shirt. "Ah, Amanda." The insistent hand reached inside, brushing her stomach lightly. "Oh, God. We can't." Amanda's mouth attached itself to her throat, as the hand began moving upward. "Mmm. No! What if someone, ahh." The warm hand found its target, taking the firm flesh and kneading gently.

"How about," Amanda whispered into Lex's ear, "we continue our conversation upstairs?" She nibbled on her trembling partner's earlobe. "I want you. Right now." She pulled back a little, enjoying the flushed look on Lex's face. "Come on." Amanda slowly removed her hand, then buttoned up Lex's shirt. "I want to try out that huge bed in the guestroom." She stood up and pulled a slightly rumpled Lex to her feet.

Walking back into the house, Amanda giggled when Lex stumbled as they stepped through the kitchen doorway.

"Don't laugh. It's all your fault, you know." Her knees weak from the make out session in the garden, Lex wrapped her arm tightly around Amanda's waist.

Amanda guided them through the kitchen and back into the main foyer. Just as they were reaching the large staircase, a voice stopped them.

"I've been looking for you, Amanda. I thought we had a conversation to finish." Michael glared at Lex, noticing his daughter's bedraggled appearance, and the bruised lips on both women. "Just where exactly were you?"

Not relinquishing her hold on her lover, Amanda tried to tactfully make an exit. "We were just enjoying the peace and quiet of the gardens, Daddy." Feeling Lex tense, she added, "And I think we said all there was to say earlier."

"I don't think so. Come back into my office, and we'll try to get all of this straightened out." He turned, expecting his daughter to follow.

"I'm sorry, Daddy, but we were on our way upstairs. Maybe you and I can talk some more tomorrow." She turned, taking Lex with her. "Goodnight."

Knowing when to back off, Michael stormed back to his office. *Dismissed, like a servant, by my own daughter. All because of that...that...woman!* "We'll just have to see about that, won't we?" He sat down behind his desk, and pulled his Rolodex forward.

Finding the number he was searching for, Michael grabbed the phone.

A slightly accented female voice answered. "Richards Investigations."

"This is Michael Cauble. Put James on the phone." Michael was not in any mood for niceties.

"Very well, Mr. Cauble. Hold one moment, please." The secretary's voice was cool and professional. She was used to the rudeness of her employer's clients. Most of them were rich and rarely thought of her as anything but a means to an end.

Michael waited impatiently, drumming his fingers on his desk, as tinny strains of the song *Memories* flooded his ear. *There should be a law against Muzak.*

"Richards, here," a gravely voice intoned. "Mr. Cauble? What can I do for you?"

"James, I have a rush job for you. Double your usual fee if you can get it together before Friday." Michael pulled a pencil from his desk and doodled aimlessly on a notepad. A stick figure wearing a cowboy hat appeared beneath his sketching pencil.

"This Friday? Must be really important." Richards sounded intrigued. "What is it?"

"I want you to dig up everything you can find on a Lexington Walters. She's a rancher right outside of Somerville, Texas. I don't care what it costs, or how many men you have to put on it. I need it quick." The stick figure now stood on a wide platform.

"Not a problem, Mr. Cauble. I'll get a team out in the next hour, and send you a report by tomorrow morning." He had been under Michael Cauble's employ for the past several years and knew how well the man would pay.

"Excellent. Don't send it by courier, though. Just fax it to me. I rely on your discretion, James." Michael hung up the phone, smiling. *No two-bit dirt grubber is going to get her hands on my daughter's money.* The platform in his sketch became a gallows, and there was now a noose around the neck of the stick figure.

NOT TOO FAR away, Lex allowed herself to be led up the long staircase, her thoughts elsewhere. *Why is her family so dead set against seeing her happy? Are they really that self-centered? Or is it something else? Maybe it's because of who she's with.*

"Honey? You still with me here?" Amanda questioned, closing the guestroom door behind them. "What's wrong?" She brought Lex over to the bed, and nudged her down. "Lex?" Amanda lightly touched her face, causing Lex's gaze to sharpen.

"Huh? Oh, sorry about that. I was just thinking." Lex leaned into the touch. "What were you saying?" She guided the younger woman into her lap.

Amanda snuggled into Lex's arms, content to let the subject drop. "Nothing. I was just a little concerned." She kissed the tan throat under her lips. "Are you feeling okay?"

"I've never felt better. Why don't we get ready for bed?" Lex stood up, lifting Amanda to her feet as well. "Oh. Umm." The hands that began to unbutton her shirt again caused a delicious chill to race down Lex's spine. She reached for the rest of the buttons, intent on helping with the task.

"No. Please, let me." Amanda pushed the shirt back over Lex's shoulders and onto the floor. She unbuttoned Lex's jeans, quickly slid them down her hips, and then bumped Lex back onto the bed.

"I can—" Lex quieted when Amanda placed a hand over her mouth. She kissed the hand, which then moved to caress her face, running lightly over her upraised eyebrows.

"Just sit back. I've wanted to do this all evening." She leaned over and kissed Lex, then backed off and removed the well-worn boots from the silent woman's feet, the socks quickly following them to the floor.

Sitting back on the bed, Lex could only marvel at the gentle attentiveness that her lover showed. Deciding to just lie back and enjoy the ride, she chuckled when a hand tickled her bare foot, which she wiggled. "Hey."

"I'm sorry. You're feet are so cute, I just couldn't resist." She ran another fingertip down Lex's instep, then grabbed the end of the jeans and pulled them off. "And really sexy legs." Amanda ran her hands up the inside of Lex's calves, amazed at how strong they were. *For someone who rides horses so much, she's got incredible legs.*

"Ah, umm. Oh, God." Lex leaned back and closed her eyes, as her heart began to pound. Her eyes opened back up slightly when she heard the sound of cloth rustling nearby. Enjoying her slight bit of voyeurism, she watched as Amanda slowly removed her own clothes, unaware that she was being watched. "You are so beautiful, Amanda."

"Yeah, right." Amanda found it hard to believe that someone as beautiful as Lex would find her even the least bit attractive. *My hair's too mousy, my eyes are the color of stagnant water, and I'm not half as muscular as she is.* Her inner conversation drew her attention away from her lover as she walked back over toward the bed. When she got close enough, Lex pulled her down. "I don't think—" Her doubts were silenced by insistent lips, which claimed hers hotly. "Mmm." She wrapped her arms around Lex's neck, feeling strong hands pull her closer.

"Don't worry," Lex murmured between heated kisses. "I

wasn't expecting you to do any more thinking tonight." She rolled over to cover Amanda's body with her own.

Chapter
Ten

AMANDA STRETCHED STIFFLY, noticing with a slight frown that the sun was trying to peek in the windows. She looked down at the woman snuggled partially on top of her. Lex's dark head rested on her chest, and Amanda brushed the scatted bangs from the smooth forehead. *How did I ever get so lucky? Everything I ever wanted in someone, and in a really good looking package, too. Why can't they just see how happy I am, and leave us alone? Everything has to be connected with money, not love, as far as they're concerned.* She released a heavy sigh, letting her head fall back onto her pillow.

"What's the matter?" Lex's voice was rough with sleep. "You okay?" She nuzzled the soft skin under Amanda's cheek.

Just being asked made her feel better. Amanda glanced into Lex's eyes. "I'm great. Just thinking." She ran her fingertips across Lex's cheek. "I love you so very much, you know."

"I love you, too." Lex placed a kiss on Amanda's chest and then hugged her tight. "I don't know who to thank for sending you to me, but I'm going to spend the rest of my life loving you."

A knock on the door stopped Amanda's answer. The maid's soft voice floated through the door. "Miss Amanda? It's me, Beverly."

Lex shrugged, as Amanda gave her a questioning look. They weren't being very discreet, but neither one of them seemed to care. But, deciding to spare the maid too much of a shock, Lex climbed out of bed then padded into the bathroom, closing the door behind her.

"Come in, Beverly." Amanda had just enough time to put Lex's shirt on and climb back into bed as the maid stepped into the room.

Beverly gave the younger woman an understanding look. "I'm really sorry to bother you so early, but I thought you might want to know that your mother is searching for you." Her eyes took in the clothes strewn around the room. "And I didn't want her... interrupting, anything."

Amanda blushed. "Uh, yeah. Thanks a lot, Beverly." She

rubbed her face with one hand. "Do you know what she wants?"

"She mentioned something about choosing your outfit for Friday."

"Too bad. I've already chosen my clothes, so she'll just have to live with it." Amanda tried to look superior, then realized that the shirt she was wearing was inside out and buttoned crookedly, which caused her to blush again.

Lex stepped out of the bathroom, with a green towel wrapped around her body. "Good morning, Beverly. Is everything okay, Amanda?"

"Yeah, I guess. Beverly came up to warn us that Mother's looking for me." Amanda ducked her head, finding the pattern on the comforter quite interesting.

Lex made her way into the closet, unable to control her laughter. "Must not be looking too hard. I don't see you hiding." She stepped back out with her jeans on as she buttoned a denim shirt.

Amanda covered her head when the maid began to laugh. "Oh, God."

"I'll just let you get ready, and I'll tell your mother that you'll be down soon, so she won't be disturbing you." Beverly laughed again as another groan was heard from under the comforter. She left the room, closing the door behind her.

Sitting down on the edge of the bed, Lex pulled the comforter away from Amanda's head. "What's the matter, sweetheart? You're not shy, are you?"

WHAP!

Amanda slammed a pillow into the smirking woman's face, knocking her off the bed. But when she didn't hear anything from below, she became worried. "Lex?" She leaned over the edge of the bed, just in time for the same pillow to knock her backwards. "Hey!" Amanda felt the bed shift as a large body leaped up, straddling her hips. "You wouldn't." Long fingers began to tickle her unmercifully. "Lex!" She giggled. "Come on. Aargh!" Amanda squirmed, trying to fight back. Finally, between gales of laughter, she was able to gasp, "Stop! I'm gonna make a mess if you don't quit!"

Lex stopped tickling Amanda, and gently raised her lover's arms up over her head. Leaning down, she gave Amanda a kiss. "Bathroom's all yours, sweetheart. I'll just straighten up in here. Nice fashion trend you're setting with that shirt, by the way." She jumped off the bed, easily eluding the other pillow Amanda tossed her way.

DECIDING TO AVOID an early confrontation, Amanda asked Beverly to have breakfast served to her and Lex on the sun porch, which was right off the kitchen. With the windows open, it wasn't a usual meeting place for members of the family, because the fresh air often brought small insects with it. The sun was partially blocked by the awning that ran across the back, but Lex loved it anyway.

"That was great." Lex moaned and leaned back in her chair. She pulled her arms back over her head and stretched until her back popped several times.

Amanda reached over and scratched Lex's stomach. "You didn't eat much dinner last night. Did you get enough breakfast?"

Lex swatted the teasing hand away. "Stop that." She straightened up and grabbed her coffee cup. "Oh, yeah. I don't think I'll be ready for anything else for at least a few days. That was wonderful. What's on the agenda for today?"

"How about a drive down to the beach?" Amanda pulled her napkin from her lap and placed it on the table. "Maybe a little sightseeing?" She reached over and took Lex's hand in hers. "I thought we could just get out of the house for a little while, give my parents time to calm down." *And hopefully avoid a confrontation with Mother over my clothes for the dinner.*

Pulling their linked hands up to her lips, Lex rubbed Amanda's knuckles against her cheek. "Whatever you want, my love. It's your show. The beach sounds good. I've never seen the ocean."

Amanda closed her eyes for a moment and enjoyed the closeness. "Never? Well then, that's exactly what we're going to do." She stood and brought Lex up with her. "Why don't we go change into some shorts, then hit the beach."

Lex shook her head when Amanda began tugging her through the house. "Amanda, you packed my bag. All I have are some old cut-offs. Not exactly the thing to be running around in."

"Oh yeah? Why else do you think I packed them? I've got some, too, and I think that they'll be perfect." Amanda had gotten them almost to the stairway when her mother stepped out of nowhere. "Oh. Hello, Mother. We were just about to go to the beach. Would you like to join us?" Knowing how much Elizabeth hated anything that had to do with the outdoors, Amanda couldn't resist.

"No, thank you, Amanda. But I would like a word with you." She gave the rancher an icy glare. "Alone, if you don't mind."

Lex looked down at her companion, who looked as if she were ready to explode. "No problem. I'll just go upstairs and get changed." She gave Amanda's hand a strong squeeze, released it, then turned and moved quietly up the stairs.

"Come, Amanda. We'll go into the drawing room. I have coffee ready." Elizabeth turned and walked across the foyer, her daughter trailing dutifully behind.

Amanda waited until they were seated before she began to speak. "Mother, I know you've never approved of what I've done with my life, or the choices I've made, but I will not sit still for your rude treatment of Lex."

"Now, wait just a minute," Elizabeth sputtered.

"No. You wait." Amanda held up a hand for forestall her mother's tirade. "I resigned myself a long time ago to the fact that I was a disappointment to you and Daddy." She took a deep breath then continued. "I'm never going to be one of your snobbish little society girls, like you wanted."

Elizabeth grasped the younger woman's arm. "Amanda, that's not completely true. Your father and I respect the fact that you have a mind of your own." She released her hold to pick up a dainty coffee cup and saucer. Taking a small sip, the regal woman put it back on the table in front of them. "Where did we go wrong? Your sister seems happy." She looked her daughter in the eyes. "What did we do to make you this way?"

Amanda blinked, unsure of the question. "What exactly are you talking about, Mother? Is this about me being gay?"

"I refuse to accept that, Amanda. You were raised in a good home." She searched her daughter's face for a clue to her questions. "It's because of Frank, isn't it?"

Amanda's mouth dropped open. "What?"

Elizabeth nodded to herself, pleased with her deduction. "You and he were quite an item, and then your sister Jeannie stole him right out from under your nose." She tapped her chin with an elegant nail. "I should have seen this before. This is your way at getting back at all of us for giving your sister our blessing with him, isn't it?"

Amanda jumped up, too agitated to sit still. "Oh, for crying out loud, Mother." She paced over to the piano, then turned back to face the older woman. "I told you I was gay when I was still in high school. Frank has always been just a very good friend." She walked over to stand in front of Elizabeth. "I was the one who set him up with Jeannie. He's like a brother to me!"

"Calm down, dear. Come back over here and sit." Elizabeth patted the spot next to her on the loveseat. "We'll forget about your little outburst for now." She waited until Amanda was once again seated. "Now, about this woman you've brought with you." Elizabeth raised her hand to silence her daughter. "Just a minute. From what Michael's parents have told us, she saved your life a few weeks ago, correct?"

For the first time since they stepped into the room, Amanda was able to smile. "Yes, she did. Lex had no idea who I was, but she jumped into that flooded creek and pulled me to safety, getting herself hurt in the process."

"And you stayed with her at her ranch, afterwards?"

"Yes. The bridge was partially destroyed, so Lex offered me a place to stay until it could be repaired." Amanda's eyes sparkled with remembrance.

Elizabeth grasped Amanda's hands with her own, leaning forward slightly. "She's quite a strong looking woman. Now tell me the truth, Amanda. We can protect you here." The older woman looked around the room cautiously, then whispered, "Did she force herself on you? Are you afraid of what she might do if you don't stay with her?"

Amanda couldn't help it. She laughed. "Lex? You've got to be kidding." She jerked her hands away from her mother and leaned back in the loveseat. "Somebody should ask her that question. I practically threw myself at her."

Watching her daughter's body language, Elizabeth came to a decision. *No, I don't think she feels threatened by that woman. Perhaps another tact.* "You threw yourself at her? Amanda Lorraine. I'm—" Another idea sprouted itself in the older woman's mind. "Hero worship," she stated smugly.

"Excuse me?"

"That's it. Since you're not being forced to stay with her, that's the only logical explanation." Elizabeth took another sip of her coffee. "You feel beholden to her for saving your life and then taking care of you. So you naturally show your gratitude by staying with her."

Amanda jumped to her feet again. "That's bullshit," she yelled, then stopped when she saw the look on her mother's face. "I'm sorry, Mother." She lowered herself into the loveseat again. "You're wrong. It's not fear, hero worship, or misplaced gratitude that keeps me with Lex."

"Then what—" Elizabeth began, only to be cut off by Amanda.

"It's love. Plain and simple." Amanda looked into her mother's eyes, hoping to see understanding there. "I can't explain how it happened, or why. But I fell hopelessly, deeply in love with her almost instantly." She stood up and slowly walked to the door. "Why is it so hard for you and Daddy to understand that?" Amanda shook her head and left the room, closing the door behind her.

Elizabeth Cauble sat immobile, staring at the closed door. *We'll just see what her father has to say about this. Michael always has a few tricks up his sleeves.*

LEX STOOD AT the bedroom window, staring at nothing in particular as the voice through the cellular phone wound down.

"Lexie, don't you let those folks get to you," Martha pleaded, after hearing what Lex had reported to her so far. "You're just as good, if not better, than any of them."

The rancher released a heavy sigh. "You say that, Martha, but you haven't seen this place. It's straight out of one of those silly television shows you used to watch. I keep expecting to see Joan Collins step out of a room any minute now."

"Now that would be a sight. How's Amanda handling all of this? Poor thing's probably as flustered as you are, I'll bet."

"She's doing a lot better than I am, I think. Although it's been one fight after another for her ever since we got here." Lex ran a hand through her hair, then leaned forward until her forehead was pressed against the cool glass of the window. "She's a hell of a lot stronger than I thought she was, that's for sure."

"I could have told you that, Lexie. That young lady may look like the sweet quiet type, but she's got the heart of a lion," Martha stated, matter of fact. "You tell her I said hello and to not take any bunk from anyone. And make sure she knows she always has a home here, no matter what."

"Yes ma'am. I was kind of thinking along those exact lines, myself."

"I knew I didn't raise a fool. Now you take care of yourself, and her, too. We'll have a nice barbecue when you girls get back home."

"That sounds like a wonderful idea, Martha. I'll talk to you tomorrow."

"All right, sweetheart. Goodbye."

Lex had just closed the phone when the bedroom door opened. Turning away from the window, she crossed the room quickly when she saw the upset look on Amanda's face. "What's the matter, sweetheart? Are you—" Lex stopped her questioning when Amanda wrapped her arms around her and buried her tear-streaked face into her denim shirt. "Hey." She instinctively returned the embrace, running a hand through the soft hair. "You okay?"

Amanda sniffed, then looked up into worried eyes. "Yeah. I just needed to connect with you for a minute." She felt a kiss on the top of her head. "I love you so much, Lex. Why can't my parents understand that?"

"Your mother gave you a hard time, huh?" Lex guided Amanda over to the bed to sit. "They just want what's best for you." She pulled Amanda into her lap. "So do I."

"I don't think that's it. They want what's best for them.

They've never even bothered to ask me what I wanted." Amanda raised her arms to wrap them around Lex's neck, pulling her close for a kiss. "Mmm." She turned to face Lex, then straddled her thighs.

"Is that what you wanted?" She bent down and captured Amanda's lips again. "Better?"

"Oh yeah. Much." Amanda snuggled close, then ran one hand lightly down Lex's side, feeling the jean-clad leg beneath her. "I thought you were going to change?"

Lex waved the cell phone in front of Amanda's face. "I was, but I decided to call Martha instead."

Amanda swatted the phone away. "Oh yeah? How's she doing?"

"Ornery as ever. She sends you her love, and said for you not to let them get to you." She paused. "And, umm, she said to tell you not to forget that you have a home there," Lex finished quietly.

"I do, huh?" Amanda questioned just as quietly, looking up into Lex's face.

Lex looked down, lost in Amanda's sparkling eyes. "Yeah. You know, I've been thinking a lot about that. And I realize that we haven't known each other that long," Lex babbled, unsure of herself. "But I was wondering if—"

Amanda could feel the rancher's heart pounding under the hand she placed on Lex's chest. "Lex, honey, what are you trying to say?" She tried to calm the nervous woman by gently massaging her neck and shoulder.

"Well, um, I know you value your independence, and I'm not trying to rush you, or push you into something that you're not ready for. And it's really not that far from town," Lex continued, still flustered.

Understanding dawned on Amanda. "Wait." She covered the rattled woman's mouth with her hand. "Are you asking me to move in with you at the ranch?" Seeing the telltale flush on her companion's face, she smiled brightly. "You know, I was wondering how I was going to survive when I have to go back to work next week."

Lex looked at her, trying unsuccessfully to keep a silly grin from erupting on her face. "Does this mean—"

"Do you think that you could handle having me under foot all the time?" Amanda grunted as the breath was suddenly squeezed from her.

"Yes!" Lex whooped, hugging Amanda to her tightly. She buried her face Amanda's hair. "Under foot? I should be so lucky," she mumbled happily. "You can either redo the guest room, or just move into the master bedroom with me. I'll try to make space in my closet."

Amanda laughed. "Let's worry bout it when we get home, okay? I'm just going to have the movers put everything into storage right now. We can sort through it all later."

"We've got a pretty good-sized storage shed up by the bunkhouse, if you'd rather use that. I cleaned it out about three years ago because it had a bunch of Dad's junk in it. I don't think there's even anything in there right now." Lex kissed Amanda. "Thanks," she whispered when they broke apart.

"For what?" Amanda asked, searching the face so close to hers.

Lex cradled Amanda's cheek with one hand. "For bringing more happiness into my life than I ever thought was possible." She captured Amanda's lips again, this time with more fervor.

Amanda returned the kiss, threading her hands through Lex's hair, rolling onto her back and pulling her companion over on top of her. She retreated just far enough to speak. "Why don't we wait until this afternoon to visit the beach? I can think of better things to do around here." She guided Lex's face back down to hers.

With a wicked chuckle, Lex couldn't agree more. "You're the boss."

THE BREEZE BLOWING off the ocean was cool, but not cold as the two women walked side by side on the nearly deserted beach. When Lex had questioned Amanda about the sparse crowd, she was told it was the wrong time of the year. "Most people just spend their time in the nearby shops during the off season."

"This is great." Lex bent over and picked up a small shell, then, like a child, crammed it into the pocket of her faded cutoffs.

Amanda looped an arm through Lex's, bumping her with her hip. "Yeah, it is." She stopped and picked up another seashell. "Here, I think you missed one." She handed the treasure to her companion, who blushed slightly.

"Thanks." Lex sheepishly put it in her pocket. "Thought maybe Martha might like them." Then she grinned at the look on Amanda's face. "Yeah, yeah. Okay. You caught me. I like 'em." She pulled Amanda into an impromptu hug. "Thanks. I'm really having a good time today."

"You haven't seen anything yet. Wait until we hit the shops. Now, *there* are some interesting sights." Amanda was totally charmed by the child-like glee Lex displayed at all the sights and sounds on the beach. She had dragged Amanda playfully into the surf when they first arrived and threatened to throw her into the ocean until she surrendered a kiss. "Come on, you silly thing. Let's take your little treasures back to the car, and we'll have lunch. Then we'll do a little shopping." Amanda took her friend back toward the parking lot.

After a light lunch of corn dogs and potato chips, Amanda showed Lex a row of colorful shops, slinging a large, brightly decorated straw bag over one shoulder.

"What's in the bag?" Lex asked, trying to peek inside as she walked beside her friend.

Amanda gave her a quirky grin. "Nothing, yet. But I like to be prepared." She pushed her wide sunglasses up on her nose.

Lex laughed, and tugged down a little further over her eyes her just-acquired aqua baseball cap that stated 'Life's a Beach'. "If you say so, sweetheart." She glanced down at Amanda's legs. "You've got a really nice tan, you know that?"

"Thanks. I used to spend a lot of time at the beach when I lived here. Just to get out of the house. You know." Amanda studied her companion with a less than clinical eye. "I've never really noticed before, but *you* have a good tan. How did you manage that? All I've ever seen you in, besides nothing," she leered, "is jeans." Lex not only had a nice tan, but long, very muscular legs as well.

"Well, when I'm putting the colts through their paces in the summertime, I sometimes wear cutoffs so I don't pass out from the heat." Lex admitted. Then she stopped, sidetracked by several girls jumping multiple ropes. *How in the hell do they do that?*

Amanda wandered ahead a few yards, intrigued by a man making brightly colored sand sculptures. Just as she turned to get Lex's attention, a teenager grabbed at the bag on her shoulder, backhanding her across the face to make her release the purse.

Lex looked up just as Amanda was hit. "Hey," she yelled, grabbing one of the long jump ropes without a second thought. She ran up to Amanda, who was sitting up holding her hand against her cheek. "Are you okay?" Lex asked, looking her over carefully.

"Yeah, just caught me off guard." Amanda tried to smile, but winced instead.

"Okay. Sit tight, I'll be right back." Lex patted Amanda on the knee, then took off, sprinting after the thief.

"Lex, wait!" Amanda sat in the sand and watched Lex's long legs shorten the distance between herself and her quarry. Before Lex was out of sight, a small crowd had begun to gather around Amanda, some complaining about the lack of security, while others asked her if she was okay. A boy, about ten years old, stepped over to Amanda and handed her a small bag filled with crushed ice. She placed it on her aching cheek and tried to smile. "Thank you."

As she chased the thief down the paved path, Lex fashioned a loop on one end of her confiscated rope. She never broke pace as she dodged the endless throng of people in her path. When the youth looked back at her in fear, a primal part of Lex growled. "That's right, you little shit, you'd better be scared." It wasn't long before she made progress in catching up to the purse-snatcher, who quickly decided to take an alternate route toward the beach.

Knocking a few pedestrians down, the thief took off across the sand, not even realizing when his pursuer got closer. Lex was only about ten yards away when she began swinging the rope over her head in a wide loop, closing in on him quickly.

The teenager gasped as the rope dropped over him and tightened around his chest, stopping him in his tracks. He wheezed again as he fell onto his back in the sand, hard.

Lex skidded to her knees and straddled him, while he gasped for breath. She tangled her hands into the front of his sweat-stained tee shirt with a dark and angry look on her beautiful face. "You son of a bitch." She pulled him up slightly, then slammed him back into the sand. "I ought to kill you right here, and save the state some money." Before she could do any damage, two police officers jumped from their bicycles and pulled her off the terrified youth.

"Easy there, miss." One of the cops grabbed hold of Lex's shoulder as his partner handcuffed the frightened thief. "Must have been something pretty important in that bag," he commented, handing the item back to the still heavily breathing woman.

"No," Lex gasped, still on her knees, as she worked to get her breathing under control. "It's empty." She gave the subdued man a nasty look. "The little bastard hit my friend." As if that explained everything.

The other cop grinned as his partner handed the rope back to Lex. "Nice job, by the way. We're going to need to get a statement from you, though."

"Can I go back and check on my friend first?" Lex asked, standing up and brushing sand from her knees.

"Sure," Cop number two agreed, leading the teen to a nearby police car. "We'll even have someone give you a ride back, since we need to collect a statement from your companion, too." He opened the front passenger side door for Lex, then pushed the dazed thief into the back seat. "Johnston here," he nodded toward the burly officer behind the wheel of the car, "will drop you off on his way to the station, and we'll meet you there, okay?"

"Thanks." Lex shook his hand and got in the car, still shocked at what she almost did. *Damn. I could have killed that guy. And he was just a kid. Thank God the police showed up when they did, or I'd be the one in the backseat.*

Back further down the beach, Amanda was dealing with her own problems. *If I have to ward off one more kind person, I swear I'll scream!* Ever since Lex chased after her assailant, concerned bystanders, offering her everything from a glass of water to a dinner date, bombarded her. Some helpful soul had even brought her a folding lawn chair to sit in as she fretted over the whereabouts of her companion. *Lex, why did you go after that guy? You knew there was nothing in that damn bag.*

When a police car pulled up into the parking lot beside the area where Amanda sat, she immediately thought the worst. *Oh, no, what's happened to her?* She fought to keep the tears at bay, when a tall form blocked the sun in front of her.

Concerned eyes looked directly into her soul, as Lex knelt down in front of her friend. "Amanda?" She placed a warm hand on Amanda's knee. "You okay, sweetheart?"

"Oh, God. Lex—" Amanda broke into tears, then launched herself out of the chair and into the arms of her lover. She wrapped her arms around Lex's neck, ending up on her knees in front of her.

"Easy there, Amanda. Shhh." Lex continued to murmur words of comfort into Amanda's ear, rubbing her back with a comforting motion. She slowly stood up, bringing the sobbing woman with her.

Amanda leaned back slightly, tears still running down her face. "Are you okay?"

"Yeah, I'm fine. How about you?" Lex ran her fingertips lightly over Amanda's jaw where a bruise was already beginning to form. *That son of a bitch. Kid or not, I should have killed him when I had the chance.*

"I'm okay," Amanda assured her, then slapped her hard on the side.

"Ouch!" Lex jumped.

"Don't you *ever* do that to me again," Amanda demanded in a shaky tone, anger and fear in her eyes.

"What?" Lex stepped back away from Amanda, whose eyes were sparkling with emotion.

"Take off after a thief like that. Dammit, Lex! That stupid bag wasn't worth risking your life for!"

Lex moved toward Amanda cautiously. "Him? Aw, Amanda, he's just a scrawny two-bit little purse-snatcher."

She really doesn't get it. "Lex," Amanda said patiently, "he could have been a junkie looking for quick money and carrying a knife or gun for protection." She put her hands on her lover's waist. "And I don't want to lose you this soon after finding you, okay?"

Understanding raced across Lex's tan features. "Oh. I never really thought about that. I just saw him hit you, and kind of lost it." She pulled Amanda into a hug. "I'm sorry." She reluctantly released Amanda when a throat was cleared discreetly behind her. Turning, Lex kept her arm about Amanda's waist as she greeted the two bicycle cops. "Oh, hi, officers." Although she realized that their afternoon was about to get even longer, Lex didn't care as long as Amanda was by her side.

LEX STUDIED HER companion's profile with concern as Amanda drove them back to her parents' house. "Oh, Amanda," she said quietly, touching the side of Amanda's face, "that is going to be one hell of a bruise."

The side of Amanda's face was already purple, from her cheek down across her jaw. "I guess." She tilted her head to peek into the rear view mirror, then grimaced. "Well, at least there's not much swelling. The ice really helped. I can't believe you actually roped that guy. Wish I had seen that."

Lex rolled her eyes. "Those cops exaggerated, I think. I'm sure it looked a lot more impressive than it actually was." Lex thought back to the group of people on the beach, all of whom had followed them both all the way to their car. "Thought we'd never get away from your fan club, though."

"Don't remind me." Amanda decided to bring up Lex's own adventure with the police. "Although I think you had your own admiration society with those two cops. The look on that one's face when you turned down his dinner offer was priceless."

When the taller of the two police officers had approached Lex for a date, she politely declined, stating she didn't think her girlfriend would approve. The embarrassed officer apologized, then offered to take them both out, which they also turned down, saying they had to leave for Texas.

"Yeah. I wasn't really thinking. But it was pretty funny, wasn't it?"

Amanda shook her head. "What am I going to do with you?"

"Oh, I'm sure you can come up with something creative."

"We'll see about that, my little thief roper." Finally home, Amanda pulled up to the familiar security box. Before she reached out to punch in the security code, she edged over the other way and grabbed Lex by the back of the neck. "I'll show you creative."

Lex obeyed willingly, allowing Amanda to take control of the situation, as chills chased down her spine. "Damn, Amanda," she wheezed as they broke off. "How in the hell do you do that?" She leaned her forehead into Amanda's as her entire body trembled slightly.

Amanda took a deep, shaky breath as well. "Whoa. That sure got the old blood pumping, didn't it?" She gave Lex another, shorter kiss. "Oh yeah. Whoo!" She grinned, then released Lex and punched the code into the gate.

When he spotted Lex and Amanda walking across the main foyer toward the stairs, Michael Cauble went ballistic. "What in the hell did you do to my daughter?" He stormed directly over to them with his fists clinched at his side.

"Daddy, wait!" Amanda stepped in front of Lex, holding her hand out to block her father's path.

Shoving his daughter aside, Michael slammed Lex up against the stairwell, his face red with rage. "You like hitting defenseless women, dirt grubber?"

Amanda squeezed between the two of them, pushing her father back. "Stop it! Lex didn't do anything to me, Daddy. I was mugged at the beach."

"What? You were mugged?" Michael backed off, but only a step, glaring at the rancher. "Where the hell were you while my daughter was being assaulted?"

Lex wisely kept her mouth shut, allowing Amanda to handle Michael. She knew if she said anything, it would only hurt the woman she loved, so she kept quiet. *Stay calm, Lexington. Let Amanda take care of him.* She took a deep breath and released it, feeling Amanda's hand pat her gently on the arm.

"Lex was only a few steps away, and she caught the guy, then turned him over to the police." Amanda stepped back and put a hand behind her to make contact with the silent woman, whose anger she could almost feel as Lex reached to put her hands on her waist.

Michael prudently decided to let the matter drop. "Very well." He looked at their matching ragged shorts and frowned. "Is it too much to ask that you two change for dinner? We're not having a clambake."

Amanda felt Lex stiffen behind her, the hands on her hips tightening slightly. "Is it too much for me to ask that you and Mother act civil tonight? If not, Lex and I can go out for dinner, then fly out first thing in the morning." She halfway hoped his answer would be negative. *Please. Give me a reason to get out of here.*

Amanda watched a mix of emotions cross her father's face, first surprise and then a look of pride. . "Of course, dear? We just got off on the wrong foot, didn't we, Lex?" He reached forward and offered his hand to the quiet woman. "No hard feelings?"

"Sure, Mr. Cauble." Lex took his hand in a firm grasp. But she couldn't help but believe that the man was up to something. *Probably up to no good, but we'll just play it by ear for now.*

"Thanks, Daddy." Amanda gave her father a hug. "We'll be cleaned up and changed in time for dinner." She wasn't fooled either by his sudden capitulation, but decided to accept the cease-fire for now. "Come on, Lex." She took Lex by the arm and led her up the stairs.

Once they were safely ensconced in the guestroom, Amanda locked the door and studied her quiet companion. "Are you okay?" She ran her hands searchingly over Lex's body. "My father didn't hurt you, did he?"

"I'm fine." Lex grabbed the wandering hands and pulled them behind her back. "He just pushed me, no damage done." She felt Amanda's hands tuck into her rear pockets, and she raised an eyebrow in response.

"Just checking for bruises," Amanda explained unrepentantly. "Maybe I should take off your clothes and double check? No sense in taking any chances."

Lex laughed. "Sure. But let's take a shower. The lights are much better in there." She pulled Amanda into the bathroom and closed the door behind them.

Chapter
Eleven

AFTER A SHORT argument with Elizabeth, which she won—Amanda had Lex's place setting moved from next to Frank's to across the table beside hers. The entire meal was spent in tense silence, only broken by the occasional attempts of Jeannie and her husband to clear the air.

"Good grief, Mandy. Daddy told us about what happened to you today. But he failed to mention that you looked like you got into a fight with a heavyweight boxer and lost." Jeannie was shocked at the large bruise that covered her sister's cheek. "So come on, tell us the whole story."

Amanda's explanation about the day's events further antagonized her parents, especially when she painted her companion's part in the tale so heroically. "The police officers said the look on that thief's face was really funny when Lex pulled the rope tight and he hit the ground. They were trying to catch up on their bikes and saw the whole thing."

Michael glared at Lex. "Sounds rather foolish to me, chasing down a criminal when you're unarmed." He took a sip of wine. "People have been killed for less."

"I really wasn't thinking. I saw him hit Amanda and totally lost it. I just wanted to make sure he paid for what he had done to her."

Jeannie knew her parents wouldn't let the subject drop and could see that both Lex and Amanda were uncomfortable. In just the short amount of time that she had gotten to know the quiet rancher, Jeannie had come to like her and felt a bit protective of her sister's friend. *Uh-oh. Time to change the subject, I think.* "So, my lovely sister, give me all the juicy gossip from Somerville." She purposely ignored the glare from her mother and winked at Lex. "Or maybe you can fill me in, Lex."

"Sure. What do you want to know?" Lex flinched slightly when Amanda poked her leg under the table.

"Got anything on my sister? She never likes to talk about herself."

Lex almost yelped out loud as her leg was pinched. "Ow!" She quickly cleared her throat to cover up her slip. "Excuse me. Well, did Amanda tell you about her promotion? She's now the manager of the real estate office."

"Really? That's great news, Mandy." Jeannie almost squealed with excitement. "But what about that Neanderthal, Rick? He's always so rude when I call Amanda's office. Someone needs to knock him down a peg or two, in my opinion."

Lex almost choked on the water she was drinking. "Well," she coughed, "there's actually a really funny story about that. Ow!" Amanda had stomped Lex's foot, and the sharp pain effectively halted her in mid-sentence.

Frank, who had been silent up until now, couldn't help but grin at Lex. "You okay, Lex?" His smirk let her know he knew exactly what was wrong.

"Yeah." She glared at Amanda, who smiled innocently. "Sudden cramp, I guess." She felt a hand rub her leg in a soothing manner.

"So, what's the story?" Jeannie asked, missing the glare her sibling threw at her.

Feeling the hand on her thigh tighten into a claw, Lex decided that discretion was the better part of valor. "Seems poor Rick not only got fired, but ended up receiving a bruised jaw and got thrown into jail for disorderly conduct." The claw straightened out and gave her a loving pat instead.

Amanda quickly decided to change the subject. "So, Mother, have you decided on a cruise or a tour of Europe this year?" She knew Elizabeth had one real passion in her life, and that was travel.

"I believe I'll do Paris. The last cruise was such a disappointment to me. People actually brought children on board!" Elizabeth's disgust was evident to all by her tone of voice. "And they let the little heathens run wild. It was absolutely disgraceful."

Lex started to say something, but closed her mouth and concentrated on her plate instead, *thinking there was no sense in giving them any more reason to make Amanda's stay here miserable.*

Michael had seen her begin to speak, then stop. "Do you have something you'd like to say, Lex? I'm sure that we would all be interested in whatever is on your mind."

Amanda looked at her father in surprise, but didn't speak up.

"I really don't think you want to hear my opinion, Mr. Cauble."

"Don't be ridiculous." He gestured toward everyone else seated at the table. "Please, share with us."

Feeling Amanda's comforting touch on her leg, Lex gave her partner an apologetic look. "I was just going to say that those folks probably worked and saved for years to go on a cruise, so they had just as much right to be there as anyone."

"Are you saying that I don't work for my money?" Elizabeth gave Lex a nasty look, daring her to answer.

"No, ma'am, not at all. I'm just saying that most folks don't take a real vacation every year. But when they do, they have as much right to relax and enjoy themselves as the people whose biggest concern is where they'll go, not how much it will cost."

Sensing that his mother-in-law was preparing herself to attack, Frank jumped into the conversation. "Have you ever been on a cruise, Lex?"

"No. I've never really had the time. As a matter of fact, this is the first time I've been away from the ranch in several years." Lex gave Amanda a meaningful look. "But I wouldn't mind going on one, someday."

"Frank and I are taking an Alaskan Cruise as a second honeymoon next spring," Jeannie shared. "Maybe you should consider going on one, too. It's certainly a great way to beat the summer heat. I didn't visit as often as Amanda did, but the Texas summers stand out as extremely wicked in my mind. I don't know how you're able to handle it."

Lex shrugged. "I guess I'm just used to the heat. It doesn't really bother me any."

Elizabeth saw her opportunity. "I suppose it's like the migrant workers in the Valley. They don't know any better than to stay in the hot sun all day. They're quite used to it as well, I suppose."

Amanda glared at her mother. "I can't believe your attitude."

"It's okay, Amanda." Lex placed a hand on her lover's arm, trying to calm her down.

"No, it's not," the furious woman snapped, then saw the hurt in Lex's eyes and immediately dropped her voice. "I'm getting tired of listening to my parents take potshots at you."

Lex slipped her hand beneath the table and took a firm grasp of Amanda's fingers. "We'll talk about this later, okay?" She gave the hand in hers a squeeze. Looking up at Elizabeth, she cleared her throat. "And I have to agree with you, Mrs. Cauble. If a person works all day, every day in the heat, it's much easier for them to handle it." Then, with a slight twinkle in her eye, she continued, "Unlike the poor folks that have to sit in an office all day long. They break out into a sweat just walking to their cars at the end of the day."

Touché, Mother. Amanda winked at Lex, then noticed the partially eaten plate of food in front of her lover. "Are you full?"

"Yeah. I'm just not real hungry, I guess." The truth of the matter was that Lex's stomach was still in knots over what happened earlier in the day.

"Do you two have any plans for tonight?" Frank asked, after a not-so-subtle poke in the ribs from his wife.

Amanda looked at Lex, who shrugged. "Not really. What do you have in mind?"

"Lex, you can't come to LA without going out at least for one evening. Isn't that right, Amanda?"

"Umm, that's really nice of you, but I didn't bring anything to wear for a night out on the town." Lex hadn't gone out much since she was younger, and the thought of doing so in a strange town made her extremely uncomfortable.

Frank could see the worried look on Lex's face. If he knew his wife, they'd hit a few less crowded, certainly more relaxed, clubs. "Actually, you'll be more suitably dressed for where we're going than Jeannie or I will."

"Okay, then, why not?" Lex turned to check with Amanda. "Do you feel up to it?" The tone in her voice made it clear that Amanda could just say no.

Amanda patted Lex on the arm. "Sure." She touched her bruised jaw with her fingertips. "I know this looks bad, but it really doesn't hurt."

Elizabeth Cauble sighed heavily, drawing everyone's attention back to her. She gave Amanda a pitiful look. "I guess it's too much to ask that you actually spend some time with your father and me before you leave us."

"Now, now," Amanda's father said. "I'm sure Amanda will be glad to spend some quality time with us in the morning." Michael gave Lex an unreadable look. "And you too, Lex. I'd really like the opportunity to get to know you a little better." The smile on his face sent chills down Lex's spine.

Why do I suddenly feel like a man at the gallows being told to jump? Lex wondered. "Sure, Mr. Cauble, if you really want to." She gave Amanda's hand a firm squeeze. "But I'm sure I can find something to occupy myself if you need to spend a little time alone with Amanda."

"That won't be necessary, Lex." He smiled, and again, Lex felt a warning bell ringing in the back of her mind. "If my daughter is determined to be with you, I'd really like for us to become better acquainted."

Jeannie stood up. "Great. We'll get ready and meet you two in the sitting room in an hour." She grabbed her husband by the hand and hurried from the room.

Amanda released Lex's hand and stood up as well. "I guess

we'd better go get ready, huh?" she asked her lover. "We'll see you both in the morning," she assured her parents as Lex joined her by the door. "Goodnight."

Halfway up the stairs, Lex pulled Amanda to a stop. "Do you have any idea where we're going tonight?"

"Sure. But I'm not telling." Amanda continued up the stairs, with a laughing woman at her heels.

LEX STOOD AWAY from the pool table, watching as Amanda lined up her shot. She couldn't help but smile as her lover's tongue slightly poked from her mouth, in the perfect picture of intense concentration.

"Don't let that innocent look fool you," Frank whispered. "She's a shark. The first time we played, she beat me so badly I had to carry her books to class for a solid week. Do you know how demeaning it is for a high school senior to be enslaved by a fresh-man?"

"Amanda said you were her best friend." Lex took a sip of her beer, enjoying the relaxed atmosphere of the bar, and the camara-derie of the people she was with. "How long have you known each other, if you don't mind me asking?" She shook her head as Amanda sunk her shot, dancing around and waving her hand in front of her sister's face. "Uh-oh."

Frank watched, as his wife good-naturedly threatened her sis-ter with her cue stick. "Don't worry. Amanda can take her." He laughed out loud at the look of shock on Lex's face. "I'm kidding. Well, not completely. Mandy *can* take her, but they don't actually fight anymore." He took a strong swallow of his third scotch and water. Lex was still nursing her first beer, which she surprised them all by ordering. She told them she didn't drink much any-more, which was okay by him and Jeannie, since the last time they were out they got carried away and had to call a cab. "Mandy liter-ally ran me over on my first day at her school." He shook his head in remembrance. "I had just transferred from a small school south of Sacramento and was completely and totally awed by this huge school. I had run myself ragged trying to find my classes and had bent down in the hallway to tie my shoe. Then this little whirlwind came flying around the corner and knocked me flat on my face."

The mental picture that Frank painted caused Lex to crack up. "I'll bet that was a sight. But it's nice to know she's always been like that, running from place to place." She felt a hand on her arm.

"What's so funny?" Amanda asked, reaching across Lex to grab her vodka Collins.

"Frank was just telling me how you two met."

Amanda rubbed her face. "Umm, it's your shot, Lex." She really didn't want to get into what a brat she was back in high school, and knew that her brother-in-law had a lot of tales he could tell.

"You look really happy, Mandy." The big man studied his sister-in-law closely. "I don't think I've ever seen you smile so much." He nodded toward the pool table, where his wife was trying to ruin Lex's shot by making faces and slinging silly comments at her.

"I'm very happy." Amanda saw what Jeannie was doing and tossed a pretzel at her. "Stop cheating," she yelled, getting a nasty look from her sibling. Turning her attention back to Frank, she smiled warmly. "She's the one, Frank."

"I kinda figured that by the look on your face, kiddo." Frank couldn't help but remember the long talks the two of them used to have. Amanda had sworn she would find her one true love and not settle for anything less. Frank was the only person she had shared that with. Not even her sister knew the high standards she had set for a mate. He had understood, since he had fallen completely in love with her sister the moment he met her. "Even I can see she's special, Mandy. Don't ever let her go." Frank spoke quietly, and his eyes suspiciously sparkled in the smoky light of the bar.

Amanda wrapped her arms around his neck, giving him a light kiss on the lips. "Thanks, Frank. I knew you'd understand."

"I guess this means I get to take Slim here home with me." Jeannie walked up from the pool table, wrapping an arm around Lex's waist. "No offense, Frank, but I think I got the better end of the deal." She wriggled happily as a long arm draped across her shoulder.

Lex drawled, "I've heard about some of the wild things that go on here in California." Her eyebrow rose as Amanda spun and Frank placed his chin on her head, wrapping his arms about her protectively with an innocent look on his face. "You think you can handle her?"

Frank appeared thoughtful. "I dunno. Since you met her, Lex, you nearly drowned, got your ribs banged up, were shot, and attacked by rustlers." He stepped back and pushed Amanda forward. "Give me back my wife. Please!"

Lex impulsively caught Amanda who nestled happily into her arms, much to Frank and Jeannie's amusement. "Fickle, ain't she?" Lex muttered to the other couple, only to receive a slap on the arm. "What'd I say?"

Jeannie watched, an approving look on her face. *The more I'm around her, the better I like this mysterious woman who has stolen my little sister's heart.* She watched them for a moment longer, then said, "Okay, gang. Now that I whipped Slim at pool—"

"What?" Amanda leaned back so that she could look Lex in the eye. "How could you lose? We only had to make one shot." She turned back around and glared at her sister. "What did you do?" The strong arms that wrapped tightly around her calmed Amanda, if only for a moment.

Lex shook her head. "I didn't think she could actually do it." She propped her chin on Amanda's shoulder. "I said she couldn't distract me into blowing my shot."

Amanda frowned. "I'll ask again. What did she do?"

Jeannie laughed. "I tried dancing around the table like a fool, which didn't work. I even blew in her ear." She saw Amanda's eyes widen. "Nothing. So, while she was bent over about to shoot, I pinched her on the butt." At this startling confession, everyone burst out laughing.

With and embarrassed grin, Lex admitted, "Damn near knocked the guy at the next table out with the cue ball, too."

Amanda pulled the arms around her tighter. "I'm sorry I missed that. Are you ready for our next stop?"

Lex released a heavy sigh. "Do I want to know where we're going?"

Jeannie reached over, grabbed Lex by the hand, and dragged her toward the door. "Dancing," she explained, as Amanda and Frank followed closely behind.

A short time later, Lex found herself in a new club quite different from the first. "What in the hell is *that* supposed to be?" Lex grumbled as a young person walked by. Bright purple spiked hair and multiple face piercings shocked the more conservative rancher.

Amanda pulled Lex through the crowd of people, right behind Frank and Jeannie. "I think it was a he, but don't quote me on that."

They found a table near the crowded dance floor where loud music with a strong beat made Lex's teeth hurt. The lights flicked and flashed all around them in time to the beat of the music. She ordered another beer and then focused her attention on the dozens of people dancing. Men dancing with women, men dancing with men, and women dancing with women, all having a good time. There were even a few wildly dressed people dancing alone, which caused a smile to cross Lex's face.

"See anything you like?" Amanda asked, her lips close to her lover's ear. She could tell Lex was a little overwhelmed by a lot of things she would never come across in a small town. Lex looked particularly entranced by a young woman wearing white makeup with black across her eyes and lips and studs and hoops adorning her eyebrows and nose. "Maybe I should get my nose pierced," Amanda whispered, then playfully licked Lex's ear.

"Huh?" Lex jumped, then smiled. She knew she wouldn't get

another chance like this for a while. "Come on," she grabbed Amanda's hand. "Let's go join the crowd." Lex stood and pulled Amanda along with her, just as a slow song began. She quickly claimed a piece of the dance floor with her partner. "Perfect."

Amanda linked her hands behind her lover's neck, snuggling her face into Lex's chest. *I really like this,* she thought blissfully, as Lex pulled her even closer.

Closing her eyes, Lex gently swayed to the music, enjoying the feeling of holding Amanda in her arms. Her peaceful thoughts were interrupted by a strong hand on her shoulder.

"Mind if I cut in?" yelled a short, pudgy woman. She was clad in leather pants and a leather vest, with slicked back hair and more attitude than good sense.

"No, thanks." Lex gripped Amanda tighter and turned away, not wanting her evening spoiled.

"Hey." The woman, grabbed the taller woman's arm and swung Lex to face her. She took in Lex's jeans and denim shirt, glaring at the obvious tourist. "Look, cowboy," she hollered over the music, "I'd like to dance with the cute one there." She looked Lex in the eye. "Why don't you go feed your horse, and I'll show the lady a good time."

Thinking fast, Amanda stepped between the two women. "Lex, honey," she said loudly, putting her arm about her partner's waist. "You remember what your parole officer said. The next person you hospitalize can get you sent back to prison." She almost laughed out loud at the look on the pushy woman's suddenly pale face.

Lex leered at the intruder, then glanced down at her lover. "Aw, come on, baby. Just this once?" She took a menacing step toward Amanda's would-be suitor. "Please?"

Deciding to find someplace else to be, the leather-clad woman whirled off, hastily making her way back through the crowd, all the while muttering under her breath.

"Thanks, sweetheart." Lex wrapped Amanda into a hug, kissing her lightly on the forehead. "I really didn't want to ruin tonight by getting into an argument with Motorcycle Mama."

Amanda chuckled. "I was tempted to just smack her one, but I was afraid she'd scream lawsuit." She wrapped her arms back around Lex's neck. "Don't we have a dance to finish?"

Lex kissed her lightly on the lips and rested her hands on Amanda's waist. "Yeah." She pulled Amanda to her and closed her eyes, slowly rocking once again to the music.

Later, at the table, Frank gestured to the crowd. "I thought for sure we were going to have a brawl on our hands. We saw that woman try to cut in."

Jeannie nodded. "Why didn't you just slug her, Lex?" she asked the smiling woman. "I know I probably would have, the rude little turd."

"Nah. I really couldn't blame her any." Lex put her arm on the back of Amanda's chair. "She has great taste in women." She enjoyed seeing her lover blush. "Besides, I knew Amanda would be coming home with me."

For the second time that night, Jeannie found herself smiling. *Mother and Father are so wrong about her. She's the best thing that's ever happened to Mandy.* "You guys about ready to leave? I think Frank has had about all the fun he can stand for one night." She gestured to her husband, whose eyes were beginning to droop.

Frank stifled a yawn. "I'm sorry about that. I guess I'm not used to all this excitement."

"I'm pretty pooped too," Amanda admitted, leaning back against Lex's arm. "How about you, honey?" She turned her head and gazed into her lover's eyes. "Ready to go home and go to bed?"

Lex couldn't help but grin. "Is that an offer from the *cute* one?" She stood up, offering her hand to Amanda and pulling her to her feet. "I thought maybe I was just getting old. I can barely keep my eyes open."

"You? Old? Yeah, right." Frank took Jeannie's hand, and they followed Lex and Amanda through the still raucous crowd to the front door. "If she's old, then I'm ancient," he grumbled to his wife.

Jeannie patted him on the rear lovingly. "Whatever you say, grandpa."

LEX DIDN'T NOTICE when Amanda borrowed Frank's cell phone on the drive back to the house and was confused when she was escorted around the back, while the other couple went in the front door. "Where are we going?"

"Trust me," Amanda whispered. She took them along a cobbled path past the fountain until they came upon a white wooden gazebo, which was fenced in by decorative garden trellises. Opening the gate slowly, Amanda looked over her shoulder and grinned. "I thought it would be fun to relax a bit before we went to bed, so all that dancing wouldn't make us sore." She loved the look on Lex's face when she realized where they were.

"So this is the infamous hot tub, huh?" Lex moved closer to Amanda and circled her arms about Amanda's waist, propping her chin on her shoulder. "I hate to break this to you sweetheart, but we don't have any swimsuits."

Amanda reclined into the embrace. "What makes you think we need suits? It's not like there's a lot of people here." The silence from her partner almost made Amanda laugh out loud. "Honey, really. I called Beverly while we were on the way home, and everything we need is in the cabana over there." She pointed to a small building a few yards away. "Towels, robes, and suits, I promise."

"Ah." For all her attempts at appearing worldly and uncaring, Lex knew she would always be a conservative country girl at heart. *I've got to remember that Amanda was raised in California. She's probably laughing to herself right now.* That thought didn't make her feel any better, and Lex wished, for the first time in her life, that she had grown up somewhere besides a ranch.

"Lex?"

"Hmm?"

Turning so she could face her, Amanda tried to see why Lex had suddenly gotten so quiet. "Are you all right?" The dim light around the gazebo made it hard to read the expression on Lex's face.

"Yeah, I'm fine."

"You don't look fine." Amanda touched the side of the tense face. "Talk to me."

Lex closed her eyes at the touch. "I think I'm just overtired. It's nothing, really."

Not convinced, Amanda decided to let the subject drop. *For now, anyway.* "Do you want to just go to bed? We can always try the spa another time."

"No. I think this is exactly what we need." Lex placed a quick kiss on Amanda's lips. "Now what were you saying about swimsuits?"

Since there were several small dressing rooms in the cabana, both were able to change at the same time, but they couldn't see what the other was wearing until they emerged. Lex stood next to the tub in a white terrycloth robe when Amanda finally joined her, wearing a similar outfit. The California nights were getting cooler, and neither one of them wanted to catch a chill.

"Well, aren't we the pair?" Amanda joked, as she unbelted her robe. She removed the garment and placed it within easy reach, revealing a bright pink bikini. Reaching over the tub's edge, Amanda traced her fingertips through the water. Assuming that Lex was following her lead, she climbed up the steps and into the spa. "Perfect."

You can say that again. The view of her lover's backside disappearing into the frothy water made Lex's mouth go dry. She had seen Amanda in—and out of—many different outfits, but she could now say without a doubt in her mind that the bikini was in the top two. Lex stood there silently, replaying over and over the enticing view, unable to move.

"Lex? Are you coming?" Amanda waved her hand, not certain what was up with her partner. "Hello?" She stood, and the water sluiced off her body, the cool air making her nipples visible beneath the suit.

Lex's eyes widened at the sight, and she felt her legs go weak. She fumbled with the tie on the robe until she was finally able to get it loose and allowed it to fall to the ground, forgotten. Her shaky legs struggled up the steps, and she nearly fell as she leaped over the side of the hot tub.

"Whoa there, Slim." Amanda caught her partner before Lex could plummet beneath the water. "Watch your step."

"I can't see anything but you," Lex murmured, her eyes never leaving her lover's face. "You are an absolute vision." She lifted her hands and ran them across Amanda's cheeks. "I've never seen anyone, or anything, more beautiful in my entire life."

Amanda sank lower in the water, bringing Lex with her. "Thank you." Her arms went around her partner's waist as their lips met, gently at first, then with more passion. It wasn't long before urgent hands reached behind her and untied the top of her suit, and Amanda couldn't help but tilt her head back when Lex broke off the kiss and followed the curve of Amanda's throat with her lips.

It was if she couldn't get enough of Amanda's skin. Lex wanted to touch her everywhere at once, yet savor each and every inch of her lover. The warm, bubbling water only served to heighten the experience, which became more heated by the moment. Lex felt the straps to her navy one-piece bathing suit slide from her shoulders as the quiet gurgling of the spa covered up their moans. They continued to explore each other in the water, and as the day's troubles disappeared, Lex found out you really *didn't* need a suit in a hot tub, after all.

Chapter
Twelve

The four late-night revelers ended up sleeping in, so they spent the latter part of the morning enjoying each other's company during breakfast.

Frank couldn't help but tweak the rancher. She was quiet until you got to know her, then she gave as good as she got. "So, Lex. Are you ready to go back out dancing? Maybe we can find your little friend again."

"Think I'll give it a miss. I don't want to end up bailing Amanda out of jail."

"Me?" Amanda said. "I have no idea what you're talking about." She tried to look innocent, but failed miserably when Lex cut her eyes over at her. "Now, stop that."

Choking on her coffee at her sister's attempt to feign innocence, Jeannie couldn't help but gasp and wipe tears from her eyes. "Mandy, you know darn good and well what Lex is talking about. You've still got a bad temper, though I was hoping that staying with Gramma and Grandpa would have had a positive effect on you." She changed her focus of attention to Lex. "Has she taken a swing at you yet, Slim?"

"No, not—" Lex shook her head, then stopped. "Well, actually, just yesterday, she slapped me."

Amanda looked shocked. "I did no such—" She paused, then rolled her eyes. "Oh, for God's sake. You deserved that by scaring me half to death, chasing after that guy." She glared at Lex. "And I'll do it again, if you ever pull another stupid stunt like that."

"Yes, ma'am," Lex teased, then sobered. She ran gentle fingertips over the purple bruise on her lover's face. "How's that feel today? Looks like all of the swelling is gone." She barely controlled the urge to lean over and kiss the contusion.

Capturing the hand with one of her own, Amanda happily leaned into the touch. "Fine. It doesn't even hurt today." *Of course, soaking in a hot tub doesn't hurt, either.*

Jeannie sighed. *They are just so cute together.* "Well, I hate to leave such wonderful company, but I promised Mother that I'd go by and check on the gallery." She tossed her napkin onto the table and touched her husband's arm. "Are you ready, darling?"

"Sure. I've got a couple of last-minute things to pick up before the dinner tonight, anyway."

Lex gave Amanda a look. "Yeah, I still have to get something, too, I guess." She missed the wink her partner gave Frank.

Beverly stepped quietly into the dining room, with a subdued tone in her voice. "Miss Amanda, I'm terribly sorry to interrupt you, but your father has requested that you join them in the library."

"Our cue to run." Jeannie hooked her arm with Frank's and moved to the doorway, waving a hand. "Good luck, guys."

Amanda smiled at the maid, to show her that she didn't blame the messenger. "Thanks, Beverly. We'll be right there." As the woman turned to go, Amanda added, "What kind of mood is he in, or dare I even ask?"

"That's just it, Miss Amanda. He's in a really good mood. It's very strange." Beverly tipped her head in acknowledgment and then left the room quietly.

Amanda frowned. She certainly didn't want to subject her lover to whatever games her family was playing, and she was afraid that Lex would have enough of her parent's bitterness and leave. "I don't think I like the sound of that. You sure you want to go with me?"

"I'm with you, sweetheart, for as long as you'll have me."

"Forever sounds pretty good to me, at least to start with." Amanda leaned in and covered Lex's lips with her own, sharing a kiss full of love and promise. Releasing a heavy sigh, she forced a smile. "Let's go 'visit,' then we'll go shopping, okay?"

"Right." Lex stood up, then brought her friend into a strong hug as soon as Amanda got to her feet. "One for the road. I love you, Amanda." She spoke quietly, savoring the moment. "With all my heart and soul."

Amanda felt her partner tremble slightly. "I love you too, Lex." She returned the embrace, kissing the collarbone that peeked through the v-neck of the shirt Lex was wearing. "And I always will."

"COME IN AND have a seat, you two." Michael motioned the two of them into the library. Elizabeth was comfortably perched on the loveseat, while he stood at the bar, holding a sheaf of papers in his hand.

Amanda brought Lex to the sofa, which was at a 90-degree

angle from the loveseat, and directly across from the bar. She sat down next to her, close enough to touch if she needed to. "Good morning, Mother."

"It's almost afternoon, Amanda. But I hear you had a late night last night." She gave Lex an almost civil look. "Lex."

Lex tipped her head slightly. "Mrs. Cauble."

Michael interrupted. "Coffee? Oh, I'm sorry Lex." He raised a decanter filled with amber liquid. "I hear whiskey is more to your liking in the mornings." He poured a glass. "I'm afraid that all I have right now is scotch, but we can send one of the servants out for something a bit less civilized, if you would prefer." Michael watched with hidden glee as his daughter's face showed confusion.

"What are you talking about, Daddy?" Amanda turned to face her lover. "Lex?"

Lex stared at her feet with a resigned look on her face. Then, taking a deep breath, she looked up and locked gazes with Amanda's father. "No thank you, Mr. Cauble. I haven't drunk hard liquor in years." She turned and met her lover's eyes. "Remember I told you about Linda?" she asked softly.

Amanda frowned, thinking. "Yes. But what does that—"

"After that, I got a little wild for a while, but Martha straightened me out." Lex felt the reassuring presence of Amanda's hand on her leg. "I'll tell you all about it later, I promise."

"I'm not worried, love."

Michael frowned, and from the look on his face, Amanda knew things weren't going as he had planned. "My mistake, Lex." He conceded the point to his daughter's lover, although he was obviously far from finished. "So, do you have family back in Texas, Lex?"

Confused by the sudden change in topics, Lex nodded. "Yes. I have an older brother, Hubert."

Stepping away from the bar, Michael sat next to his wife on the loveseat. She took a sip from a China cup as he asked, "How about your parents?" He leaned over and poured three more cups of coffee, keeping one for himself and offering the others to Lex and Amanda.

Lex accepted the offering politely, even though the thought of ingesting anything right now made her stomach cramp. "Thank you." She balanced the cup and saucer on one thigh. "My mother died when I was four, and my father...travels a lot." *No lie there, but I guess I could just say he's a drifter who would rather wonder where his next meal is coming from than have to look at his daughter.*

Elizabeth's face was calm and unreadable. "And does your brother work with you at your ranch?"

"No, ma'am. He's an accountant in town. He's not much for

the ranch life."

"A professional, then. I'm sure you're very proud of him." Elizabeth gave her daughter a look. *Much more suitable than a common cowhand.* "You only have one sibling? Must have been lonely growing up."

Lex swallowed the lump that had formed in her throat. "I had a younger brother, but he died...about nine years ago." She felt Amanda grasp her hand for support.

"I'm terribly sorry to hear that. It's always so tragic when a child dies." Michael shook his head sadly. "Especially when it can be avoided. Wait, I seem to recall a boy named Walters that was killed at the lake around that time." He looked at Lex, trying to convey understanding on his handsome face. "That was your brother, wasn't it?"

"Louis." Lex nodded, trying to keep her emotions under control. *Almost ten years ago, and it still hurts as much as the day it happened. Why can't I get past this?*

Michael adjusted his glasses slightly and looked down at the papers in his hand. "That's what I thought. If I recall correctly, there was a boat full of kids, and they were hit by another boat, right?" Seeing the quiet woman nod slightly, he continued. "Absolutely horrible. The whole affair could probably have been avoided with the proper adult supervision." Seeing Lex pale, he went in for the kill. "Don't you agree, Lex?"

"That's it!" Amanda stood up. "Let's go, Lex." She pulled the silent rancher to her feet. "We've got things to do, if you'll excuse us."

Lex allowed Amanda to lead her through the doorway, her mind a million miles away. *He's right. I should have been there. If I had been driving the boat, maybe the entire accident could have been avoided.* Numbly, she followed Amanda, feeling a small amount of comfort in their linked hands. The cool breeze on her face brought Lex back to her senses. Looking around, she found herself standing in the garden under Amanda's favorite tree.

"Come here and sit down, love." Amanda took a seat under the Eucalyptus and patted her leg. She waited patiently until the blank look faded from Lex's face, and then she held out her arms. "Please?"

Forcing a weak smile to her face, Lex dropped down in front of Amanda and stretched out. She ended up lying on her back between Amanda's legs, her head resting against her lover's chest.

Amanda gently ran her fingers through the thick, dark hair, her motions finally causing Lex to relax. "I'm calling the airline. We're going home on the next flight out."

"No."

"Yes! Dammit, Lex, there's nothing here worth putting you through this. I'm tired of defending my actions to them, and having them try to get to me through you." She absently straightened the bangs on Lex's forehead, a gesture that not only calmed her lover, but Amanda as well.

Lex turned slightly so she could look into Amanda's face. "Don't let them win, sweetheart. They'll never let you live it down." She had been around bullies of one sort or another most of her life and knew how they worked. The last thing she wanted was for Amanda to succumb to her parents' whims, when it wasn't in her best interest. She raised a hand and caressed the side of Amanda's jaw that wasn't bruised. "I can handle this. They just kind of caught me off guard."

Leaning down until their noses were almost touching, Amanda dropped a kiss on her partner's mouth. "Are you sure about this? We can be home before it gets dark tonight."

Lex raised her head slightly to make the kiss more prolonged. "Mmm." *Home. I think I like the sound of that, but we've got unfinished business here. I don't run from assholes like that, even if they are Amanda's parents.* "Yeah, I'm sure. We've got a dinner to sit through tonight. But it won't hurt my feelings if you decide you want to leave Saturday morning."

"That's a great idea. I'll call and change our reservations." Amanda wrapped her arms around the reclining woman and squeezed hard. "Have I told you lately just how much I love you?" she whispered into the ear next to her face.

"You may have mentioned something about it a time or two," Lex teased, raising up slightly to return the embrace. "I'm sorry about all that stuff with your father. I guess I should have told you about that mess before you heard it from someone else. It was just a matter of time before somebody told you."

"No, Lex. I don't expect a day-by-day account of your life before you met me. What I don't understand is how he knew so much about it." Amanda had pulled back enough so she could look Lex in the eye and was angered by the barely hidden pain she could see there.

"It's a small town, and my little 'binge' was certainly no secret." Lex closed her eyes at the gentle touch on her head. "I spent over a month drunk out of my mind, being thrown out of quite a few bars, and was even picked up by the law a time or two. I imagine everyone in town knows all about it."

Amanda continued to run her fingers through Lex's hair, once again using the motions to calm them both. "You were young and had been terribly hurt emotionally. Didn't anyone try to help you, talk to you?"

"Yeah, right." Lex looked up into her lover's eyes, wanting to somehow make Amanda realize just what kind of person she had been. "You've got to understand, Amanda. It's true that I was young, but I was so full of anger and hatred at how unfair I thought my life was, that most folks steered clear of me." She blinked, then looked down, afraid to see the look on the other woman's face. "Even Martha threatened to leave me because I had been so nasty to her." She took a ragged breath. "I think the fear of losing her was what finally snapped me back to reality."

"Oh, sweetheart. I don't think Martha would ever leave you, no more than I could." She gave her partner another kiss.

After returning the kiss, Lex's heart felt pounds lighter for the talk. "God, I love you." She ran a shaky hand down Amanda's face, then let out a wry chuckle. "I don't think she was actually going to leave, either. But she did toss a bucket of muddy water on me while I was passed out on the front porch one morning."

"I'll bet that went over well." Amanda could almost picture the younger face as Martha dished out her own brand of 'tough-love.' "Wish I had been there to see that."

"If you'd been there, I wouldn't have been in that situation," Lex murmured, as she made a move to get to her feet. "Let's go. I think we've got some shopping to do."

"You're right. I need to pick up a few things for tonight." Amanda jumped up first, then pulled Lex up with her.

Lex kept her hold on Amanda's hand as they walked back to the house. "A few things," she mumbled, feeling the hand in hers tighten. "I thought you were going to help me get something more suitable to wear." Personally, she really didn't care what she wore, but even though she knew she was going to be a fish out of water at the affair, Lex was determined not to embarrass her lover with her choice of clothing.

"Actually," Amanda led the way through the house and up the stairs, "you're all set. I have to find just the right thing to go with what you're wearing." She pulled Lex into the guestroom. "Just let me get my purse, and we'll go." She started to step away, then found herself back in her lover's arms.

"Aren't you forgetting something?" Lex asked, bringing Amanda into a firm embrace.

Amanda unconsciously clasped her hands behind Lex's neck, smiling up into her twinkling eyes. "Hmm. You know, you're right. I need to grab the car keys, too."

"Ah. I see." Lex ran her hands lightly up her partner's ribs.

Amanda giggled and squirmed. She tried to back away, but found herself suddenly lifted into the air, cradled in Lex's arms like a small child. "Lex, stop that!"

"Seems to me someone needs her memory refreshed." Lex slowly carried her cargo toward the bed.

Kicking her feet, Amanda unsuccessfully tried to break the hold the other woman had on her. "You're going to hurt yourself, you nut." Then she squealed when she was tossed in the air. "Lex!" Amanda landed on her back in the middle of the large mattress, bouncing slightly. Before she could say a word, she was covered with a long, lean body, and her wrists were held together above her head with one hand.

"You know, I could do this one of two ways." Lex bent closer and took a small nip at Amanda's earlobe.

The hot breath on her skin made Amanda shiver, although she was far from being cold. "W..w..what's that?" she gasped out, trying to get her breathing under control and failing miserably.

Lex allowed her free hand to slowly trace down Amanda's trembling body. "I could just torture you until you begged." She kissed just below her lover's ear.

Amanda wiggled, causing Lex to straddle her waist. "Uh-huh. And just what sort of torture, oh, God!" She felt a warm hand slip inside her shirt and begin to lightly stroke her belly.

"Hmm." Lex sat back a bit, so she could look into Amanda's flushed face. "Just how much 'torture' can you stand, my impudent friend?" She leaned back down and traced Amanda's lips with her tongue before deepening the kiss.

Amanda accepted the kiss greedily, trying to pull her hands free so she could tangle them in Lex's hair. "Mmm, Lex." She still squirmed, but now for an entirely different reason.

Lex pulled away from Amanda's mouth, then kissed and licked her way down the slender throat. "You know..." She slowly used her free hand to unbutton the bright green shirt. "I bet I can make you beg for mercy." She kissed the skin just above Amanda's bra.

"Oh, ummm." Amanda closed her eyes, breathing heavily. "I'll never beg, you...oh, God." She felt a warm tongue lick lightly at her chest. All thoughts of trying to play the game flew out the window.

"Won't beg, huh?" Lex placed a series of small bites on Amanda's exposed stomach. "You sure about that?"

"No, you can't make me...ah, Lex." Amanda was panting heavily now, as Lex continued to work her way across her belly. Suddenly she squealed, and her eyes popped open as Lex's fingers began to tickle her ribs. "Lex, stop it!" Amanda wiggled back and forth, working in vain to escape the touch.

Lex continued her assault, knowing that she'd won the game. "Say it, Amanda." Her lover was giggling almost uncontrollably now.

"Oh, God, Lex. Stop," Amanda sputtered out between gales of

laughter. "Please! I'm begging you!"

With a triumphant grin on her face, Lex relented. "Told you I could make you beg." Then she laughed as she was pulled down for a heated kiss, which caused the world to slip away.

Chapter
Thirteen

Shopping, Lex decided, had to have been invented by some poor slob trying to occupy his bothersome wife and keep her out of his hair, because no sane person would actually volunteer for such torture. Slouched in a highly uncomfortable chair, she sighed again as her companion tried on yet another item of clothing. She was stationed directly outside the dressing room door, mumbling replies to Amanda's questions, as she had been for the last couple of hours.

"Now, before you say anything," Amanda warned, still behind the door, "I know that this is too formal for tonight, but I just couldn't resist trying it on."

Suddenly, standing in front of Lex was a vision in aqua. The long satin gown hung by spaghetti straps, draped seductively over Amanda's lithe figure.

"Uh." Lex swallowed several times. She tried to get words from her brain to her mouth, but she couldn't form any words. *Wow.*

Amanda turned around and glanced at herself in the mirror, not noticing the look of complete awe on her lover's face. "So, what do you think?"

Lex blinked, inhaled deeply, and struggled to find words. "Beautiful." That didn't seem to even touch how Amanda looked, so she tried again. "Absolutely stunning." She stood up and walked over until she was directly behind her, then looked over Amanda's shoulder into the mirror and whispered into her ear, "You've got to get this, sweetheart."

"It's too dressy for the dinner tonight. I checked with Jeannie, and she said that most of the guests would be coming in straight from the office. Mother was going to make it a formal affair, but something came up this past week, and everyone had to put in extra time."

"I don't care." Lex put her hands on her friend's shoulders and turned Amanda around to face her. "I'll find someplace elegant to take you, but you look too beautiful in it *not* to have it. Please? Let me buy it for you."

Considering the request, Amanda looked at the price tag. *Six hundred dollars? Oh no, I don't think so, my love.* She covered one of Lex's hands with her own. "Honey, I really appreciate the thought, but this dress is too expensive for you to waste your money on."

Picking up the tag and peering at it, Lex shrugged. "It can't hold a candle to what you're worth to me. How about if I make it a birthday present?"

"My birthday isn't for several months. Not that I don't appreciate the thought." Amanda blushed, not being used to such bold compliments. "And I really appreciate the sentiment behind it as well." She turned back toward the dressing room. "Could you come in and help me with the zipper, please?" This was asked in a voice loud enough for the circling saleswoman to hear.

"Sure." Lex followed her into the small room, latching the door shut behind them. "Turn around and I'll—" She quickly found herself the recipient of a long, loving kiss.

Once they broke apart, Amanda looked into her lover's eyes. "I love you, Lexington Marie Walters. No one else has ever made me feel as loved and special as you do." She turned so that her back was facing her friend. "Now unzip me and we'll get out of here."

Happy to oblige, Lex did as she was asked. She ran a fingertip down the exposed back and enjoyed seeing the squirm it caused. "We're finally through?"

"Well," Amanda pulled the dress off, slipping back into her comfortable khakis. "We can always look around some more, if you want." She looked down shyly as Lex knelt, offering her help with her shoes, then plucked at her green polo shirt. "I feel a little bit like Cinderella, going from that gown back into this." Stepping into the loafers, she watched as Lex tied them for her. "You're going to spoil me, you know."

"All part of my plan to keep you happy, sweetheart." Lex massaged a strong calf. "Besides, I enjoy it, too." She stood up and allowed Amanda to exit the dressing room first, grabbing the dress on her way out. "You almost forgot something."

Amanda shook her head. "I'm not going to win this one, am I?" she asked, watching as her lover handed the dress to the now beaming saleswoman.

"Nope." Lex turned to the woman at the cash register. "She's gonna need shoes to match, right?"

The painfully thin woman nodded enthusiastically. "Of course! I can tell you're a woman of refined tastes, Madam." Considering that Lex was dressed in her usual jeans and a taupe button down shirt, the comment was almost comical. She turned and looked at

Amanda, her eyes gleaming at the thought of an additional sale. "What size, dear?"

Amanda stepped back a pace. "Oh, no, that's really not necessary. I'm sure I have shoes to match somewhere."

Leaning up against the counter with her arms crossed, Lex grinned. "Size?" She had noticed the size of the loafers when she put them on her friend, but she enjoyed watching Amanda squirm.

"Six." Amanda gave up, knowing she'd just have to pick her battles, and this was one she was bound to lose.

Leaning over to the saleswoman, Lex whispered, "I don't care what it costs, make sure they're the most comfortable shoes you can find, okay?"

Dollar signs practically lighting up her eyes, the saleswoman scurried away. "Right away, Madam."

"I'll get you back for this," Amanda muttered, watching as the saleswoman hurried back with a shoebox under one arm.

"Oh, yeah?" Lex handed the clerk a credit card. "You can try, but I wouldn't waste money on a fancy dress for me." She signed for the purchases. It was more money than she had spent on clothes for herself in the past several years, but Lex didn't mind. *And I don't care if we have to go out to some fancy-assed restaurant or club to show her off because she looked too damned good not to get that dress.*

"Thank you for your business, Ms. Walters. I look forward to serving you again."

The saleswoman handed the shopping bags to Lex, who added them to Amanda's collection. *Damn things are multiplying faster than coat hangers in a closet.* Lex grunted as she shifted her weight in order to take on the ever-increasing load.

Amanda couldn't help but chuckle at the look on Lex's face as she tried to hold the bags without dropping them. "No dress, huh?" She bent down and picked up her other shopping bags, then started out of the store. "That's too bad. I could really see you in a slinky red number."

"Oh, no. That would clash with my boots."

THEY WERE ALMOST back to the car when Lex stopped in front of building with a decades-old façade. The sunlight played across a necklace in the window, and she couldn't seem to take her eyes off of it. The knick-knack shop wasn't like most on the block. It was less pretentious and appeared to be privately owned, and the tiny storefront could barely been seen where it was squeezed in between two fancier businesses. It looked out of place among the trendier shops on the street.

It didn't take Amanda long before she realized she was alone, and she turned to see where Lex had gone. She retraced her steps, and soon was next to Lex. "What'd you find?"

"I'm not sure." Lex tapped the glass with one finger. "Check out that necklace."

"Which one?"

"That one down at the front, with the red stone in it."

Amanda squinted against the glare. "Oh, yeah. I see it." She turned to Lex. "It doesn't really look like you, though."

"Not for me, for Martha. Remember when I told you I wanted to do something for her?" Lex shifted the dress bag to her other shoulder. "Do you think she'd like it?"

"Honey, Martha would like anything you gave her. That much I know for a fact."

"You think? Because I really wanted to pick up something for her while I was here, and I didn't want it to be something cheesy, like a tee shirt, or something." Lex continued to stare at the necklace, almost mesmerized by the way the light bounced from it.

Amanda couldn't help but smile at her lover's thoughtful nature. "Let's go inside and see it up close."

The small bell above the door jingled softly as they entered, barely announcing that customers had just arrived. Once inside, both women had to wait until their eyes adjusted to the light. When they were able to see, it was apparent that the store was *much* different from the ones they had just visited, and Lex felt immediately comfortable in the clutter. Tables of all shapes and sizes were scattered about, holding everything from vases and lamps to worn out children's toys and odd bits of dinnerware. The scent of mothballs filtered through the air along with the musty odor of old trunks and even older furniture.

Lex and Amanda stood rooted in place while their senses adjusted to all the sights and smells around them.

A voice from the back of the store beckoned them further inside. "I won't bite, you know." The voice belonged to a shrunken old woman, dressed much like the shop herself, in flowing silk garments that had seen better days. Her wiry gray hair stood out on her head, looking like it hadn't seen a comb for many years.

Suddenly shy, Amanda allowed her friend to take the lead. She was more than happy to stay as far away from the strange little woman, who was a good half foot shorter than she.

"Excuse me, ma'am, but I saw a necklace in your front window, and—"

"You're not from around here, are you, child?" The woman edged around the counter she had been standing behind and walked right up to Lex, craning her neck to look up into the younger woman's face.

Lex shook her head. "No ma'am."

The shop proprietor cackled, proud of her deductive reasoning. "Didn't think so. You're much too polite. From the accent, I'd say you were from the south. Texas, maybe?"

"Yes, ma'am."

"That's lovely." Looking behind Lex, the woman said, "Don't look now, honey, but you've got a cute little gal on your back. I'm Sally, by the way. This is my little piece of heaven."

Lex laughed, and put her arm around Amanda's shoulder. "It's a pleasure to make your acquaintance, Sally. My name's Lex, and this 'cute gal' is my partner, Amanda."

"It's nice to meet you," Amanda offered, feeling a bit braver and coming out from behind her partner.

Sally clapped her hands together with glee. "I haven't had anyone come in for months. Would you like some tea? Or maybe coffee? I can even whip up a batch of cookies, if you're not in any hurry."

"We'd love some coffee, although I'm afraid we don't have time for the cookies," Amanda answered for them both. Once she'd gotten a closer look at Sally, she could see that the woman was harmless. Not quite all there, but harmless.

After Sally returned with the coffee, she showed Lex and Amanda to a cramped sitting area in the rear corner of the shop, then swept away once again. "I'll be back in a jif, kids. Just start without me."

Lex watched her leave. "She's sweet."

"Yeah." Amanda was ashamed of the way she had acted when they first walked into the shop. "A little scary, at least at the beginning, you'll have to admit."

"Scary?"

"You know, the hair, the clothes, that laugh." Amanda shivered in remembrance. "And this place, with all the dusty, old stuff. It's a bit creepy."

About to reply, Lex stopped when Sally returned, holding the necklace. "Is this what you were talking about, dear?" She handed it to Lex, while Amanda nervously watched.

I don't like this place. She turned her head and could see a stuffed buffalo's head on a nearby wall. *And I'll bet he doesn't like it much, either.* Seeing Lex's eyes light up when Sally handed her the necklace, Amanda shoved her misgivings back and tried to appear interested in their conversation.

"I just put that piece out this morning," Sally was explaining, as she leaned over Lex's shoulder, their faces only a few inches apart as they studied the jewelry. "As you can see, the quality of the stone is perfect, and the setting is pure sterling silver." She looked up and winked at Amanda. "At least that's what my grandmother told me years ago, and I don't think she'd lie to me."

Lex started to hand it back to Sally, who had moved around and sat between her and Amanda at the round table. "Your grandmother? This is from your family?"

"Sure is, sweetie. Been in my family since before the turn of the century. The last one, that is," Sally added hastily, pushing the necklace back to Lex.

"But that means it's very valuable. Don't you want to keep it?" Lex thought to herself that if the woman needed money that badly, she'd find something else in the store to buy.

Sally sipped her coffee. "Why should I?"

"Family is very important," Lex murmured. She looked at the glittering stone in her hand and wondered about the women who had worn it before, what their stories were, their dreams, how they lived their lives, and if they were happy. She shook her head, surprised by the turn of her thoughts.

"I'm the last of my line, Lex. No sense letting the state have something that might make someone else happy." From out of the folds of her dress, Sally produced a hand-sized wooden box, stained a deep cherry. "Here's something to put it in. I'm assuming it's a present for someone?"

Accepting the box, Lex nodded. "I was thinking about getting it for my, umm, mother." It would have taken all day to explain her own family dynamics to the storekeeper, and Lex knew they didn't have that much time. And, as far as Lex was concerned, Martha *was* her mother. "Are you absolutely sure you want to part with it? Because if you're not, I'll be more than happy to find her something else."

Sally watched as the young woman carefully packed the necklace into the box. "If the two of you are any indication, this family heirloom is going to a good and loving home. Take it, with my blessing. I think Grandma Caraway would be proud."

"Okay." Lex started to pull her wallet from her back pocket. "Thank you. I'm sorry, I forgot to ask you how much you wanted for it."

Reaching out, Sally waited until Lex's hands were in hers, and they were looking each other in the eye. "I want nothing for it except that you give your mother a hug from me, and tell her to wear it in good health. Maybe she'll pass it along to her *own* grandchildren, someday." As she spoke the last words, Sally turned to smile at Amanda.

No longer frightened, Amanda cast a shy grin at the old woman. She could see the gentle soul that Sally was and was glad that Lex had found the little shop. "Maybe so," Amanda agreed quietly.

Lex persisted, "Are you *sure* you won't take anything for it? I hate to—"

"Don't argue with me, child." Sally stood up, and with Lex sitting, could finally stare her down. "Now I think you said when you came in, that you were in a bit of a hurry." She brushed at her silk dress. "I've got things to do, too, so why don't you just give an old woman her peace?"

"Yes, ma'am." Lex rose, and before the storeowner could move away, bent and kissed her on the cheek. "Thank you, Miss Sally." She reached into her wallet and brought out a business card. "If you're ever in Texas, look us up."

Sally took the card and touched her cheek. "Go on now, before I change my mind," she gruffly ordered. She looked at the card as they made their way to the door. "You're nice kids. I'll bet your mothers are proud of you."

Amanda led them out the door and to the rental car, struggling with the packages she carried while she tried to reach into her purse. "That was certainly an experience."

Lex helped her with the bags. "Wasn't it, though? Here, I'll hold these, while you unlock the trunk."

"Thanks, honey." Amanda playfully piled all the bags into her friend's arms.

Lex juggled the packages, trying to keep from dropping any of them. "Good grief." She barely kept one of them from falling to the ground. "I don't remember seeing you buy this much stuff." She balanced a bag on her raised thigh, praying that she'd be able to keep her equilibrium long enough to save whatever was inside. A high-pitched female voice squealed from behind her, and a woman brushed by Lex.

"Mandy Cauble? Is that really you?"

Amanda spun around just in time to be wrapped up in an embrace from a tall woman with dark blonde hair. "Darla?"

The woman stepped back a pace, smiling broadly. "Oh, my goodness, I can't believe it. You look absolutely fantastic!" She kept a firm grasp on Amanda's hands as she bounced up and down excitedly. Stopping to look at the car, she commented, "I'm glad to see you finally retired that old heap you were driving."

Unable to keep her juggling act up any longer, Lex dropped a couple of packages to the pavement. "Ah, hell." She squatted to gather them back up and didn't notice the close scrutiny of Amanda's friend.

Darla eyed Lex with a speculative eye. "I see at long last you've got a driver. Did you knuckle under to the pressure from your mother? I should have known you'd pick a nice-looking woman. But isn't she dressed a little casual?" She eyed the taller woman in appreciation.

Amanda released Darla's hands to help Lex with the strewn-about packages. "I'm sorry, honey. Let me help you get them to the car." She turned back to a slack-jawed Darla. "Would you mind opening the trunk? The keys are still in it." Amanda picked up a couple of bags and then nodded in her lover's direction. "Darla, I'd like you to meet Lex Walters, the love of my life." She dumped her packages into the trunk, unloading Lex's arms as well. "Lex, this is Darla Cummings, a really good friend of mine since high school."

Lex held out a hand. "It's nice to meet you, Darla." Feeling as if she were on display, Lex almost blushed at the other woman's close perusal of her.

"My pleasure, Lex." Darla gave her a slow once over, then winked at Amanda. "Honey, if I could find someone like this, I'd dump my husband. I take it you're only visiting? Something tells me Lex isn't from around here."

"Nope. We're leaving tomorrow. What gave her away?" Amanda stood next to the blushing rancher and patted her on the arm in an attempt to comfort her.

"Well, she has the most darling accent. And yours seems to have picked up quite a bit, too."

"It's probably because I've spent the last seven months in Texas," Amanda acknowledged, as she turned back to face her old friend.

Darla suddenly noticed the bruise on Amanda's jaw. "Goodness, what happened to you? And what does the other guy look like?"

Amanda ruefully stroked the side of her face, careful of the bruise. "I got mugged at the beach yesterday. But Lex caught him, and it doesn't even hurt, now."

Darla stepped between the two women, linking an arm with each of them. "Now this sounds like a story I want to hear. Let's go have a cup of coffee and you can tell me all about it." She led them down the sidewalk, babbling the entire time.

"YOUR FRIEND WAS really nice," Lex observed quite some time later, totally relaxed as she lounged on the bed in the guestroom. "Chatty as hell, but nice."

Amanda stepped out of the bathroom, clad only in a black slip and matching lace bra. "Yeah, I know. She's one of the few friends I had in high school who didn't dump me when they found out I was gay." She sighed and sat down next to Lex.

Lex put an arm around her and pulled her close. "I'm so sorry, Amanda. I suppose in that respect, I was a lot luckier than you."

"Really? Why?" Amanda scooted back for a moment, looking into Lex's eyes.

"I didn't have to worry about what anyone thought. I pretty much stuck to myself and didn't have anyone I really considered a friend. Except for Martha and the guys at the ranch – and none of them ever judged or ridiculed me." Lex brought Amanda into her lap. "I'm glad that you had Darla, and even Frank."

Amanda wrapped her arms around Lex and sighed. "I had a couple of friends who stuck by me, although there were quite a few more who acted as if I had the plague. And of course I also had Gramma and Grandpa Jake. They were the absolute best. Telling my grandparent's was the scariest because I respected the two of them more than anyone else, including my mother and father. I must admit, they were a bit shocked and confused, but I was so lucky. They said there wasn't anything I could tell them that would keep them from loving me."

"I take it your folks were in the not-so-happy-to-hear-it crowd, huh?" Lex asked, feeling warm breath on her chest.

"I guess you could say that. They *still* think it's a phase I'm going through. Daddy blames the liberal school system I attended. Meanwhile, Mother thinks I'm gay because Jeannie married Frank, and I'm trying to get back at all of them because of that."

Lex laughed out loud at that revelation. "You poor thing, pining away for your sister's husband." She flinched as she received a sharp poke from a sharp finger. "Ouch! Jeannie was right."

Amanda sat back a little. "Huh? My sister was right about what?"

"You *are* a bully!" Lex captured Amanda's swinging hands in self-defense. She fell back onto the bed, allowing her friend to straddle her hips.

"And *you* are lucky that it's almost time for us to go downstairs for the dinner." Amanda leaned down to bedevil Lex with a near kiss. "Otherwise, I'd show you just how much of a bully I can be." She jerked back just as Lex raised up to catch her lips. "Teach you to tease me." She bent back down and dropped a quick kiss, then rolled to the side quickly.

Lex lay on the bed and closed her eyes. "Okay, you win." She released a heavy sigh and let go of Amanda's hands.

"I win? You've got to be kidding. You never give up without a...aaaaaah!" Amanda found herself suddenly on her back with a grinning woman over her body. "You cheated," she muttered.

"Me? Cheat? I can't help it if you let your guard down like that. You shouldn't be so trusting." She gave Amanda a kiss. "Let's

get dressed for this shindig, before your mother bursts in here looking for you."

Amanda allowed Lex to help her off the bed, then headed for
the closet. "I'll just get your clothes together, then." She stepped
back out, carrying several items on hangers. "Here you go."

Lex looked at the clothing. "Are you sure about this? I really
don't want to upset your parents any more than they already are."

"I'm perfectly sure. It will go very well with what I'm wearing,
and I want you to be comfortable." Amanda handed her the hangers. "Trust me. You'll look great." She went over to the shopping
bags sitting in the corner. "Let me slip this stuff on, and you'll see
what I mean." She carried two of the bags into the bathroom and
closed the door.

Resigned, Lex took the clothing off the hangers and slipped out
of her shirt. *I hope she knows what she's doing.*

MILLING AROUND THROUGH the dozen or so people, Jeannie searched for her husband, murmuring her apologies to yet
another nosy business associate of her father's. "Yes, Amanda is
here, Mr. Cross. She should be arriving any moment now." She
quickly stepped away from the large, sweating man, who had
always seemed quite enamored with her younger sister. *Like she'd
ever give your creepy butt a second look.* Jeannie flinched away from
his hand as it came perilously close to her rear end.

A warm voice whispered in her ear, as another hand lightly
patted her bottom. "There you are, sweetheart."

Spinning quickly, Jeannie almost slapped her husband. "Frank,
where on earth have you been?" Forgetting her anger immediately,
she eyed her husband's sturdy form with appreciation. The black
denim hugged his hips and legs well, and the gray tab collar shirt
fit his broad shoulders like a glove. *Everyday I love him more and
more. Amanda isn't the only one who was struck by love at first sight.*
Jeannie thought back to when her sneaky little sister had brought
Frank home one evening to "help him study for a history test."
Even though she was a freshman, and he was a senior, they were
both in the same class. Jeannie had been studying in the library
when the two of them came into the house. Neither Frank nor she
realized until much later that Amanda, who thought they'd be a
perfect match, had set them up. They had been together ever since.
And for that, I will be eternally grateful. Jeannie caught the adoring
look her handsome husband bestowed upon her. "You look great,
honey."

"Thanks, baby." He leaned over and kissed his wife's lips.

"You look absolutely gorgeous yourself."

Jeannie was wearing a knee-length dark green skirt complemented by a pale yellow silk top, which had already brought her mother's wrath down upon her. Elizabeth had demanded that she go back upstairs and change, citing that the evening was a dinner, not a "sock-hop." Knowing her mother would get over her fit soon enough, Jeannie apologized, slipped by her, and had been busily avoiding her ever since. "I'm glad someone thinks so. Mother wasn't quite so impressed."

"I saw the look she gave you." Frank pulled his wife to him and put his arm around Jeannie's waist. "Don't let her get to you. You look fantastic." Seeing a movement by the door, Frank turned his head. "Whoa."

"What?" Craning her head over the others in the room, Jeannie followed his line of sight. She finally was able to see what caused her husband's comment. "Oh, wow."

Amanda had stepped into the room, her partner following close behind. She was wearing a black denim skirt that fell to just below her knees, and a slightly oversized dark red silk shirt, the color lighting up her face. She reached behind her body and grabbed Lex's arm to bring her into the room. Jeannie's jaw almost hit the floor when she studied Lex. She was wearing pressed black denim jeans, shiny black boots, and a deep green satin shirt that complemented her skin tone, too.

Frank gave out a low whistle. "They make a nice looking couple, don't they?" he whispered into his wife's ear. He caught Amanda's eye and waved them over.

The two women made their way across the room, stopping ever so often so that Amanda could speak to one of her father's associates, and introduce Lex to them. After what seemed like forever, the two women were finally next to Jeannie and Frank. Amanda nodded at the couple's clothing choices. "Hey, guys. You both look great."

"Damn, Mandy, you didn't tell us that you two would be looking so stunning." Frank enjoyed the blush on Lex's face that his comment caused. He could also see the adoring look she bestowed on Amanda and knew that his sister-in-law had finally found the right person. "Have you two seen—"

A low, hissing voice came in from behind them. "It's about time you made it downstairs. People have been asking about you for the past twenty minutes," Elizabeth Cauble snapped, stepping between her youngest daughter and Frank. Looking at Amanda's clothes, she gave a long-suffering sigh. "Are you and your sister trying to ruin this family's reputation? How much is it to ask that you dress properly for a social function?" She was about to continue when a distinguished older gentleman stepped into their little group.

"Elizabeth, don't tell me these two lovely young women are your daughters?" He took Amanda's hands into his and brought one to his lips. "Amanda Cauble, I swear you look more and more like your lovely grandmother Anna Leigh every time I see you." He gave her a wink as he peered over her knuckles.

Amanda stepped into his arms for a hug. "Uncle John, it's so good to see you again." She pulled back and grabbed Lex's arm. "I want you to meet my close friend, Lexington Walters. Lex, this is John Grayson, an old friend of my grandparents."

The tall, gray-haired man held out his hand, which Lex took and gave a hearty handshake. "It's a pleasure to meet you, sir." Out of the corner of her eye, she saw the look of disgust on Elizabeth's face. *Gee, sorry about that, Mom. It seems like everyone else here likes the way that Amanda looks.*

"So you're the young lady who saved Amanda's life. I spoke to Jacob just last week on the phone, and he told me all about Mandy's latest adventures."

Lex felt the heat from her blush rise up her neck. *Word spreads around these people quicker than a brushfire.* "I just happened to be in the right place at the right time."

"And modest, too. Well, whatever you want to call it, you have our deepest appreciation, Ms. Walters."

"Please, call me Lex, Mr. Grayson."

"Only if you'll call me John, young lady." He grinned at her, knowingly. "Perhaps I'll see you at Anna Leigh's big pre-Christmas get-together this year, Lex."

Lex glanced over at Amanda, who was nodding. "Umm, you just might, sir."

"Excellent!" He patted her on the shoulder, before turning his attention back to Amanda. "Mandy, I'm sure I'll see you later." Grayson accepted another hug from the young woman and then took a gentle grasp of Jeannie's arm. "Come on, young woman. Tell me what you've been up to lately." He walked off with Jeannie and Frank in tow.

Elizabeth glared at the retreating man's back, then stepped up into Lex's face. "Don't think that you can fool everyone here," she whispered. "My husband will find out what you're after, sooner or later." She spun around and made her way into the group of people, greeting them with insincere words.

"What did she say to you?" Amanda asked, seeing the look of resigned acceptance cross her lover's face.

"Nothing important." Lex gestured to the other end of the room, desperately trying to change the subject. "It looks like they're moving everyone out."

"Good. Then we'll have a minute to ourselves." Amanda waited until the room had cleared, then led Lex over to the loveseat. "Sit down with me for a moment, okay?"

"Are you sure? I'd hate to make your mother angrier at you right now." Lex was concerned about the matriarch's attitude. She could handle Elizabeth's wrath as long as it was directed at her, but she didn't want to subject her partner to any more of the woman's hateful outbursts.

"It's going to take her at least ten minutes to get everyone seated like she wants, so she'll never miss us." Amanda reached out and pulled her lover to sit beside her. "Lex, please don't shut me out. Anything that has to do with you is important to me." She brought their linked hands to her chest. "I know my mother said something completely out of line to you. Please tell me, or I'll just ask her myself."

"No." Lex shook her head adamantly. "I don't want you to get into another argument with her because of me." She looked at their hands, which were now in Amanda's lap. "She said your father will keep trying to find out what I want with you. They seem to think I'm after your money," Lex finished quietly.

"Damn them!" Amanda jumped up, only to be held back by the strong grip Lex still had on her hand. "I'm going in there right now and give them both a piece of my mind."

Lex pulled her back down. "As much as I appreciate you defending my honor, let me handle them." Forestalling another outburst from Amanda, she continued, "And even though I don't want to sink to their level, I've got an idea about how to answer their questions. So don't worry. I'll take care of everything."

Amanda looked into Lex's eyes, then tilted until their foreheads were touching and gave Lex a kiss. "Okay, I'll let you handle it. But don't expect me to stand by and watch them continue to treat you badly." She gave Lex another kiss. "Because I can't do that."

"Do you think you two can control yourselves long enough to join us for dinner?" Michael Cauble's disgusted voice carried across the sitting room.

Lex stood, then calmly led Amanda through the room, not releasing her hand. At the doorway, Lex stopped to look down on Michael. She gave him a cold smile. "Thank you for coming to get us, *Michael*." She stressed his name, daring him to say something. "I know that you usually have one of the servants do that, but I really appreciate the personal touch." Lex patted him on the shoulder with her free hand as she and Amanda stepped past him and started for the dining room.

"What was that all about?" Amanda whispered, as she and Lex walked down the quiet hallway.

"Just the first part of my plan, sweetheart." *No more Ms. Nice. It's time to play some hardball, and I'm gonna enjoy every damn minute of it.*

Before stepping into the dining room, Lex tried to release Amanda's hand, but her lover held on stubbornly. With a mental shrug, Lex decided to stir things up a little. Reaching their designated places, she gave Amanda a quick grin and pulled out her chair for her. The eyes of over a dozen curious people were on them.

Blushing slightly, Amanda accepted the gesture. "Thanks." Out of the corner of her eye, she saw her mother narrow her eyes. *Uh-oh. I don't know what Lex is up to, but I think it's working.*

Lex traded nods with Frank, who was seated directly across from her. Looking around the table, she could tell that the only person who 'dressed' for the dinner was Elizabeth, as most of the guests were wearing business suits. She gave the smirking Jeannie a wink and sat down beside her partner.

Michael Cauble stood at the head of the table and addressed the group. "Since we are *finally* seated, I would like to thank everyone for attending this evening."

As his voice droned on, the man sitting next to Lex muttered under his breath, "He threatened us with the loss of our jobs if we didn't show up for this little function. Jeremy down there," he nodded toward a thin, nervous looking young man who kept checking his watch, "his wife went into the hospital late this afternoon. She's in labor with their first child." Michael finished his remarks and sat while Mark shook his head in barely disguised disgust, and then offered his hand to Lex. "My name's Mark Garrett. I handle all of the accounts in the Southwest."

"Lexington Walters, but you can call me Lex. I'm a friend of Amanda's." Lex gave the dark haired man's hand a firm shake. "You say you're in charge of the Southwest? Where are you based?" *I didn't know that. I thought that Cauble only had the one office here in Los Angeles. That is interesting.*

"Santa Fe, New Mexico. For the moment, at least. But I've been trying to talk Mr. Cauble into moving the office to Dallas. The weather's a little milder there." Mark lowered his voice. "You'd think that since he has family in Texas, that he'd be thrilled to have an office nearby."

Lex nodded. "Have you worked for Mr. Cauble very long?" It was nice to have a friendly face at the dinner table tonight. Glancing back at her partner, Lex could see that Amanda was engrossed in a conversation with her sister.

"About six years. I'm hoping to open my own office someday. I've been offered a job here in Los Angeles, but if I'm going to relocate, it will have to be someplace without smog or crime."

"I don't blame you a bit, Mark. I can't wait to get back home myself." Lex pushed her food around on her plate. "What is this stuff, anyway? Looks like it isn't quite dead yet."

Amanda noticed that her partner had "fenced off" the main course with her vegetables. "Lex, quit playing with your food."

Lex put her fork down. "It still looks alive, Amanda. I just didn't want it to get away."

"At least try to eat some of it. We'll raid the refrigerator later, I promise." Glancing around the table, she was somewhat relieved to see that Lex wasn't the only one not eating the dinner. *I hate when Mother decides to experiment with the menu. The last time she did that, I broke out in hives. Yuck!*

Missing the entire conversation over the food, Mark politely asked. "Lex, are you in the real estate business too?"

She almost choked on her water. "Uh, no. What made you think that I was?"

"Well, you said you were a friend of Amanda's, and you seem too 'normal' to have come from the same social circles Mrs. Cauble usually frequents. I just assumed you had met her through the real estate office, that's all."

Lex returned his smile with a somewhat mischievous one of her own. "As a matter of fact, we did sort of meet that way. She came out to try and put my ranch on the market." Pausing to let that sink in, she then continued, "It was just a shame that I didn't know I was supposed to be selling it at the time."

Mark admired Amanda's profile, before turning his attention back to Lex. "Tenacious, is she?"

"Yeah, she is. But it wasn't her idea. Her manager sent her on a wild goose chase."

"Really? So, you're a rancher? No offense, Lex, but I was under the impression that most ranches today are run by corporations because there's not enough money in it for the average person to make any kind of profit from it." The icy glare he received caused Mark to try and back pedal his position. "No, wait." He held up a hand to placate her rising temper. "I honestly didn't mean anything by it. I was just curious. My mouth tends to overrun my mind, most of the time."

"No, that's okay. It's just that I'm a little...sensitive...on that subject right now." Feeling a gentle touch on her leg, Lex turned back to face Amanda.

"What's up?" Amanda had felt Lex tense up and could tell that the conversation with Mark upset her.

"Nothing. Mark and I were just discussing the ranching business." She reached under the table and covered Amanda's hand with her own. "Are you doing okay?" Glancing around, Lex noticed that most of the people had finished eating, or at least finished pushing the food around on their plates. "Is this all there is to their damn dinner? You had to fly all the way across the country for half-cooked—" she looked down at her plate, "—

whatever the hell this is supposed to be, and a few insults?"

"I think it was more of an excuse to get me home than anything else. I wouldn't be here if I hadn't already planned to come and pack my stuff up, especially with the way they've been treating you." Amanda squeezed the hand that she held. "I'm really sorry about all of that."

"Don't worry about it. I'm just glad you didn't have to face them alone." Lex felt her lover lean up against her. She enjoyed the contact since she had been feeling quite out of sorts since this entire evening began.

CLINK, CLINK, CLINK!

All heads turned toward the front of the table where Michael Cauble stood tapping his wineglass with a knife to get everyone's attention. "Ladies and gentlemen, once again I would like to thank all of you for attending our dinner this evening and for making this another very successful quarter." He held up his glass of wine. "I'd like to propose a toast to each and every one of you for a job well done." Waiting until everyone raised his or her glass, he took a sip, then lifted the wine into the air once again. "And I would also like to express my gratitude to my wonderful family because without their love and support I would not be the man I am today." He gave Elizabeth an insincere smile. "To my beautiful wife, and my two lovely daughters," he nodded to Jeannie and Amanda, "who are the greatest blessings a man can have."

Lex covered her mouth with her napkin, stifling a chuckle. *He's spreading more fertilizer than we have in the entire south pasture.* Flinching at the elbow in her ribs, she coughed, then gave Amanda an innocent look.

"Behave."

Finishing his little speech, Michael stepped away from the table. "If you will all excuse me, I have some unfinished business to attend to. Feel free to have coffee or brandy in the sitting room." Once he left the room, everyone at the table breathed a sigh of relief. For some, conversations began in earnest, while many other guests prepared to leave for the evening.

Lex leaned over to whisper into Amanda's ear, then kissed it discreetly. "I'll see you in a bit, okay? I want to have a word or two with your father."

"Okay, but if you're not out of there in ten minutes, I'm coming in after you. Remember, we need to leave pretty early in the morning, so you have to be in bed at a decent hour."

Lex's allowed her gaze to roam over Amanda, head to toe, as she smiled longingly at her. Then, in her most sultry voice she said, "I certainly plan to. See you in a little bit, okay?" Amanda blushed under the appreciative eye. Then Lex left the room before Amanda could say anything else.

MICHAEL SAT AT his desk, studying the latest fax from his private investigator. *Bank statements. Now we're getting somewhere.* He thought he had finally got his hands on the proof he had been waiting for. But before he could examine the numbers, a loud knock came at the door.

"Who is it?" he snarled, angry at the interruption. *Stupid servants. When will they learn 'not to be disturbed' means to leave me the hell alone!*

The door opened, and Lex walked into the room. "There you are. I think we have some things that need to be cleared up." She strode over to one of the chairs in front of his desk and sat down.

"Make yourself comfortable, Walters," he snapped sarcastically, hiding the papers he had been trying to study. "What is it that you want? I'm a very busy man, you know."

Lex smirked, then stretched her legs out in front of her, crossing her booted feet at the ankles. "I think it's about time we come to an understanding, *Michael*." She enjoyed the way he flushed with anger.

"Really? And just how to you propose that we do that? Are you planning on leaving my daughter alone?" Michael tore off his glasses and tossed them onto the desk. He felt a sudden surge of fear as she jumped suddenly to her feet, then leaned forward with her hands braced on the desk.

"Let's quit playing stupid little games, Mike. Just what in the hell is your problem with me?" Lex continued to lean forward until she was just inches away from Michael's face. "Is it because I'm a woman? Or is it the fact that I actually work for a living? What is it about me that bothers you so damn much?"

Michael stood and stepped around the desk, trying to distance himself from the imposing figure. "Because you're a woman? No." He went to the bar and poured himself a shot, gulping down the amber liquid with a single swallow. "Unlike Elizabeth, I have resigned myself to the fact that my youngest daughter is unnatural. There's not much I can do about that. But," he pointed the empty glass in Lex's direction, "I can try to make her see reason when it comes to dirt-poor farmers trying to sink their claws into her bank account." He filled the glass again, then drained it quickly.

Lex leaned back against the desk and crossed her arms over her chest. "Dirt-poor farmer?" The terminology he used was more amusing than insulting, and she couldn't help but laugh. "Number one, I'm a rancher. Second, I have no designs on Amanda's money." She stood up straight and walked over to him, standing only a step away from the shorter man. "Third, I have more than enough money of my own, and I certainly have no need of yours." She got right into his face and added, "Last, but not least, I love her with everything that I am and nothing can change that." Hands grabbing her shirt took Lex by surprise, and she felt Michael pull her even closer.

AMANDA STOOD AT the door to the office, trying to listen to the sounds within. Not hearing anything, she opened it just in time to see her father grab Lex by the shirt and slam her into the bar. Before she could say anything, Michael punched her lover in the face. "Stop it!"

Amanda scrambled across the room and grabbed her livid father to pull him off Lex. "Daddy Let her go, now," she begged, tugging at his sleeve and collar.

Michael shook his head to clear it, and then pushed Lex back again. Her lower lip was bleeding, and he smirked, obviously happy to see he'd done some damage before his daughter interfered. "You damned arrogant piece of trash." He stuck out his jaw and looked like he was hoping the rancher would try and retaliate. "Go ahead," he whispered. "Let Amanda see you as I do."_

Lex stepped back and wiped her mouth on the sleeve of her green shirt. The blood left a dark smear. Her eyes bored into him, but she didn't say a word.

"Get out of my office," he muttered. "You're not welcome here. And you get the hell out of my house by tomorrow."

"Gladly." Lex pushed by him, again wiping her bloody mouth and chin with the back of her hand. She started for the door, doing all she could to control her anger. *Narrow-minded bastard. If he wasn't Amanda's father, I would...*her thoughts ended there as she felt a hand touch her arm.

Amanda was able to stop Lex before she got to the door. "Oh, honey." She took a firm grip on her partner's arm and led her from the office, not bothering to acknowledge her still-seething father's presence. "Come on. Let's go upstairs and get you cleaned up."

Lex allowed Amanda to lead her up the back stairs, away from prying eyes, and to the guestroom, not even realizing it when she was pushed down onto the bed. *That son of a bitch. He's more worried about his damn money than he is his own daughter! I should have throttled him when I had the chance. No, he is her father. I can't do that to her.* Lex's mind whirled as her partner stepped into the bathroom, then returned with a damp washcloth which she placed against her bleeding mouth. After a moment, Lex realized where they were, and she could see the concern etched on the face above her. "Amanda?"

"I'm here, love." Amanda dabbed at the oozing cut, wincing at the swelling and redness that indicated it was going to bruise. "Are you okay?"

Lex took stock of her body. "I think so." She was still shaking from the effort it had taken not to strangle the obnoxious man. *I have got to get this under control.* "How about you?"

Amanda sat down on the bed, pulling Lex close to her. "I'm fine. But why did my father attack you like that?" She leaned back against the headboard of the bed and brought Lex into her arms, allowing her lover's head to rest on her chest. "I've never seen him so angry. He's never been the violent type before."

Lex sighed, allowing the anger to seep slowly away, leaving behind a sad weariness. "I guess I pushed him a little too far. I just wanted to find out why he hated seeing us together." She relaxed as she felt a gentle stroking of her hair. *It's taking every ounce of control I have not to go back in there and toss him on his ass, after that arrogant bastard called his own daughter 'unnatural.'*

"What did he say?" Amanda whispered gently, continuing her stroking as she felt the body lying partially on her tense up again. "It's okay, Lex. Nothing he said could change what I feel for you." She leaned over and kissed the top of Lex's head. "Or what you mean to me."

Closing her eyes, Lex allowed herself to absorb the love emanating from Amanda, then she moved the washcloth away from her face. "He's bound and determined that I'm after your money. I guess the only way I can change his mind about that is to send him my bank statements or something." She took a deep breath, then released it slowly. "I'm sorry about this, sweetheart. I wish you didn't have to be a witness to that little scene."

"Lex. Look at me, please." Amanda stayed silent until their eyes met. "What would you have done if I hadn't pulled my father away?" She searched Lex's sad eyes, trying to find a clue as to what she was thinking. "Would you have fought back?"

"I don't know." Lex saw the quiet look of love and determination in the face above her and then looked back down. "God knows I wanted to toss him across the room for what he said about you, and for the way they've treated you." She felt the hand on her head stop moving, then tug her closer to Amanda's body.

"What did he say? Although I probably don't want to know."

"No, you don't. It was the same ol' crap. I don't know how you have survived this all these years."

Tears trailed down Amanda's face as she realized just how much Lex had figured out about her early home life. *They say it's the quiet ones you have to worry about the most, because they usually notice all the little things.* Her voice was hoarse with emotion, and Amanda felt her defenses shatter completely. "It doesn't matter, anymore. I don't care what they say, or do, as long as we're together. It just doesn't matter." She began to cry in earnest, then felt their positions reverse, before she was lifted and cradled in Lex's strong arms.

SITTING AT HIS desk after his daughter and "that woman" had left, Michael shook his head. *I've lost. That damn bitch has my daughter, and I'll never make the girl see reason about her.* He angrily shuffled through the papers on his desk. *Guess there's no real sense in keeping these, now.* Michael was about to throw the entire mess in the garbage, when he stopped. "What the hell. I paid good money to see this, might as well look at it." Letting his eyes scan the pages, he suddenly felt lightheaded. "This can't be right."

The door creaked, and he looked up to see his wife framed in the low light. "Michael, you simply *must* come out of this office and tell our guests goodnight." Elizabeth stood, arms crossed tightly in front of her, with a pained look on her face. "They've finished up all the good brandy and Scotch, and are getting quite tipsy." She saw the expression on his face and moved further into the room. "What is it?"

The pale businessman looked up at his wife. "We were wrong, Elizabeth."

"Wrong? What in heaven's name are you babbling about?" She walked over to the desk and stood next to him. "Quit sounding like an idiot and tell me." Elizabeth accepted the papers he handed her. "What?"

"Read that." Michael rubbed his eyes with one hand. *Dear God. That ridiculous hick could ruin me.*

Elizabeth looked over the papers, and the more she read, the more her hands began to shake as reality slammed her hard. "You mean to tell me that uncouth farmer actually *owns* major stock in one of your subsidiaries? How is this possible?" She felt her legs weaken, as her husband stood and guided her to the loveseat nearby.

"From what I've read, it seems that her mother was a very wealthy woman before she married. When she died, her holdings were divided between her three children. After the youngest child died, his portion was split up between the two remaining offspring. It appears that Walters," he still choked on the name, "turned the majority of her money over to an investment broker, and he made several wise plays on the stock market. Just happens that one of the investments is in my business." Michael shook his head. "If she finds out about this and cashes in her investments, I could go under."

"If this is true, I wouldn't be able to show my face again. Imagine the humiliation!" Elizabeth glared at her husband. "What are you going to do about it?" She glanced down and noticed a red stain and scrape on his knuckles. "That looks like blood." Her eyes narrowed. "What happened to your hand?" His guilty look and the speed with which he pulled out a handkerchief to wipe at his hand was all she needed to put the equation together. "Oh, no. You didn't."

Michael stood, paced to the bar, and poured two glasses of Scotch. Silently he walked back to the loveseat and sat down, handing his wife a glass. "I'm afraid I did. The damned woman made me so angry, I didn't even think about it." He tipped the glass up and drained it. "But I have to admit it felt really good, punching that smirk off her face."

Elizabeth took a sip of her drink, then let out a heavy breath. "Damage control, that's what we need now." Her eyes shot a murderous gaze in his direction. "You should apologize immediately."

"No. That would probably make her realize that something's up. We need to be subtle about all of this. " He chewed his lip in concentration, looking much like his youngest daughter. "I found out from the upstairs maid that they're planning to leave first thing in the morning. We'll just let them go and hope to God that she doesn't realize the power she holds." Michael nodded to himself, believing his plan would work. "If worse comes to worst, we'll get Amanda to keep her in line. For some reason, that clod seems to listen to our daughter."

"Very well. But you'd better be ready to beg for forgiveness from this woman if she finds out." The small smile she bestowed on Michael was anything but friendly. "Because money isn't the only thing that you would lose if she destroys you, dear." Elizabeth patted her husband on the cheek, then stood and left the room, feeling his eyes on her as she closed the door.

Chapter
Fourteen

BRIGHT, EARLY MORNING sunlight beamed down on the silent figure placing bags in the trunk of the red convertible. Lex gave the last bag a shove, wondering how in the hell they were able to get them in there to begin with. *I thought she sent most of her things back with the movers. We didn't have this much stuff before, did we?*

"Everything about loaded up? Frank and Jeannie should be out to say goodbye in a few minutes." Amanda came up behind Lex and circled her arms about her lover's waist.

Lex turned around and linked her hands behind Amanda's back. "Yep, that was the last of it. Although we may have to pay freight charges for all the luggage." She leaned down and placed a light kiss on Amanda's lips, careful of her own sore mouth. The two of them sported similar bruises on their faces, and Lex could just imagine how they looked to others. "Did you run a final check for any missing underwear?" she teased, seeing her lover blush.

"How was I supposed to know that you threw them behind the chair? I swear Sophia giggled for hours after finding them." Amanda continued to blush after she thought about the note from Beverly that stated she needed to keep better track of her 'unmentionables' so as not to distract the rest of the household staff. Looking up, she saw Lex trying not to smile. "You're going to make your lip start bleeding again." She raised one hand and ran her thumb lightly across Lex's bruised lip. "Maybe you need a stitch or two."

Kissing the thumb offered to her, Lex shook her head. "Nah, it'll be okay." She was about to prove her point when a voice echoed through the cool, still morning.

Jeannie walked through the front door, Frank close behind her. "You two never seem to get enough, do you? I guess it'll just be us seeing you off. Mother is upstairs with a migraine, and Father is on an overseas call."

Amanda stepped away from Lex to embrace her sister. She felt a twinge of sadness at leaving. "It's probably for the best, anyway. Thanks for everything, Jeannie. I really appreciate how you've accepted Lex."

The auburn-haired woman held her sister tightly. "I'm just glad you finally found the person you've been looking for, Mandy." When she realized that this was probably the last time she'd see her little sister for quite a while, she murmured, "I know you probably won't be coming back to this house any time soon." *If ever.* "But Frank and I have plenty of room, if you two would like to come and visit."

"Thanks." Amanda pulled back a bit and glanced over her shoulder. Seeing Lex's nod, she gave them an invitation of their own. "The next vacation you two get, why don't you come out to our ranch and stay with us." *Our ranch. I think I really like the sound of that.*

Lex moved closer to the women. "That's a great idea. We've got quite a bit of room ourselves, and I won't even make you muck out any stalls." The last part of her statement was aimed at Frank.

The big man stepped forward and pulled Amanda into a fierce embrace. "Take care, Mandy. We'll try to stop by and see you two real soon, okay?"

Amanda felt her heart surge with love for her brother-in-law and dear friend. "That would be great."

"What are your plans for Christmas?" Lex asked, shaking hands with Frank. Seeing the happy look on Amanda's face, she mentally patted herself on the back. *Good one, Lexington. You just might figure all of this out yet.*

Frank looked over at his wife, who shrugged. "Well, I was planning on hiding." The holiday parties Elizabeth threw were almost as dull as her dinner parties, and the food actually seemed worse. "Why do you ask?"

Lex put her arm around Frank and escorted him over to the two sisters. "Well, since it's going to be Amanda's first Christmas out at the ranch, I thought maybe you two would like to join us. I'm hoping to have a houseful."

"A houseful, huh?" Amanda stepped away from Jeannie and nearly flew into the Lex's arms. "Anyone I know?"

"Well, you, me, Martha and Charlie, your grandparents, the Wades." Lex glanced over at the other couple. "And of course Frank and Jeannie, if they're willing."

Jeannie laughed, then pulled her sister away from Lex. "I don't know about Frank, but I'd love to be there!" Feeling Lex pull her close, she whispered into her ear, "Thank you, Lex. I've never seen my sister so happy." She pulled back a bit, then kissed a very embarrassed Lex on the cheek. "Welcome to the family, Slim."

Lex sighed, then grinned mischievously. *Why not? She* kissed Jeannie full on the mouth. "Thanks, sis." Lex almost laughed out loud at the deep flush covering the woman's face.

Frank laughed so hard he had to hold on to Amanda to keep from falling down. "Damn, Lex, are you trying to kill me?" His wife stalked toward him, and he raised his hands ineffectually against her attack. "Honey, wait!" he pleaded, as Jeannie slapped at him.

"Sorry, Frank. But any woman who pinches my butt gets a kiss." Lex took Amanda into her arms, and then led her to the car. "I hate to kiss and run, but our plane leaves in less than two hours." Before she climbed into the vehicle, Lex turned around. "We'll make up an extra spot in the barn at Christmas for y'all, okay?" She ducked the shoe that Jeannie tossed at her, then got in the passenger seat and closed the door behind her.

LEX TOOK A panicked breath as she boarded the plane, and a cold chill ran down her spine. *Come on, Lexington, you can do this. It's no different than the last time.* She let Amanda take the seat by the window, which enabled Lex to stretch her long legs out in the aisle of the plane. Sitting down, she felt a hand grasp hers and hold on tightly.

"Are you doing all right?"

"No problem." Lex gave a tiny smile, then took a deep breath as the flight attendant closed the door on the plane. *Breathe, dammit.* She listened as the air conditioner pumped oxygen into the plane. *See? You're not gonna suffocate, so just get over it, idiot!*

Amanda brought one of Lex's hands closer, until she was able to cradle it against her chest. Kissing the knuckles, she whispered, "It's okay, Lex. Look at me, honey." She waited until Lex complied. "Listen to my voice, okay? It's just you and me." Amanda felt the plane taxi down the runway, but Lex was totally transfixed on her. "Have I told you about the time I accidentally locked Jeannie in the trunk of the limousine? Mother nearly had a cow." She told her partner about the tale of two young girls, playing hide and seek, and of the complete embarrassment of a well-to-do woman who had sent her driver to meet an important artist at the airport only to have the artist greeted by a crying girl in the trunk of the expensive limousine.

The story took up almost half of the flight, with Amanda embellishing it several times to make it last. When she noticed Lex's eyes droop, she finally snuggled up against her lover and closed her eyes.

Lex couldn't help but smile at the top of Amanda's head. *Poor thing. This week has been real rough for her. Maybe I can do something to make up for that.* She didn't even realize when her head dropped and she fell asleep.

"Ma'am? The plane has landed." The lovely young flight attendant gently jostled Lex's shoulder, trying to wake her up.

Opening her eyes and seeing the empty plane, Lex gave the woman an embarrassed smile. "Thanks. We'll be out of here in just a second."

"There's no real hurry. I just wanted to make sure you didn't have another flight to catch." The attendant folded up a blanket from a nearby seat before moving down the aisle. "If you need anything, just let me know." Then she passed along a look that promised more than just good customer service.

Oh, boy. It's a good thing Amanda slept through that. Lex returned her attention to the woman still sleeping next to her. "Sweetheart? Amanda, we've landed." She kissed the head snuggled against her and used her free hand to brush the hair away from Amanda's eyes.

"Mmm." Amanda leaned up and placed a kiss on Lex's mouth. As she stretched, she realized where they were. "Oops. Did you say we've landed?" She looked around, very glad that they appeared to be the only ones left on the plane. "I was having the most incredible dream." She released Lex's hand and rubbed her face.

"Obviously." Lex stood up and raised her arms over her head and leaned backward, which caused her back to crack several times. "I hate sitting for that long." She noticed her appreciative audience as Amanda's eyes followed her every move. "See something you like, ma'am?"

Amanda stood up and ran a hand through her disheveled hair. "You could say that."

She caught the look that the flight attendant was still giving Lex. "And I don't think I'm the only one, either." Not caring where they were, Amanda hugged her lover. "But she'll just have to be content to enjoy you from a distance, because I'm not sharing."

Lex chuckled. "Fine by me." She returned the hug. "I love you, Amanda."

"I love you, too." Amanda ran her hands up and down Lex's back, before taking a step away. "Let's go home. Um, would you mind too much—"

"If we went to see your grandparents first? I was just going to suggest that." Lex carefully guided her lover down the narrow aisles and out of the plane. "We can let them know you survived, and then tell them you're going to be moving in at the ranch." As they walked through the jet way, Lex turned back to Amanda, who was about half a step behind her. "I enjoyed your story, by the way. Made me forget all about the plane."

Amanda hitched her purse up on her shoulder, then took an

extra step to be directly next to her lover. "Really? Thanks. I'm sorry I fell asleep on you, though." She looked up to see an amused look on Lex's face. "What?"

"Don't feel bad. I fell asleep, too. The flight attendant had to wake me up after the plane was already empty." Lex looked around, trying to read the signs. "Where the hell do we pick up the damn luggage?" She spotted a map of the airport and walked over to check it out. When she found her destination, she shook her head. "You've flown quite a bit, right?" Lex asked her partner, as they made their way to the baggage claim area.

"Yes, although the last time I was so worried about Grandpa Jake, I don't remember much of the flight. Jeannie and Frank had my car shipped up to me." Amanda followed the long legged rancher, struggling to keep up. "Why do you ask? Hey, honey, do you want to slow it down to at least a reasonable jog?"

Lex stopped and turned around. "I'm sorry. I keep forgetting that not everyone can cover as much distance as I can." She waited for a moment until Amanda caught her breath. "Anyway, I was just wondering, why do they seem to make you walk all the way to the other side of the damn airport to pick up your luggage? Especially since they won't let you carry much of it with you? Seems rather ridiculous to me."

Amanda laughed. "I think travelers have been asking that same question since the first commercial flight." She wrapped her hand around Lex's upper arm to lead her through the milling crowds. "Come on. We're almost there."

"MANDY, YOU'RE BACK early," Jacob exclaimed as the two women stepped into his kitchen. He had barely opened his arms before his granddaughter practically knocked him down in her exuberance. "Hey, there. Easy, honey." He hugged her tightly, looking at Lex over her head. Seeing the bruise on her mouth, Jacob frowned. "Are you two okay?"

Amanda moved back in order to look into her grandfather's concerned eyes. "We're fine, Grandpa. It was pretty exciting, actually." She felt his callused hand gently trace the bruise on her face, and decided to try for a change of subject. "Where's Gramma?"

"Right here, dearest." Anna Leigh stood in the doorway, where she had an arm around Lex. "You two look like you've been in a fight." She led Lex over to where Amanda and Jacob were standing. "You are going to tell us why you look like this, right?"

"Sure." Amanda rubbed her jaw. "It's really quite a good story, too." She winked at Lex. "But do you mind if we raid the refrigerator first? Lex's stomach growled all the way back from the airport, and I couldn't even hear the radio half the time." Amanda stepped away from her grandfather and pulled Anna Leigh into a hug. "I really missed you, Gramma."

The older woman held her granddaughter tight. "We missed you too, Mandy." She looked over Amanda's head to met Lex's gaze. "And while you're at it, you can also tell us what kind of trouble you got into."

"Don't blame me. Trouble just seems to find her." Lex pointed at her lover, and then started backing up as Amanda stalked toward her. "Well, it's true." She held her hands out in front of her, trying to ward off the pending attack.

"Just you wait, Slim. I'll take care of you later, when you least expect it." Amanda loved the light blush that the nickname brought to Lex's face.

Jacob pulled several items from the refrigerator. "I hope a sandwich sounds okay."

"Let me help you with that, Mister, um, Jacob," Lex offered, maneuvering quickly around her amused friend. She took some of the things from his hands and placed them on the table.

"AND THEN LEX ropes the guy with a kid's jump rope," Amanda related, waving a potato chip around in circles to emphasize her point. "The police officers said she looked just like John Wayne. Then she sat on him, and the two cops had to pull her off."

Anna Leigh put a hand on Lex's arm. "Goodness, Lexington. That was a very brave thing to do. Is that how you got hurt?" She was surprised when Lex looked down at the table.

"Uh, no. He didn't touch me." Lex looked up at the older woman. "And it was pretty stupid, actually. I just didn't think. But I tend to have that problem around your granddaughter."

Amanda chuckled, then realized what had been said. "Hey, wait a minute. What did I do?"

Jacob loved watching the teasing that went back and forth between the two younger women. "Okay, so now you've explained how Mandy ended up looking like she does. But what happened to you, Lex?" He didn't miss the exchange of guilty glances between them. "Oh, come on. It can't be that bad, can it?" Then a thought occurred to him. "Mandy, you didn't do it, did you?" He knew his granddaughter had a fiery temper and had been known to explode quite easily when angered.

"No, sir, she didn't. Her father did." Hearing Anna Leigh's shocked gasp, Lex turned to face her. "It was pretty much my own fault. I kind of pushed him into it."

"That's the biggest load of bunk I've ever heard. There's never an excuse to hit a lady." Jacob looked ready to do battle in Lex's behalf, and if his son were anywhere nearby, he might do just that.

"I'm no lady, Jacob. And I really did keep at him until he lost control."

Amanda put her hand on her grandfather's arm to try and calm him, but looked at Lex. "You did no such thing, Lex. You were just trying to protect me."

"Protect you?" Anna Leigh was still in shock over the revelation that her son could strike a woman. "Dear heavens, don't tell me he was going to hit you, Mandy."

Lex took a deep breath. "No ma'am. I went into his office last night to find out why he was so hostile toward our relationship." She looked at her lover with sad eyes. "She never said anything, but I could tell it was tearing Amanda up inside." Turning back to Anna Leigh, Lex swallowed hard. "Anyway, I asked him if it was because I was a woman, and he said no, that he was pretty much used to the idea that Amanda..." and here she paused. *I really don't need to bring that part of the conversation out, do I?* "Well, that she was gay. So then, I asked if it was because I worked for a living. That kind of set him off. He thinks I'm after Amanda's money."

Jacob looked at her quizzically. "You? After Mandy's money?" He burst into laughter. "Oh, that's too funny!"

"Did you enlighten him, dear?" Anna Leigh covered Lex's hand with her own.

"No, ma'am. I didn't think it would do any good, because he'd probably think I was lying. But I did tell him I loved Amanda, and no amount of money could change that, and I couldn't help myself—I got right up in his face and stood over him." She touched her mouth with her free hand. "That's when he lost it and grabbed me."

Amanda picked up the story. "I opened the door to the office and saw Daddy grab Lex and push her back against the bar. He hit her before I could stop him." She exchanged a tender look with Lex. "I'm glad we decided we were going to leave this morning, instead of tomorrow, because I don't think either one of us could have handled another day there."

Jacob sighed. "I thought we raised him better than that. I really want to turn that boy over my knee." He looked at Lex. "I'm sorry about his behavior, child. I hate the fact that you were hurt by someone from our family."

"I don't blame you, or your family, Jacob." Lex looked at the older man with respect. "Amanda and I talked about it last night. Even though he's her father, you and Anna Leigh are a whole lot more of a family to her than they are." Smiling at Amanda, she continued, "And speaking of families, that reminds me of something we need to tell you, right, Amanda?"

"Hmm?" Amanda asked, then her face lit up when she realized what Lex meant. "Oh, yeah. That's right. Umm...well...Lex asked, and...I..." She began to stammer. "You see...it's—"

Feeling sorry for the tongue-tied woman, Lex stood and circled the table until she was standing directly behind Amanda, then placed her hands on her shoulders. "What my friend here is so eloquently trying to say is that I asked her to move into the ranch house with me, and she accepted."

Anna Leigh clapped her hands in delight. "That's wonderful, isn't it Jacob? We were just discussing that very thing this morning."

"You were?" Amanda was hard pressed to keep her jaw from hitting the table. She raised her hands and covered Lex's. "It's really not that far from town, and we'll still visit with you often."

"Honey, I think it's okay." Lex wasn't very surprised, but she was delighted at the Caubles' acceptance. "And you know that you have an open invitation, right?"

Jacob stood up. "We'll be sure and take you up on that offer, young lady." He helped his wife rise and move away from the table as well. "Now we've got some errands to run. Why don't you go on upstairs and get a little rest? You both look completely worn out."

"That's a wonderful idea, love." Anna Leigh said, as her husband wrapped an arm around her. "We'll see you girls for dinner tonight?"

Amanda stood up as well, letting Lex wrap long arms around her. "Wouldn't miss it." She stifled a yawn. "But I think you're right about needing a nap. We'll see you guys later, I think." She blushed as her grandfather winked at her, just as they left the room.

A sultry voice whispered in her ear, causing chills to chase down Amanda's back. "They're just too much, sometimes."

"Mm hmm."

"What was that about a nap?"

"Nap? Who said anything about a nap?" Amanda turned around in Lex's arms. "I didn't say nap, did I?" Meeting her lover's face halfway, they shared a long, passionate kiss. "The hell with the nap. Let's just get upstairs." She took one of Lex's hands and led her to the stairs, the exhaustion from their trip forgotten.

THE NEXT MORNING'S sun was hot against Lex's back as she rearranged a bag in the bed of the pickup. *Dinner last night was interesting to say the least. Jacob knows some pretty good tales about Amanda.* Lex chuckled as she tossed another bag into the back of the truck. *And I had no idea she was such a hellion when she was a kid.*

"What's so funny?" Amanda asked, bringing the last bag with her and handing it to Lex. "You're still thinking about those stories Grandpa Jake told last night, aren't you?"

"Yep. I had no idea you were such a...scamp, growing up. Remind me not to let you unsupervised anywhere near the cattle."

Jacob had related a tale of a young Amanda using the neighborhood dogs as dolls for a tea party, complete with clothes and hats. It seemed funny to everyone until it was found out that the clothes were from her grandmother's closet, and Amanda found herself grounded for over a week during that particular summer. Anna Leigh admitted there were several hats that she never wore again, since the dog smell never quite left them. That little bit of information caused her granddaughter even more embarrassment.

"I'm going to have to find some way of getting even with him for telling that one, aren't I?" Amanda took another step until she was wrapped up in warm arms. "Mmm."

Lex enjoyed the embrace. *I don't think I will ever get enough of this.* "We'd better get a move on. Martha's expecting us for lunch." She kissed the top of Amanda's head, and then released her.

Jacob and Anna Leigh met them at the front of the truck. "You two will be back over for Jacob's birthday next weekend, right?" Anna Leigh asked, giving Amanda a hug.

"We wouldn't miss it for anything," Lex replied, shaking Jacob's hand. She reached out to Anna Leigh, but was surprised when the older woman wrapped her arms around her and squeezed.

"Thank you for making our little girl so happy, Lexington." Anna Leigh's whispered gratitude was just between the two of them. She felt Lex return the hug enthusiastically. Pulling back slightly, she said in a louder voice, "Welcome to our family, dear."

Lex held Anna Leigh close as a lump formed in her throat. "You—" she had to stop and clear her throat, "both have always made me feel like part of the family. Thank you for raising such a wonderful granddaughter." She stepped away and ran a hand across her face. "Umm, yeah." Taking a deep breath, Lex finally got herself together, at least for the moment. "Thanks for everything." She was grateful when Amanda moved in close and put an arm around her waist. "We'll, ah, see you next weekend, right?" Lex knew she was quickly losing her composure. *We've got to get out of here before I start bawling like a baby.*

Amanda understood the emotional fine line Lex was treading and decided it was time for a retreat. "We've got to get going. Martha is probably getting ready to call out the National Guard by now."

"You two go on. We'll see you Saturday, if not sooner." Jacob pulled his wife to him as the two women climbed into the truck. "Those two are something else, aren't they, sweetheart?"

Anna Leigh looked up into his eyes lovingly. "Yes, they are, my dearest. Let's go into the house and discuss it, shall we?"

Jacob loved when they had discussions, especially the kind his wife was hinting at. "Why do I have the distinct feeling that we won't be doing much talking?" He followed the woman of his dreams, the love of his life, into the house and allowed her to pull him up the stairs.

THE DRIVE TO the ranch was unusually silent, as both women were deeply occupied by their own thoughts. Lex was worried about Amanda and how she would be able to adjust to the life they were about to embark upon together. The fact that Amanda's parents disapproved didn't matter to Lex, but she knew in her heart that the younger woman was devastated by their hateful words. Looking sideways as she drove, Lex noticed with surprise that there was a slight smile on her companion's face. "Penny for your thoughts?"

Amanda turned away from the window. "Think you can afford it, Slim?" She noticed the concern etched on her friend's face and reached over to bring one of Lex's hands into her lap. "Actually, I was just thinking about how happy I am right this very moment."

"Really?" Lex wanted to be reassured. She wanted to know that Amanda was happy with her decision, happy with the opportunity to start a life with her. "I was just thinking, that if you wanted, we could always build a house in town, if you don't like living on the ranch." She braced herself for the answer. *I'll go anywhere, be anyone, just for the opportunity to be with you. I hope you know that.*

"But you love living on the ranch." Amanda frowned and wondered what on earth was going through Lex's complex mind.

"What good is the ranch without you?" Lex stopped the truck just before they were about to cross the old bridge. She unbuckled her seatbelt and turned so she could give Amanda all of her attention. "I love you, Amanda. And I want to do everything in my power to make you happy. If that means living in town, fine." She took Amanda's hand in hers and chafed it with her fingertips while she spoke. "If that means pitching a tent in the middle of the woods, that's fine too."

"Lex—"

"No, wait. Please. I've got to get this out now." Unused to sharing herself with anyone, Lex blinked, shedding a tear that then rolled down her cheek. "I'm not real good with stuff like this, but I want you to understand what a difference you've made in my life. I love you, and I hope we can have a long and happy life together." Lex looked deeply into Amanda's eyes and saw a strong love reflected back to her.

Amanda gently pulled her hand free and wiped the tear away with her thumb. "I love you too." She looked around and realized where the truck was parked. "It's kind of fitting that we should start our life together here." Hoping that some fresh air would help settle her partner, Amanda opened her door. "Come on. Let's stretch our legs for a minute, okay?"

Lex followed her lead, and soon both women were standing on the shore of the creek, looking down at the peaceful stream of water that flowed beneath the bridge. "Full circle, huh?" Lex felt at peace for the first time in her life. The woman standing with her made her feel complete.

"Full circle, love," Amanda whispered, her lips meeting Lex's in a life-affirming kiss.

Other books in this series available from
Yellow Rose Books

Destiny's Bridge

Rancher Lexington (Lex) Walters pulls young Amanda Cauble
from a raging creek and the two women quickly develop a
strong bond of friendship. Overcoming severe weather, cattle
thieves, and their own fears, their friendship deepens into a
strong and lasting love.

ISBN 1-932300-11-2

Hope's Path

In this next look into the lives of Lexington Walters and Amanda Cauble, someone is determined to ruin Lex. Attempts to destroy her ranch lead to attempts on her life. Lex and Amanda desperately try to find out who hates Lex so much that they are willing to ruin the lives of everyone in their path. Can they survive long enough to find out who's responsible? And will their love survive when they find out who it is?

ISBN 1-930928-18-1

Love's Journey

Lex and Amanda embark on a new journey as Lexington rediscovers the love her mother's family has for her, and Amanda begins to build her relationship with her father. Meanwhile, attacks on the two young women grow more violent and deadly as someone tries to tear apart the love they share.

ISBN 1-930928-67-X

Strength of the Heart

In the fifth story of the series, Lex and Amanda are caught up in the planning of their upcoming nuptials while trying to get the ranch house rebuilt. But an arrest, a brushfire, and the death of someone close to her forces Lex to try and work through feelings of guilt and anger. Is Amanda's love strong enough to help her, or will Lex's own personal demons tear them apart?

ISBN 1-930928-75-0

Also from Carrie Carr
and
Yellow Rose Books

Something To Be Thankful For

Randi Meyers is at a crossroads in her life. She's got no girlfriend, bad knees, and her fill of loneliness. The one thing she does have in her favor is a veterinarian job in Fort Worth, Texas, but even that isn't going as well as she hoped. Her supervisor is cold-hearted and dumps long hours of work on her. Even if she did want a girlfriend, she has little time to look.

When a distant uncle dies, Randi returns to her hometown of Woodbridge, Texas, to attend the funeral. During the graveside services, she wanders away from the crowd and is beseeched by a young boy to follow him into the woods to help his injured sister. After coming upon an unconscious woman, the boy disappears. Randi brings the woman to the hospital and finds out that her name is Kay Newcombe.

Randi is intrigued by Kay. Who is this unusual woman? Where did her little brother disappear to? And why does Randi feel compelled to help her? Despite living in different cities, a tentative friendship forms, but Randi is hesitant. Can she trust her newfound friend? How much of her life and feelings can Randi reveal? And what secrets is Kay keeping from her? Together, Randi and Kay must unravel these questions, trust one another, and find the answers in order to protect themselves from outside threats—and discover what they mean to one another.

ISBN 1-932300-04-X

"An excellent story about two women who've gone through the School of Hard Knocks. You can't help but root for Kay and Randi as they try to make sense of their lives. This is Carrie Carr's best novel yet!"

~Lori L. Lake, author of *Gun Shy* and *Different Dress*

Carrie is a true Texan, having lived in the state her entire life. Newly married to her partner of four years, AJ, they make their home in the Dallas/Ft. Worth area with their teenage daughter, Karen. Easily bored, Carrie has done everything from wrangling longhorn cattle and buffalo, to programming burglar and fire alarm systems. Her spare time is spent traveling and trying to corral the two smallest members of their household, a Chihuahua named Nugget, and a Rat Terrier named Cher. Check out Carrie's website at www.CarrieLCarr.com for the latest news on personal appearances and information on how to get autographed bookplates.